DOUBLE DOG DARE

E.J. COCHRANE

BELLA
BOOKS
2018

Bella Books, Inc.
P.O. Box 10543
Tallahassee, FL 32302

Printed in the United States of America on acid-free paper.

First Bella Books Edition 2018

Editor: Ann Roberts
Cover Designer: Judith Fellows

ISBN: 978-1-64247-006-2

PUBLISHER'S NOTE

Other Bella Books by E.J. Cochrane

Matilda Smithwick Mystery Series
Sleeping Dogs Lie

Acknowledgments

This book wouldn't exist if not for a wonderfully supportive team of people who helped me take it from ideas to the page. The initial inspiration came from my dear friend Heather L. Mathes, but the plot was born over a series of beer-fueled consultations with my sisters Jennie Tyderek (my Knowledge Sherpa) and Heidi Krystofiak (my Professional Nag). They help me stay focused and keep me on track, even when my schedule gets less author-friendly than usual. There's a small chance I could do this without them, but I really don't want to try. Likewise, my partner (in the truest sense of the word) Sue Hawks somehow manages to silence my inner critic, lift me up, troubleshoot, problem solve and support me, all without losing patience. She lets entire weekends of potential fun pass uneventfully by while I do battle with words, and she never complains. I'm truly blessed. Thanks also to my brother-in-law Mike Tyderek, my Czar of Technology and Creative Violence. Not only did he save my laptop from its destiny at the bottom of a ravine, but he's also like a walking encyclopedia of weaponry (traditional and otherwise). And Tom Scrip, ballistics consultant and weapons enthusiast, thank you for your patient instruction. I've barely scratched the surface of your teachings, but their time will come. As always, my beta readers took what I gave them and helped me turn it into something much better. Thank you Amy Cook, Kathy Rowe, Erin Dunn, Jamie Lee Winner, HLM, Lynda Fitzgerald and Diane Piña. Your feedback was invaluable. I'm deeply indebted to the best editor on the planet, Ann Roberts. Thank you for teaching me so much in such a short time, and I promise I'm working on that pronoun thing. Finally, to the amazing women of Bella Books, I'm honored to put my work in your hands. Thank you for all you do.

About the Author

In addition to teaching college English, E.J. Cochrane has had just about every job imaginable, including running her own dog walking company. When she's not writing, teaching, walking dogs, or distracting herself with yet another employment adventure, she's one of those awful people who enjoys running (and somewhere in her closet has the dusty collection of marathon finisher medals to prove it). She and her partner live in Chicago with their cats and an elderly plecostomus.

Dedication

For Heather L. Mathes—it was good living with you.

PROLOGUE

Lindsey stepped onto her balcony, lit a cigarette and watched, fascinated, as the plume of smoke she exhaled swirled in the breeze off the lake. She didn't know why she continued to smoke outside. Habit, she supposed, but Terry wasn't around anymore to complain about the smell, and the kids spent more and more time at their father's house. It was a quiet she'd have to adjust to if Ray won the custody battle. He was such a bastard. Even after Terry died, he hadn't relented. She needed time to grieve, but he refused to give her even the tiniest break from attorneys and courtrooms. If anything he seemed to be taking pleasure in her suffering, like her current anguish was some sort of payback for ending their marriage all those years ago.

She took one last drag off her cigarette before stubbing it out on the railing and flicking the butt onto the pavement twenty stories below. She hoped Mrs. Snodgrass, the old busybody next door, wasn't hiding behind her curtains, watching Lindsey and waiting to witness her latest infraction of the rules. That woman lived to complain about her. She probably got a kickback from the management company for all the violations she reported. Lindsey groaned at the thought of another fine she couldn't afford. On top of the endless legal fees and the astronomical rent she had no money for. Now that she didn't have Terry's income to depend on, she wondered how many corners she would have to cut if she wanted to hang on to this place.

She supposed she should go back inside to the emails she'd been slogging through before Leigh's surprise visit. Not that she'd minded the interruption. Anything was better than dealing with the correspondence she'd neglected for the past two weeks, and Leigh was so eager to please these days. She felt momentarily guilty about moving on with her life so soon after Terry's death, though it was less a betrayal than her infidelity in the weeks beforehand, and it could eliminate her financial worries. Still, her recent activities with Leigh might raise some eyebrows, especially with the police, and since they had talked to Old Lady Snodgrass (whose favorite pastimes were eavesdropping and gossip) at least once already, she needed to be careful. She didn't want to take any unnecessary risks. She had to be patient, at least for a little while longer.

She knew Leigh had never gotten over her, and if their reconciliation stayed on track, she would be taken care of. Leigh made good money, and that kind of security was worth the potential backlash over her truncated widowhood. She would lose this place, she realized with a twinge of sadness. Even lovesick Leigh couldn't be convinced to pay for the home she and Terry had shared. Remembering that Terry had also shared this home with her ex mitigated her sorrow considerably. A fresh start would be good for her.

Thinking she should remind Leigh of the importance of discretion, she reached for her phone and sighed when she remembered that she'd left it in the bedroom. She stepped back inside but stopped short when she saw a familiar figure standing in her living room.

"What are you doing here?"

"I came to check on you. I wanted to see how you're handling your loss."

"How did you get in?"

"The door wasn't locked."

She'd meant to lock up behind her earlier visitor but had decided to languish in bed instead, a choice she now regretted. "You can't just barge into other people's homes."

"You're not really in a position to make demands."

The trespasser stepped closer, and she backed away, again wishing her phone was nearby.

"What do you want?" She feigned boldness, but it had no effect on her unwanted guest, who took another step forward. She now stood in the open door to the balcony.

"I want to give you a present."

Reluctantly, she opened the manila envelope the intruder handed her. She read the typed note she found inside and gasped. "This is a suicide note. I'm not going to kill myself."

"I can work around that."

A surprisingly strong shove sent her back into the railing, and as she struggled to regain her balance, the note slipped from her hands, and a second, more forceful blow sent her tumbling twenty stories below.

CHAPTER ONE

Matilda Smithwick squinted in the bright sunlight streaming through her open Jeep. If not for her adopted Great Dane Goliath deciding that her sunglasses made a perfect chew toy (for the third time) she would have been fine, but thanks to his penchant for destroying protective lenses (which he always seemed to find, no matter where she hid them), she had decided to stop wasting money on them. Until she found an alternate way to shield her eyes from the sun or figured out how to turn his tastes to something more dog appropriate, she would have to squint and hope for the best.

Searing eye pain aside, Maddie had no complaints about the day. She didn't know how, in late October, Chicago had been blessed with a sunny, sixty-five-degree day, but she would take it. Given the city's contentious relationship with Mother Nature, by tomorrow Chicagoans could be buried under a foot of snow (making Maddie regret waiting to put the hard top on her car), but for now she would enjoy the remainder of the lingering fall.

Finding a rare parking space in the overcrowded neighborhood where Patrick Walker, her right-hand man and favorite employee lived, she pulled in and almost wished she would be there long enough to make this victory worth celebrating. But since she was in Lakeview only long enough to pick Patrick up, this minor and short-lived stroke of luck seemed more like a cosmic tease from whatever deity ruled parking in Chicago than an actual godsend.

"What are we in for today, boss?" Patrick asked as he hopped into the passenger seat and buckled up. He focused his blue eyes on her for a moment before sliding his sunglasses into place, causing Maddie to scowl briefly before leaving her glorious spot to the next recipient of the parking god's benevolence.

"Honestly, I'm not sure."

Maddie blew out a frustrated breath. She so didn't want to be squandering this gorgeous Saturday (possibly the last one until June) on a fruitless mission for real estate. Considering her entire lack of success thus far, Patrick had graciously agreed to join her for the latest installment of the hunt for a larger space to accommodate Little Guys, her rapidly growing pet care business. And even though it was partly the fault of his marketing prowess that they needed more room, she still felt bad dragging him away from outdoor fun to help her find the potential in a musty abandoned building.

"I think this place used to be a bakery. Or maybe it was a bank. Harriet sent me all the information." It looked exactly like the information on every place she had already rejected. "I don't remember much. This is probably going to be a giant waste of your time."

"Or it will be perfect." Patrick's optimism fell on deaf ears and not only because Maddie, who was trying to merge onto Lake Shore Drive, wasn't fully listening to him.

So far, the whole endeavor had been an exercise in disappointment and frustration, and she suspected it was for Harriet, her older sister and real estate agent, as well. Over the last month and a half, Harriet had shown Maddie no fewer than twenty spaces, all of them adequate in size, decent in price and not too far from perfect in location. She really should have found something by now, but not one of the places she'd seen had been what Maddie wanted. She couldn't explain it to her sister except to say that none of them felt right. She knew from the second she saw the exterior and a sinking feeling in her chest told her the building was all wrong, but she still let Harriet take her inside to do the realtor thing, hoping the interior would change her mind. That strategy had yet to work, but by the fifth rejected building, Maddie had made a game of counting her sister's use of the word "nice" to describe their surroundings. If nothing else, it distracted her from her growing annoyance.

Harriet showed no signs of losing her patience (a skill Maddie suspected she'd honed during her years of dealing with the indecisive public), but that just made Maddie feel worse about her lack of eagerness. In truth, she should have felt more enthusiastic that her business had outgrown its current home (and if not for a fear of growing too big too fast and failing, she surely would have), but a small part of her wanted to ignore the demands of her burgeoning pet care empire and devote her weekends to regular life. Things like yardwork and laundry, tending to her dogs and visiting her grandmother. But not dating. She wondered if her life would ever be that uncomplicated again.

"Is Harriet handling your new house too?" Patrick asked.

Maddie clenched her jaw and nodded as she downshifted to accommodate the timid driver in front of her (who really should stick to side streets—or public transportation—if he wasn't willing to keep up with the vigorous flow of traffic).

"How's that going?"

"Well, I have a renter now." Her answer sounded clipped and harsh to her own ears.

"You're not happy about that? I thought that's what you wanted."

"What I want is to get rid of it, but I can't."

Not long ago, she, already a perfectly content homeowner, had inherited a house from her former client. Technically, Howard Monk had left his home to Goliath, his beloved (and rather disobedient) Great Dane, but since she had been the only one willing to take Goliath in after Howard's brutal murder in his own living room, she was now the unhappy owner of a grisly murder site. She couldn't sell it as long as Goliath lived, and she couldn't afford to leave it sitting empty, but she had less than zero interest in taking up residence in the place where Howard had died.

"But given my limited options of living in a house where I stumbled upon a murder scene or moving Little Guys to said murder house or leasing it so someone who doesn't mind the gruesome history, renting seems like the way to go. Renting to my best friend and largest source of torment, however, was not what I'd hoped for."

"Ms. Hunter is your tenant? I thought she was strictly Lincoln Park."

"She's 'grown tired of that element,'" Maddie explained in her best Dottie voice.

"She doesn't object to living where her friend was killed?"

"According to her, Howard's ghost will protect her as thanks for catching his killer." Not that Dottie was the one who cracked the case, but the less recognition Maddie got for her naïve and foolhardy attempt at detective work, the better.

"I like Ms. Hunter a lot, but I can't imagine being her landlord. That's got to be, um, interesting."

"So far she's been quiet—a little too quiet if you ask me. I've tried checking in with her, but she hasn't answered my texts or calls. I'm expecting an itemized list of her demands any second now."

"You really think it will be that bad?"

Compared to her, Patrick had known Dottie for roughly a nanosecond, and he wouldn't have to deal with her ridiculous requests, so of course he could indulge his hopefulness.

"I'm anticipating a stipulation for proper grass length or that she'll want the whole house repainted by tomorrow in whatever colors are trending in interior design right now, or she'll tell me her acute sense of smell can still detect traces of Howard's blood so I'll have to replace the floors."

"Maybe she'll surprise you."

"She always does," Maddie said as she slowed with the traffic approaching the end of Lake Shore Drive. "That's what I'm worried about."

She turned onto Sheridan Road and a block and a half later regretted her decision. Both northbound lanes had come to a complete standstill, a not uncommon occurrence on this short stretch of road between Lake Shore Drive and Rogers Park, the neighborhood where she lived and worked. Though it was too late to turn around, and she was too far from a side street to change course, she wasn't worried yet. They'd been making great time, so she didn't think they'd be late. Once the congestion—probably from some considerate driver trying to turn left right next to a moving truck parked in the right lane—cleared, they'd be on their way and meet Harriet with plenty of time to spare.

And then she heard the sirens.

"What now?" she muttered and waited for any indication they would start moving again soon.

CHAPTER TWO

"See anything?" Maddie asked Patrick, who stood on his seat trying to get an idea of what lay ahead of them. Almost a foot taller than Maddie, Patrick's chances of getting an accurate visual far exceeded her own.

"One ambulance, a fire truck, at least four cop cars and absolutely nothing to indicate why they're here." He sank back into his seat, and apparently guided by his unflagging optimism about their chances of moving before Thanksgiving, refastened his seat belt.

"And not one of them can try directing traffic?" She sighed in exasperation.

She wasn't one of the many Chicagoans who viewed the CPD as a mostly necessary evil. The majority of her interactions with the police had been positive (bordering on enjoyable if she focused on the day the stunning Officer Murphy had strolled into her living room), and she was intelligent enough to understand that the entire police force was greater than the sum of its few unsavory parts. At this particular moment, however, she cursed their refusal to do something—anything—to alleviate her suffering.

They'd been stuck for twenty minutes, Maddie watching her generous cushion of time slipping away all the while. The last time they moved was five minutes into their ordeal, when she (oddly proud of her progress) lurched forward half a foot. Since then there hadn't even been cause to hope they would move again, and as the automotive impasse dragged on, she contemplated turning off her car. It didn't look like they'd be getting anywhere anytime soon. Why waste the gas?

"Should you call your sister?"

"Probably." Even if their path were cleared by every car in front of them magically disappearing in the next thirty seconds, they still had no chance of making their appointment on time. Admitting defeat, she groaned and reached for her phone.

Normally, she refused to touch her phone when driving. Nothing was so urgent that it couldn't wait until she pulled over. And for all she knew, she currently sat in vehicular purgatory because some fool thought a call or text was more important than operating the two-ton machine at his disposal. In her present state, however, she was as good as parked. Where was the harm?

"She's never going to let me live this down," she grumbled as she waited for Harriet to pick up.

"I'm walking up to the building right now, and you're ten minutes early. Do not give me grief about being late," Harriet said by way of greeting.

"Considering that we're not there yet and probably won't be for at least half an hour, I wouldn't dare give you a hard time."

"What?" Harriet's sharply barked response rang in her ear, and she imagined that her sister's purposeful stride came to an abrupt halt as she processed this extraordinary information. "You can't be late. You're never late. You were even born early."

"Only by a day."

"Still early."

"Well, if not for the mysterious emergency blocking our path, we would be there already, waiting for you."

"I have to call our sister. She should know about this, maybe start stockpiling canned goods and bottled water. The end times are here."

"You're hilarious. I'm ignoring you now, just so you know."

"That won't get you here any faster."

"Anyway," she set the conversation back on track, "I have no clue how long it's going to take to get out of this mess. You don't happen to have all afternoon to sit around waiting for us, do you?"

"I have about an hour before my next appointment. I could reschedule, but my client can be a little high maintenance."

"Dottie?" She recalled that her best friend had hired Harriet to help her "throw off the yoke" of Lincoln Park.

"You said it, not me."

"If she feels like you're neglecting her, she'll kill us both," Maddie said. "I guess we should just reschedule."

"Actually, now that I'm here looking at this place, I'm thinking we won't need to."

"That bad?" She was almost grateful the traffic jam had saved her from feigning interest in yet another not quite suitable piece of real estate.

"It's just not very you."

"Great. Wasn't that the last vacant building in the neighborhood?"

"I may have one more space." Harriet spoke cautiously.

"You've been holding out on me?" Her voice rose an octave. She attributed her excited tone both to surprise that she somehow hadn't trudged through every abandoned structure on the North Side and relief at the probable end of her quest for property. This building, whatever it was, would almost certainly disappoint her like all its predecessors, and once that was established, she would postpone the search for new headquarters, possibly indefinitely.

"Well, it's a bit of a fixer-upper."

"You sold me my house and have been to it since." Maddie had labored with her father for months to transform a long neglected graystone two-flat into a charming living space, one she took an extra helping of pride in, considering the effort she'd made to resuscitate it. "You know I'm not afraid of a fixer-upper."

"It's also a little…unorthodox."

"Unless it's a bomb shelter or in the center of the lake, I don't care. I just want to find something so I can go back to my regular life."

"Why? Is your laundry piling up?"

"You know I can hire a different realtor, right?" Of course, she would never fire Harriet, but the threat was the only leverage she had in the face of her big sister's teasing.

"And you would regret it," Harriet countered. "Call me if you ever get to leave your car," she said after promising to arrange a showing of her latest architectural offering.

"Don't hold your breath."

"Good news." She turned to Patrick and speaking more brightly than should have been possible when face to face with a wall of immobile vehicles, filled him in on the change of plans. "The rest of the afternoon is ours."

"I guess I'll work on my tan while we wait." Seemingly unfazed by this turn of events (or anything ever), Patrick stretched his arms and let his unperturbed head fall back against the headrest. Maddie didn't want to witness it, but she did wonder if anything ever shook his good mood.

When the cars ahead of them started creeping forward twenty-five minutes later, she allowed herself to feel a glimmer of hope. Little by little they inched toward the source of their protracted ordeal. Several drivers around her blasted their horns in pointless displays of their frustration, but she tried not to succumb further to her irritation. Honking, though it might feel good in the moment, wouldn't get anyone out of there any faster, and she could already feel the dull throb of a fledgling headache. Besides which, it seemed obvious that someone was having a much worse afternoon than she was.

As a rule, she ignored the impulse to examine the scene of an accident as she passed by—they were called gapers' blocks for a reason, and she refused to allow her curiosity to contribute to the delay. But when she and Patrick finally neared the end of the congestion and the source of their ordeal, her eyes scanned the area without her consent (or resistance). She instantly wished she'd had the willpower not to deviate from her normal conduct.

The ambulance and fire truck had left. She didn't remember hearing any sirens, so she hoped this had been a disastrously situated but minor occurrence, at least as far as injuries were concerned. The next sight she took in, however, told her that her proximity to Patrick's optimism had somehow clouded her judgment. A few cop cars remained on the side of the road and in the parking lot of one of the many high-rises along Sheridan. There in the entrance to the lot stood Detective Fitzwilliam—the surly cop who had readily dismissed Maddie's input on Howard's murder investigation—shaking his head and frowning.

In her minimal experience, this was standard for the detective. Though he'd shown a softer side when it came to animals, nothing else about his dour personality could be considered friendly, happy or positive, a morose outlook reflected in his current grim expression. Still, she couldn't help but wonder how much of his obvious lack of cheer was habitual and how much was the result of whatever circumstances brought him here. She didn't know what those circumstances were (though she acknowledged a hint of curiosity), but she knew as sure as Fitzwilliam stood there that she hadn't just endured traffic hell because of a fender bender. Someone had died, and not from a collision.

Suddenly her impatience vanished, replaced by guilt over her own selfishness. How petty to wallow in aggravation over traffic and a missed appointment (one necessitated by her own success) when for someone life had just ended, and for that person's family, a nightmare had just begun.

Not that all that guilt prevented her from rejoicing—in a subdued way—once they escaped the horde of testy drivers.

"Free at last," Patrick whooped.

"And now I get to turn around and take you back home. Unless you want to let me buy you dinner."

"As much as I want to get out of this car, we should probably head back while we have a chance."

"I can't believe you're going to make me keep driving." She longed for even the tiniest break from the driver's seat. She was starting to hate her car, and if she didn't get away from it soon, she would renounce driving forever.

"Sorry, boss, but what are the odds that we'll have to sit through another hour-long traffic jam?"

"A lot higher now that you said that," she grumbled and headed back toward his neighborhood.

As it turned out, the drive back to Patrick's apartment was blessedly incident free, and aside from the usual trouble areas, she encountered almost no traffic (by Chicago standards). The whole trip took under forty minutes, and as she neared her home, visions of a relaxing evening with her dogs—a strong drink, a good book and maybe a bubble bath (if she could tire the dogs out enough that Goliath would allow her some privacy)—danced in her head. She wanted nothing more than to unwind for a while and then fall into bed.

Unfortunately, the universe hadn't finished toying with her yet. There in front of her garage sat a tow truck, its flashing yellow lights sending the message that she would never get home, not as long as the burly gentleman chatting on his phone and not doing his job continued obstructing her path with his giant vehicle. He didn't look like he'd be receptive to a friendly toot of her horn (not that she trusted herself to keep it friendly this late in her exasperating day), so she didn't even bother trying to get past him.

"I quit," she sighed, backing out of the alley and continuing to her street. So close to the peace and comfort she craved, she was forced to retreat and hunt for street parking, which she found two blocks away.

Trudging up the sidewalk in front of her house, she glanced up at the normally welcome sight and wanted to cry. There on her front steps sat Dr. Nadia Sheridan, the cause of her most recent broken heart. The adorable puppy at Nadia's feet alternately chewed on her leash and barked at leaves (reminding her that she needed to devote part of her Sunday to yardwork). Although she'd been dreaming of nothing but getting home since the traffic jam that wouldn't end, she now wished she was still trapped in a sea of unmoving cars.

Nadia looked up, locked eyes with her and smiled her irresistible lopsided smile.

"A perfect ending to a perfect day." Maddie sighed and dragged herself the rest of the way home.

CHAPTER THREE

"We didn't think you were ever coming home."

Nadia stayed rooted to Maddie's steps, and Maddie had an inkling that (improbable as it seemed) Nadia was nervous. She looked apprehensive but fantastic nevertheless. Not that she was surprised. When had she ever seen Nadia looking anything less than gorgeous? A quality she'd enjoyed in the past but found annoying at the moment.

"I really wish I hadn't," she muttered.

She'd spent weeks hoping for any contact from Nadia since she walked away from their zygote of a relationship, but today was not the day she wanted to do this. Tired and cranky, her defenses were down. Still, if they didn't talk now, who knew if they ever would? How much time would pass before Nadia felt like showing up again?

While she was in no mood to deal with the human half of her surprise visitors (no matter what the floaty feeling in her stomach had to say about it), she couldn't be expected to overlook a puppy, especially not one as precious as the creature occupying her front steps. Chances were good that Nadia understood that and had planned accordingly.

"You must be Mabel." Maddie squatted in front of the gangly gray canine, ignoring Nadia completely, a feat made next to impossible by the intoxicating aroma of Dr. Nadia Sheridan (and there went that stomach flutter again). "It's nice to meet you, Mabel."

Maddie stuck out her hand, and Mabel placed an oversized paw in her palm, executing a perfect shake before licking her chin. "You are so smart." She scratched behind Mabel's floppy ears and was rewarded with more licking. "And much more well-behaved than your father."

In defiance of almost two months of training, Goliath still refused to move beyond the basics: sit, stay, come. At times his willful nature prevented him from giving Maddie even that much. The one command he obeyed without fail was roll over, which he performed with gusto, often repeatedly and without being asked, before bounding over to her for his reward.

"What I'm wondering, Mabel, is what you and your friend over there are doing at my house. Because somebody asked for time to think about things, then disappeared for two and a half months." The puppy kept licking her face, making speech (and anger) a challenge, but she pressed on. "Last I heard, we don't really have the kind of relationship where we drop in on one another unannounced." Though they might have by then, had Nadia not walked away.

"You're not happy to see me?"

She favored Nadia with an irritated glance. "It's been a long day made a thousand times longer by a stranger's death."

"Are you going to investigate?" Nadia smiled as if to say she was joking, but Maddie glared at her for an eternity, watching as Nadia's jovial expression withered.

"I don't know. Are you going to tell me you had a clandestine connection to the deceased?"

Nadia blanched, and Maddie instantly felt awful for reminding her of her peripheral role in Howard's death.

"I'm sorry. I'm exhausted, and I wasn't expecting company. Did you need something?"

"I need to talk to you."

"Now? You've had two and a half months, and you chose the worst day since the last day I saw you to talk to me?"

"I'm sorry if this is a bad time, but you're not the only one who's been taken by surprise lately."

"What does that mean?"

"You had Goliath's records sent to your vet's office."

"He was sick."

"What was wrong?" Nadia instantly flipped into concerned vet mode, reminding Maddie of why she'd been so drawn to Dr. Sheridan (beyond the physical). "Was it serious?"

"Nothing a little boiled chicken and potatoes couldn't fix." She wanted to stay mad, but damn it, Nadia's concern for Goliath softened her resolve.

"Why didn't you warn me?"

"You asked for space."

"Not from Goliath."

"Just from me, then."

"That's not what I meant."

"What did you mean?"

Nadia, looking meek (and somehow managing to be even more attractive in her contrition), gazed at her from under a furrowed brow. "I missed you."

She jingled her keys for a moment, considering what to do. Before she realized she'd made up her mind, she unlocked the door and held it open. "You might as well come in," she said to a grinning Nadia.

Once inside, they were ambushed by Goliath and Bart, Maddie's rescued mutt, who rushed to greet and inspect the recent arrivals. After much hearty butt sniffing, excessive yowling and gleeful leaping, a spirited and vocal game of chase inspired her to banish all three dogs to her yard. With any luck, Mabel would exhaust the boys before she and Nadia left, getting Maddie one step closer to her peaceful evening.

In her kitchen as she waited for the dogs to settle down enough to come back inside, she took another step toward that relaxation and poured herself a drink. Part of her wanted to exclude Nadia from cocktail hour, but the good manners instilled by her parents and Granny Doyle forced her to at least make the offer.

"Can I get you a drink?"

"Not if it has to be that." Nadia wrinkled her nose and gestured to the bottle of bourbon in Maddie's hand.

"I have plenty of lightweight options. Can you be more specific?" she snapped and then cringed when she saw Nadia's wide-eyed, fearful expression. She turned guiltily away and, under the pretense of letting the dogs back in, made her apology to her back door. "I'm sorry. It's been a long, exhausting, horrible day."

"So you said."

"I just want to take care of my dogs, have a drink, and go to bed."

Nadia looked concerned and beguiling simultaneously. Her mouth quirked up in a lopsided half smile (the same smile that had hooked Maddie initially) while her eyebrows dipped and her brow furrowed. She hated how good Nadia looked almost as much as she hated her visceral reaction to the beautiful Dr. Sheridan.

"You don't have to do any of that alone," Nadia said.

"You can't be serious," she said despite the tightening of her stomach at Nadia's words.

"Let me take care of the dogs while you get comfortable. Take a bath, finish your drink, whatever you need. Just take care of yourself while the pups and I go for a walk."

"Really?"

"Is half an hour long enough?" She nodded, already dreaming of time in the tub without a hundred and thirty pound dog trying to join her. "Maybe when I get back, we can have a drink and talk."

She nodded again and moved to get the boys' leashes, but Nadia stopped her, a soft hand on her arm. Her skin tingled beneath the warmth of Nadia's fingers, and she kicked herself for her body's predictably traitorous response. All of this was a bad idea—possibly her worst since driving into the heart of a traffic jam—but she convinced herself that she could handle it, that contrary to her entire history with Nadia, this time she would maintain her composure in the face of Nadia's considerable charm.

"I've got it," she said, and as soon as she had the leashes in her hand, she was besieged by dancing, eager canines, who guided her (perhaps a bit too enthusiastically) out the door.

Wasting no time, she dashed to her bathroom. She hadn't had the opportunity to soak away her stress since becoming a dog mother of two, and though she didn't have long, more than five uninterrupted minutes in the bath was a gift not to be dismissed. She didn't even wait for the tub to fill before climbing in.

She sank in sighing contentment as the hot, bubbly water rose around her. Ideally, she'd have her drink and a book to complete the basking experience, but after a day like the one she'd had, the mere thought of being alone in her bathroom soothed her. Considering that she could barely clean the bathtub without sparking Goliath's interest in a bath, she realized she might not have another opportunity like this for years.

Sighing again, she glanced at her watch before letting her head rest against the back of the tub. She didn't want to lose track of time and have Nadia walk in on her in a compromising position (among other things, she doubted that would help her maintain the aloof detachment she longed for in this scenario), but the more relaxed she felt, the more her thoughts drifted to Nadia.

For weeks, she'd wanted nothing more than to see Nadia, but now that she'd shown up, she wasn't sure she wanted to hear what Nadia had to say. If she came to officially let her know what she'd surmised by week four of silence—that Nadia wasn't interested in seeing her anymore—she could handle it. It would be one more dismal event in an already brutal afternoon, but she would get through it.

But if Nadia had returned to say she wanted to try again, Maddie didn't know if that was any better. Nadia's disappearance had hurt and wouldn't taking her back send the wrong message? Didn't it say, "Abandon me whenever things get rough, and I'll just be waiting right here for you?" She wasn't sure what she wanted, but she had no desire to say that. Ultimately, though, knowing where they stood would be better than living with the constant, miserable wondering.

Her emotional quandary momentarily settled, she checked her watch again and settled in to enjoy the remaining eighteen minutes of blissful solitude.

"Sugar pie? Honey bunch?" Dottie's voice rang out. "I know you're home because your door was unlocked."

"This cannot be happening." Maddie sat upright, hoping she was hearing things. She hadn't been expecting Dottie, so of course she should have expected her.

"Where are you?"

"I'm in the bath," she called, knowing her chances of evading Dottie were nonexistent.

She was about to call out that she would be right out when Dottie burst through the door. So much for her relaxing alone time.

"Where are your beasts?"

"Please, Dottie, come in. I wasn't doing anything private."

Dottie dismissed her comment with a flutter of her fingers.

"The dogs are out," she explained.

"Out? What? Did they make a run for snacks?"

"They're on a walk."

"By themselves? Goliath's training must really be paying off." Dottie draped Maddie's towel over the toilet and perched delicately on it.

Maddie almost said, "Don't be ridiculous," but then she remembered who she was talking to.

"They're with Nadia." She attempted to sound casual and failed completely.

"Nadia?" Dottie shrieked. "The illustrious Dr. Sheridan has returned?" Her eyebrows rose to astronomical heights as she took in Maddie's bubble-strewn repose. "Well, well, well. The good doctor does move fast."

"She's here to talk. That's all," Maddie huffed.

"Of course, doll."

She rolled her eyes and sank lower in the tub since it seemed like her best friend had decided to make this an extended visit. Though she really wanted Dottie to clear out before Nadia returned with the dogs, it didn't seem likely she would get her way. Her bath had gone from relaxing to stressful in under a minute.

"Has your bathroom always been this large?" Dottie scrutinized the room.

"Uh-huh," she said, trying to calculate her odds of grabbing a new towel without giving Dottie a peepshow.

"You've never moved any walls?"

"Nope."

"Impressive square footage." Dottie rose and turned in a full circle.

"Thank you." Considering how frequently Dottie had used her bathroom in the past, Maddie wasn't sure what to make of her sudden interest in its layout.

"How difficult is it to make a bathroom larger?"

"For you? I wouldn't recommend it. Why?"

"You know my unquenchable thirst for knowledge knows no boundaries." Dottie moved to the doorway to study the woodwork.

Taking the opportunity provided by Dottie's diverted attention, Maddie stepped out of the tub and grabbed her towel. She wanted to put some clothes on before Nadia came back to an unbelievably awkward scene, but as with everything else in her life that day, fate thwarted her simple desire to be dressed when she next saw Nadia. Towel in hand but otherwise exposed, she froze when bath-crazed Goliath charged in. Nadia, tethered to the strong and willful Great Dane, followed immediately behind despite the protests from Bart, who avoided the bathroom at all costs (unless he was bound to someone being dragged there by his larger, stronger brother). All eyes turned to Maddie, who stood there, stunned and dripping. She didn't even have the presence of mind to cover herself with the towel she held.

The tiny functioning portion of her brain registered Nadia's satisfied grin before she averted her eyes and removed herself and the dogs to give Maddie some privacy. That was at least as gratifying as the experience was embarrassing. Dottie, however, didn't even flinch at her friend's nudity, but she latched on to her first brief glimpse of Nadia.

"That's your former?" she cooed as she took control and wrapped Maddie's towel around her. "I'm impressed, sugar lips. The doctor is definitely in."

"The doctor is here to talk, probably to clarify what a huge mistake she made by ever dating me." Doubting that Dottie would suddenly offer her privacy, Maddie gave up waiting and started dressing. She hadn't finished pulling her favorite soft T-shirt over her head when Dottie gasped.

"You're wearing that?"

"Just until I can get to my collection of ball gowns," she deadpanned. "Of course I'm wearing this."

"I can't allow that." She stared at her friend, eyebrows raised but saying nothing. "You can't possibly re-woo the love doctor in a worn-out undershirt."

"First, I don't know if I'm interested in re-wooing her, and second, she just saw me completely naked. I think my fashion choices have become irrelevant at this point."

"I can't abide such blasphemy, but you may have a point."

"Can I finish dressing now?"

"By all means. I'll go keep your lady friend company." Dottie started out the door. "And do something about your hair. Do you even own a brush?"

She scowled, but a glance in the mirror told her Dottie was right. Wisps of hair had escaped from her braid as she drove around the city, and now they stuck out from her head like frail red-brown tentacles. Windswept was not a good look for her.

Knowing the futility of her actions, nevertheless she attacked her hair with a brush, cringing as it grew larger, frizzier and more unruly with every pass through. Not even an industrial strength hair tie could salvage her rebellious mane. Her only recourse would be to wash it and start over.

Understanding the risk she took by leaving Dottie alone with Nadia for any length of time, Maddie embarked on the fastest grooming known to humanity. In under ten minutes, she washed and mostly dried her hair, making it resemble something close to a civilized and well-groomed human's head of hair.

Now all she had to do was get rid of Dottie (while keeping Dottie in the dark about being ousted), implement Dottie damage control with Nadia and hear Nadia out (without breaking down in either tears or wanton abandon) before she could go to bed and put this rotten day behind her. How hard could it be?

CHAPTER FOUR

Maddie wasn't sure what to make of the scene she found when she finally emerged from the bathroom (clean but no less frazzled than when she'd entered) and stepped into her living room. Bart, Goliath, and Mabel had curled up in a furry mass that spilled over the edges of Goliath's king-size dog bed. She'd given up trying to place the boys' beds close together since they always rejected the second bed in favor of crowding into one. She didn't understand it, but she thanked the gods of dog care that her pups got along so well.

Adjacent to the pile of snoring canines, Dottie had draped herself across Maddie's couch, lounging in her default seductress way. She divided her attention between the half-consumed cocktail she'd helped herself to and an anxious but politely attentive Nadia, who sat on the opposite end of the couch listening to one of Dottie's tales of high society. A mostly untouched glass of wine sat on the coffee table in front of Nadia, and Maddie offered silent thanks that Dottie had been such a gracious host with Maddie's booze.

An easy grin replaced Nadia's former neutral expression when she saw Maddie. It was entirely possible that her elevated mood sprang more from an end to alone time with Dottie than the pleasure of seeing Maddie, but she chose to interpret it in the more favorable light of delight at her presence. Maybe she would ask—if Dottie ever left, and if she got a sudden infusion of boldness.

On her way to the kitchen to freshen her drink and mix the next round for Dottie (who would pout mercilessly if she suspected Maddie of neglecting her refreshment needs), she grabbed her ringing phone. She groaned when she saw who was calling but answered anyway. It wasn't like her night could get any weirder or worse.

"Mavis, hi. It's Lester Parrish. You remember me, right?"

How could she forget? She'd met Howard's niggling, busybody neighbor shortly after Howard's death. Ever since he found out that she'd inherited Goliath (and by extension, his former house), Lester had taken to calling her regularly "to keep her up-to-date" on the neighborhood goings-on. Ignoring his calls merely increased their frequency and his worry, so leaving the work of dealing with Lester to her voice mail was not an option. Nor was quickly terminating the call. She barely had the opportunity to say anything after "Hello," so she had zero hope of ever telling him she had to go. Or her real name. Not that she wanted to cultivate a closer relationship with him.

"I was out for my evening constitutional…You know how I love to walk. It's so beneficial, especially on such a lovely evening. Can you believe what gorgeous weather we've been having? I thought those weathermen were all wrong when they said a high in the sixties—and who could blame me for that? They give an accurate weather forecast about as often as the city of Chicago operates under budget. But I guess they got it right for once."

Why couldn't he ever just get to the point? Three weeks earlier he'd called to inform her of "activity at Howard's house" (which she already knew about thanks to signing Dottie's lease just that morning), but it took him twenty minutes to get around to telling her since, as usual, he'd taken the scenic route to his point. And, figuring he'd take another lengthy detour, she'd tuned out again immediately after his big revelation. She hoped she would escape this call with at least a portion of her rapidly dwindling patience still intact.

Cautiously optimistic, she turned her attention back to Lester's endless stream of words. He seemed to be wrapping up his praise of the weather, which meant he might make sense of his call in record time. Or he might be getting his second wind.

"I couldn't help but keep going, much farther than usual. I mean, there's healthy, and then there's extreme, right Mavis?" With no pause for breath or an answer from Maddie, Lester pushed forward. "That's when I noticed the trouble at your little store—such a cute place. I love your logo."

"What trouble, Lester?" She forced her way in.

"The break-in."

"What?" she shrieked. The room started to spin, and she leaned heavily against the kitchen counter.

"Attempted break-in. I was across the street and saw someone pulling and pounding on the door. I yelled, 'They're closed,' but no one listens anymore. It's like there's a law against common courtesy. Anyway, the racket continued, so I ran home to call you—no sense calling the police. You know how they are."

"Thank you, Lester. I'll take care of it," she said with a calm in direct opposition to her racing heart and shaking hands, and then she hung up on poor Lester.

"I have to go," she told her guests as soon as she ended the call.

"What's wrong?" Dottie asked.

"Someone's trying to break into Little Guys." She grabbed her keys and headed for the door.

"Who breaks into a dog walking business? Someone in dire need of Snausages?" Dottie huffed.

"Or someone who wants easy access to all of my clients' homes."

"Do you keep the keys there?" Nadia asked, realization dawning.

She nodded. "They're locked up, but it's not Fort Knox, and my clients' addresses are all right there in my records. Put the two together and—"

"It's a cleverly planned criminal free-for-all," Dottie jumped in, her excitement obviously getting the better of her. "But you can't confront the Milk-Bone Bandit alone. I won't hear of it."

"I'll be fine, Dottie. It's probably just some drunk college kids." Maddie rushed toward the door, but her minimal progress terminated when Dottie seized her arm.

"Or it's a lunatic with a machete waiting for a willing victim to behead."

She exchanged a bewildered expression with Nadia but couldn't even begin to produce a response.

"You should take backup. I'm sure Nadia would love to be your bodyguard." Dottie thrust an unsuspecting Nadia toward her. The twinkle in Dottie's eye announced that her matchmaking tendencies refused to be tamed by inopportune timing.

"Nadia has to stay with Mabel." Maddie's already distraught mind swam with the potential wreckage the puppy version of Goliath could inflict on her home. "Unless you're volunteering to dog sit while we're gone."

Maddie's glance swept the length of Dottie's designer-clad body, painful-looking stilettos included, and she knew her friend had popped by on her way to more fruitful pursuits. No way would she be content to spend a Saturday evening monitoring a puppy's activities and intervening on behalf of Maddie's décor instead of roping in a new rich suitor.

"I would but—"

"I don't have time to sort this out." Maddie interrupted whatever excuse her friend was about to offer. "Lock up when you leave," she said to Dottie. She barely registered Nadia's concerned expression before hurrying out the door.

Living within walking distance of her business meant the drive there took under three minutes. At that time of night, especially on a Saturday, parking could be an issue, but she found a relatively close spot right away. It wasn't until that moment that she allowed Dottie's concerns to give her pause.

Blind panic had driven her out the door, but really, she had no idea what she was about to rush into. It would have been safer (and considerably wiser) to call the police. They handled situations like this all the time, and no matter what disparaging remarks Lester Parrish made, the Chicago Police were far better equipped to deal with whatever lay waiting for her. Barring the sensible approach, she really should have taken Dottie's suggestion not to show up alone. Cleaning up after the destructive antics of a bored, unsupervised puppy would be preferable to dying at the hands of a criminal mastermind caught in the act. Though the odds of coming face-to-face with a machete-wielding purloiner of pet care supplies seemed infinitesimal at best, she could be on the verge of an unpleasant and dangerous encounter. Maybe she would find drunk college students assaulting her business, or maybe it was something more nefarious. Either way, she was there now—alone and with no way to defend herself—and was about to find out.

She rushed toward her livelihood, and that's when the day's latest surprise hit her. Crouching by the thankfully undamaged front door, her head resting against the glass, sat Maddie's client and old friend Leigh Matthews.

"Leigh?"

Her friend's head bobbed up at the sound of her name. Though the dim light of the half moon and the nearby streetlamps didn't offer Maddie a clear picture of the woman sprawled in front of her business, it was enough to know that Leigh looked terrible. For one thing, she was too skinny. Leigh had never carried extra weight to begin with, but now her clothes hung loosely from her frame. She seemed frail and gaunt, more like a fading image of her former self.

Instead of styling her hair in the fun, product-heavy ordered chaos that sometimes made her look like a brunette dandelion, Leigh had covered it with a ball cap, making Maddie question if she'd even bothered to wash it recently. Dark circles had blossomed under Leigh's eyes since the last time Maddie saw her, and when she wasn't drawing in shuddering, sorrowful breaths, she was muttering something to herself.

"What are you doing here?" she asked gently and squatted near the crying and (based on the powerful aroma wafting from Leigh's general vicinity) drunk woman. "Is everything all right?"

"I'm here about the story," Leigh slurred, and Maddie wondered how far gone she was. "I need to read the story again. I need help."

"What kind of help? Is Rufus okay?" Her thoughts instantly flew to Leigh's French bulldog Rufus, a loveable little comedian and one of her favorite dogs to walk.

"He's fine. He's good. He loves me. He's a good boy." Leigh smiled, her tears abating for the moment.

"Yes, he is."

"He doesn't think I killed anyone, but I need to see the story again and get help."

"What? What story, Leigh? Who thinks you killed someone?"

"The police." Leigh sighed. "They keep asking me questions, and I keep telling them I didn't do anything to that stupid hatchet-faced lady stealer, even if I wanted to. And now," Leigh heaved another sigh as her tears started up again. "Now Lindsey's gone, and I have no one. But you can help me. You've done it before. I saw the story when I was here last time."

She groaned as at least part of Leigh's ramblings began to make sense. Undoubtedly, she was referring to the oversized framed copy of the newspaper article about Maddie's brief foray into sleuthing. Maddie hated it, hated its prominence and the reminder that she'd ever been foolish enough to pretend to be a private investigator. But Dottie had specially ordered it for her and hired a handyman to hang it. She'd even visited Little Guys headquarters to oversee the proper placement of her gift, so Maddie couldn't get rid of it without the risk of unleashing the Wrath of Dottie.

So there it hung, drawing every kind of unwanted attention, including (if she understood the current situation correctly) requests for her questionable detective skills. That was not happening again.

"You can fix this for me. Show the police I didn't do it."

"Leigh, I'm no detective."

"But I saw—"

"I was incredibly stupid and got extremely lucky. I can't help you, Leigh. I'm sorry."

"I've got no one left, Mads. I don't know what to do." Leigh dropped her head into her hands and wept, and Maddie's heart broke at the sight of her friend's pain.

"Why don't we start by getting you home?" she said and guided Leigh toward her Jeep. She didn't know what else this day had in store for her, but she knew she was in for a long night.

CHAPTER FIVE

Rufus greeted them eagerly, his small body a tawny blur as he raced around their feet and spun in excited circles. His sharp barks pierced the air, and Maddie suspected he would benefit from a good walk. Doubting that Leigh was up to the task since she'd barely been able to walk herself, Maddie took him for a quick trip around the block. She hoped she would come back to find a somewhat more collected version of her friend with an explanation that would make sense.

What she found instead was Leigh at her dining room table, crying and nursing a beer Maddie would have discouraged her from opening. The last thing this situation needed was less coherence. A vision of the remainder of the night unfolded, and she felt certain it would be a long, frustrating, unproductive affair.

"Tell me what's going on, Leigh," she said once Leigh's weeping tapered off into an intermittent stream of tears.

"I'm in trouble."

Based on the evidence strewn about the normally tidy house, evidence of one hell of a bender, she would have to agree with Leigh's assessment. But sitting across the table from her friend, who sniffled while absentmindedly stroking Rufus, Maddie needed the specifics. What had driven her friend to this state of despondency?

"What happened?"

"I don't know where to start." Leigh ran her fingers through her hair and dropped her gaze.

Maddie exhaled loudly, her frustration getting the better of her. As much as she wanted to help her friend, Leigh wasn't making it easy. Desperate to get to the point before her next birthday, she latched on to one of Leigh's more jarring comments from earlier.

"Who do the police think you killed?"

"Terry."

She had no idea who Terry was, but before she could continue her plodding interrogation with an impatiently worded question, Leigh clarified. "A former friend. The woman Lindsey left me for."

Maddie remembered the shock, confusion, and anger she'd felt when Leigh's partner of six years had jettisoned their ostensibly happy life to pursue a different relationship. Leigh had come home from work one day to find a loaded moving van at the curb and Lindsey's children from her first marriage, whom Leigh had loved and raised as her own since they were three and four years old, weeping in the front seat. The only explanation Lindsey had offered was that she'd grown too content and wanted something else. Leigh had been understandably devastated.

She hated that Leigh was reliving that pain, but at least now they were getting somewhere. Not far or fast but somewhere. At this rate she might learn what was going on by the end of next week. Over the next twenty minutes (during which Leigh finished her drink and, despite Maddie's protests, stumbled into the kitchen for another unnecessary round), Maddie learned that about a week and a half earlier Terry had died under suspicious circumstances. Not long after, the cops had called on Leigh for the first of many visits, asking about EpiPens and Leigh's whereabouts on the date in question.

"What about the EpiPen?" She interrupted Leigh's meandering drunken narrative.

"Anyone with Internet access and half a brain could tamper with an EpiPen," Leigh offered a partial explanation. "But since I'm a pharmacist with nothing but hatred for that no-neck, hatchet-faced home wrecker, I'm an obvious suspect. Never mind that I kept my distance from the she-beast—I didn't want to look at her butt face when we were friends. That didn't change after she tore my family apart. I certainly wasn't about to bake her brownies, even if they would kill her."

Leigh was getting worked up, but at least information was forthcoming. It didn't entirely make sense, but she crossed her fingers for clarity before dawn.

"Brownies?"

"Someone gave the hag with severe peanut allergies one of my special brownies."

Leigh's peanut butter chocolate chip brownies were legendary. Almost every young woman in their dorm (including Maddie) had been brought back from the brink of heartbreak by Leigh's brownies. They cured hangovers and fueled frantic cramming for finals. Their medicinal properties rivaled Granny Doyle's no-raisin oatmeal cookies, and Leigh reserved them for special occasions or extreme circumstances. While murder would certainly fall under the heading "Extreme Circumstances," she believed the brownies would only be used for good, not evil.

"But it wasn't me. The last time I made them was when Lindsey *married* that…thing."

"Who else could have made them?"

"Anyone. It's not like I kept the recipe a secret."

That was true. She had a copy though she rarely used it. The brownies tasted better when they came from Leigh's need to lift someone's spirits.

"I didn't do it, Maddie. I never even went near her."

Maddie believed her. Leigh was too kind, gentle, and generous to ever hurt someone, even if that person had hurt her. She had known Leigh since her freshman year of college when a rare stroke of good luck had paired them up as roommates in Sargent Hall. She would never believe that the young woman who had shown her around campus, introduced her to friends and helped her survive her first year of college had grown up to be a cold-blooded killer of philandering debauchers.

However, she also understood how things looked from a law enforcement perspective. Unless Leigh had an irrefutable alibi, she made the perfect suspect, and the police had little reason to doubt her guilt.

"I don't know what I'm going to do, Maddie." Leigh's voice cracked as the tears that had dried up came rushing back. "And now that Lindsey's dead, I've got no one," she wailed and then dropped her head into her hands.

"Wait." Maddie's head spun at her friend's most recent bombshell. "What happened to Lindsey?"

"She killed herself," Leigh managed to choke out before breaking down completely.

Not knowing what else to do, she gently rubbed Leigh's back and waited for another sodden, piecemeal revelation.

Eventually she learned that Lindsey's ex-husband had sued for custody of the kids. "I guess he didn't like Terry any more than I did." Leigh laughed bitterly. "With the drawn-out legal battle and Terry's death, I guess Lindsey just gave up. She jumped off her balcony."

"When?"

"This afternoon."

"Oh god," Maddie gasped, impossible suspicion dawning. Though she knew it was not the best time to press for details, she had to reassure herself that she was leaping to ridiculous conclusions. "Where did she live?"

"One of those high-rises on Sheridan."

"Oh god," Maddie said again.

"Her note said she couldn't face life without her loves. I guess that doesn't include me." Leigh sniffed and then began wailing in earnest.

As Maddie tried to console her friend, she realized that, peripheral though the connection might be, she had somehow ended up linked to another untimely and violent death. On top of that, she knew her friend was in real trouble.

What she didn't know was what she planned to do about it.

CHAPTER SIX

For a brief, beautiful moment upon waking the next morning, Maddie let herself believe that the events of the last eighteen hours had been a particularly vivid nightmare, that her Saturday hadn't gone down in flames, leaving her exhausted and apprehensive about the calamities that might befall her in the days ahead. She didn't question that her uptick in misfortune would last longer than a day. Once the turmoil started, it would keep coming and probably increase. Just the thought of dealing with the unholy mess that would likely unfurl in the coming days made her want to stay in bed for the foreseeable future.

Of course, not all of her Saturday had been dreadful—given the option to relive the last twenty-four hours, she would keep the weather. It seemed Mother Nature agreed. Goading her into meteorological optimism, the early morning sun peeked through her window, filling her head with visions of another wonderful day, at least as far as the temperature was concerned. But not even the prospect of late-season climatic perfection inspired within her a desire to get up.

Then there was the other not entirely awful scrap of her day—Nadia. Reluctantly, she admitted that, after the shock and anger abated, seeing her ex again had been an unexpected highlight. She found herself regretting the abrupt end to their incomplete conversation (and not only because of the decided downturn the evening had taken from that point). If it had ended there, her bad day would have been only somewhat irritating, a designation she happily would have accepted.

But as the fog of too little sleep lifted (aided by a pained sigh from Goliath, who rested his chin on her pillow, favoring her with a warm, steady, kibble-scented breeze on the side of her face), the bleak reality of the previous day descended on her. Her life truly had gone from mildly frustrating to disturbingly chaotic in a matter of just a few hours, and no matter how hard she wished she hadn't, she knew she really had spent the better part of her night comforting her hysterical friend, even while the details of Leigh's story made comfort seem like an impossible dream.

Worse, the more Leigh drank, the stronger her conviction grew that Maddie alone could magically fix her life by finding the real killer and proving her innocence. Maddie doubted Leigh could come up with a worse solution to her problems, but Leigh refused to believe her. She had more or less successfully evaded Leigh's begging the night before—every time Leigh had pleaded with her to search for the truth, she had changed the subject, a typically fruitful strategy made considerably more trying by Leigh's unrelenting hounding. Though she'd escaped her company without acquiescing to her endless requests, she didn't imagine that sobriety and the harsh light of day would prevent her from asking again. Maddie needed a strategy other than avoidance.

Goliath sighed again, and her hair fluttered across her face in the gust of his hot dog breath. When the normally patient Bart added a pathetic whine to the mix, she knew she couldn't loiter much longer. The boys had taken umbrage with her last night when she arrived home too late to take them on their customary nighttime walk around the neighborhood. Apparently taking grudge-holding lessons from their Aunt Dottie, they seemed no closer to forgiving her now. The doubt and judgment she read in their eyes made her momentarily question her qualifications as their guardian.

It was barely seven o'clock, and already the day felt endless.

After a quick text to let Dottie know she hadn't succumbed to a homicidal lunatic, she leashed her dogs and headed out the door. As she expected, the boys steered her to the beach (their favorite place on earth), and as they romped and frolicked and explored, her thoughts again drifted to the story Leigh shared the previous night. Certainly, her friend needed help, and Maddie would provide whatever support she could, short of volunteering to incur the wrath of the police again by interfering with another of their investigations. Not that she could offer much in the way of interference. Even if she wanted to look into Terry's death, she had no idea where to begin. She had a thousand questions but no answers.

Leigh said that Terry's peanut allergy and a faulty EpiPen had caused her death. Maddie's own allergies made her both shudder at the thought of death by anaphylaxis and praise the angels of affliction that shellfish could more easily be avoided than peanuts. Her own chances of such a wretched demise seemed minimal by comparison. But did Leigh have the facts right? More than once last night she had teetered across the line of incoherence. If that wasn't enough to call her claims into question, she hadn't been arrested. Surely if the police thought her guilty they would have acted by now. It was entirely likely that Leigh was jumping to paranoid conclusions about Terry's death based on the questions from the police.

If she was right, though, then the killer had to have been acquainted with Terry well enough to know about her allergy and have access to her autoinjector. How was Maddie to know who, in a metropolitan area of roughly ten million people, that could be? She had never even met the deceased, so she didn't have a clue who knew Terry and hated her enough to want her dead. Other than Leigh.

Her head spun from contemplating just that small aspect of Leigh's situation, and as the boys raced toward her, their feet and bellies caked in wet sand, a cluster of four or five equally beach-coated pups surrounding them, she reaffirmed her belief that this was a matter best left to the police.

Nevertheless, thoughts of Leigh and the tragedy that surrounded her plagued Maddie. She didn't have an inordinate amount of spare time on her hands—on top of laundry, housework, yardwork, and a run, assuming her schedule and the elements cooperated long enough to squeeze one in, she still wanted to talk to Dottie (while neither one of them was in a compromising position). The sooner she addressed whatever home improvement demands Dottie had in store, the better. And then Granny Doyle expected her for dinner promptly at six. Still, she thought she could spare a few moments to see what information the Internet had to offer about Terry and Lindsey—just to satisfy her curiosity. She could call Leigh for more details, but she didn't want to risk reigniting her campaign for an extreme amateur detective to solve her troubles.

When they'd been at the beach for almost an hour, Maddie attempted yet again to clear her mind of thoughts of Leigh. Deciding it was time to go home, she called Bart and Goliath to her and was pleasantly surprised that Goliath, who was about fifty-fifty on "come," actually loped toward her on her first attempt to retrieve the boys from their fun. As she leashed them again, both boys, their tongues hanging out as they happily panted, favored her with loving glances—the kind that dogs seem to specialize in and made pet parenthood especially rewarding. If she accomplished nothing else that day, at least she knew she had earned her dogs' forgiveness.

Back home, she hadn't gotten through the door when her cell phone rang. It was too early for Dottie to be awake, so she knew it wouldn't be her best friend on the hunt for the details of her ordeal. Though she hadn't anticipated this call either, it wasn't an entirely unpleasant surprise.

"At least I know you weren't dismembered, decapitated or disemboweled," Nadia said.

"I think you may have spent too much time with Dottie last night," she replied, startled by the vivid imagery.

"She doesn't lack for imagination. Even so, I was worried about you."

"You didn't need to be."

"Yes, I did. Maybe you've forgotten, but the last time you ran off to confront a bad guy, you didn't fare so well."

"I haven't forgotten." Short of an amnesia-causing blow to the head, she didn't think she'd ever forget confronting Howard's killer. "But I'm fine. Really. There was nothing even close to dangerous last night."

"Good. I'd hate if anything happened to you," Nadia said, her tone softening. "Especially since I never got to say what I wanted to say last night."

She smiled in spite of herself. She thought she might still be angry at Nadia and didn't want to give in so easily, but she liked hearing that Nadia had worried.

"I'm listening now," she said, both hoping and dreading to hear what Nadia had to tell her.

"I'd prefer to say it in person, maybe tonight over dinner?"

That didn't sound like the prelude to a let's just be friends speech, but she didn't know if that would be better or worse than an official clean break with Nadia. Fortunately, she didn't have to decide at that moment. She had an out.

"I already have plans tonight."

"A date?" Nadia asked, sounding far more insecure than she would have ever thought possible.

"Technically," she said, savoring the slight edge she had. It wasn't often (or ever) that a beautiful woman fretted over her availability.

"Oh." Nadia's dejected response hung in the air for a moment, and she almost regretted toying with her. "I'd still like to see you sometime, even if you're not totally available." That was a twist she hadn't expected.

"I'm seeing my grandmother tonight."

"Oh," Nadia said again, more brightly. "I like your grandmother."

"You've never met her."

"True, but she encouraged you to go out with me before." Unnecessarily, Maddie recalled. "Maybe she'll do it again, possibly even for dinner tomorrow."

"With Granny, anything's possible."

She knew Nadia expected a more definite answer, but at the moment semi-flirtatious uncertainty was the best she could offer. She had too many other concerns competing for her attention to devote more than a few perplexed and doubtful thoughts to Nadia's reemergence.

By the time she made it to her grandmother's house, she had managed to waste close to two hours on a futile search for more information about Leigh's supposed life of crime. While a quick Internet search confirmed the ease with which an EpiPen could be transformed from a life-saving tool into a utensil of death, she still knew next to nothing about the mysterious Terry or who would want her dead.

She wasn't sure what to make of her frustrating lack of success. On the one hand, she hated not having answers to her questions, but on the other hand, she thought it might be a good thing that this murder wasn't more high profile. The last thing Leigh needed was to be branded with some sordid nickname (like the Fatal Pharmacist) that she couldn't shake even after being proved innocent.

That her quest for details had failed miserably merely confirmed Maddie was no junior detective in the making. Somehow, she doubted that evidence would be compelling enough for Leigh, but she would have to worry about dissuading her friend after dinner with Granny.

"You've been busy lately," Maddie said as she helped Granny set the table.

She had tried to visit her grandmother throughout the previous week to no avail. Granny hadn't answered her phone, no matter when she called. If not for the fact that Granny at least returned calls, she would have worried that she would find her grandmother's supine corpse splayed on her kitchen floor.

"An old woman can't have a social life?" Granny asked, with a bit more sass than Maddie's comment warranted.

"Of course you can, Granny. I've just missed you lately. We haven't even talked in a week."

"So tell me what's going on with you," Granny said. She carried a tray of homemade biscuits to the dining room table, already laden with pot roast, salad, steamed vegetables, and mashed potatoes. Sunday dinner at Granny's was not for the weak.

"Is that a not-so-clever way of avoiding talking about yourself?"

"It's clever enough if it works." Granny raised an eyebrow at her granddaughter, a challenge Maddie didn't attempt to rise to.

"I've got appointments with three new clients this week, and we're still on the hunt for a new space for Little Guys."

Maddie had plenty more to talk about than work, but this seemed like the safest place to start. It was certainly better than, "I've stumbled on the path of another murder," or "The woman I was seeing, who bailed almost as soon as we started having sex, showed up out of the blue and seems to want to start over. And I'm actually considering it." Playful banter with Nadia aside, Maddie doubted how encouraging Granny would be about her current romantic situation. She tended to champion self-respect over potential regret brought on by cloudy judgment and suspect romantic notions.

"You'll find the right spot." Granny laid a reassuring hand on her shoulder. "Your sister is as much a whiz with buildings and property as you are with animals."

She basked in Granny's praise as she savored her meal—essentially heaven in edible form.

After a second sublime bite, she brought up another of the stressors in her life. "And then there's Dottie."

"What do you mean?" Granny asked almost before she finished speaking.

"I think she's avoiding me."

"She's probably just been busy." Granny offered a reassuring pat of the hand with her ready excuse for Dottie's recent truancy.

"She's always busy," Maddie conceded her friend's hectic schedule, though it defied logic that Dottie, who had no job or family responsibilities to speak of, should be so busy. "But she usually has time to answer my texts. I'm starting to worry about her in the house."

"Don't," Granny snapped.

"What if there's a problem? I need to know if something's wrong."

"There isn't."

"How can you be so sure?"

"If you can count on any person in this world to be vocal about problems needing fixing, it's Dottie. Now, eat your potatoes before they get cold." Granny leapt from her seat. "I forgot the gravy. I'll be right back." Without another word, she zipped into the kitchen, and Maddie knew the topic would be changed when her grandmother returned.

"You haven't mentioned anyone special lately."

Maddie called that one. "That's because there's nothing to mention."

"Should I worry about your social life?"

"Maybe not," she said and watched Granny's eyebrows rise in curiosity. "I might be going on a date soon."

"When will you know for sure?"

"Possibly tomorrow," she said before explaining, in somewhat vague detail, about Nadia's return to her life.

"And you think this Nadia is worth a second chance?"

"She's worth talking to," Maddie said, convincing herself as well as her grandmother that it was true. "I liked her a lot the last time we went out. I would have liked to see where things went. So maybe."

"Well, if she gained enough sense over the last couple of months to realize she was a fool, maybe she is worth another try."

She smiled, wondering what Nadia would make of Granny's backhanded encouragement. When a yawn crept up on her, she tried to stifle it, but Granny caught her in the act.

"I know your active social life hasn't been keeping you up at night. What's got you so tired?"

"I had a late night last night."

"Doing what?"

"An old friend is going through a rough time. I did what I could to help her, but…"

Granny scowled. "That sounds like you gave up before the problem was resolved. Did you leave your friend in need?"

"It's not like that, Granny."

"Then what is it like?" She looked stern but sympathetic. Maddie couldn't believe she faced a scolding for not obstructing justice.

"She wants me to investigate a murder." She gave Granny a brief recap of Leigh's story. "I'm not looking to add to my grievous injury collection."

"I don't want you to take risks or put yourself in any danger, but are you really going to be that selfish?"

Her jaw dropped. She had expected support from her grandmother, not counsel to rush after another killer.

"Is she a good friend?"

She nodded, reflecting on all the years she'd known and depended on Leigh.

"If the situation was reversed, would she say, 'Sorry, I can't help you because I might get hurt if I'm too pigheaded and antsy to wait for the police to go after the killer I found'?"

Properly chastised, she shook her head.

"You could help her find answers without putting yourself in danger. All you have to do is prove she couldn't have done it and let the police handle the rest. Seems like my brainy grand-daughter could have figured that out on her own." She disappeared into the kitchen again and returned with a homemade chocolate cake. "Do you think you can handle helping your friend now?"

"I think I can try."

CHAPTER SEVEN

Exhausted as she felt, sleep eluded Maddie. Though she'd been stunned by Granny Doyle's not-so-gentle nudging at dinner, Maddie knew she had a point. Though it wasn't quite as simple as Granny put it, Leigh, who had never balked at helping anyone, needed her support. And reciprocating Leigh's generosity didn't automatically guarantee Maddie would be in peril—unless she'd learned nothing from her last foray into detective work.

Rolling onto her side, she found herself face-to-face with a softly snoring Bart, his pink tongue hanging out of his partially open mouth. Goliath lay on his back at the foot of the bed, his substantial body sprawled across the lower half of her queen-size bed. Bunking with not one but two bed hogs often made for an unsatisfying night's rest, but she couldn't blame her current tumultuousness on them.

"So," she sighed, giving in to her mental upheaval, "where do we start?"

For a reply, Bart's snuffling increased in volume, and Goliath flopped onto his side, inching closer to the center of the bed and pinning her legs beneath him.

"Thanks for the feedback, boys. It's appreciated." Not that she expected much in the way of investigative enlightenment from them, but for now they were all she had.

In truth, she'd prefer to discuss this with another human, even Dottie, whose input ranged from the ridiculously off-topic to the surprisingly insightful. But Dottie still hadn't returned any of her calls or texts. If not for her best friend's intrusive appearance on Saturday night, she would have flirted with all-out panic days earlier. As it was, she remained apprehensive and concerned about her best friend's secrecy and well-being. Nevertheless, no matter the reason for her uncharacteristic aloofness, Dottie was out as a sounding board.

Nor was she eager to consult Leigh. Not only did she run the risk of inciting another emotional meltdown by saying one wrong thing, but she also didn't want to get Leigh's hopes up. If she had any chance of figuring this out, she would need to know whom to suspect. She would probably have to ask about Terry's acquaintances (sooner rather than later), but if she could make some advancements before turning to Leigh, she thought the conversation might go better.

The trouble with that plan was that she had no idea where else to start, and her peacefully sleeping pups offered absolutely no help. Maddie rolled over (a ridiculously drawn out process thanks to a hundred and thirty pounds of dog cutting off the circulation in her lower extremities) and looked to the ceiling for guidance. As she watched the moon-cast shadows creep across the room, she more fully considered a key distinction Granny made.

"I don't have to figure out who did it. I just have to prove Leigh couldn't have. How hard could that be?"

Just then, both dogs exhaled so forcefully that their lips flapped in a double raspberry that she tried not to take as commentary on her chances of success.

By five in the morning (no better rested, but oddly less agitated) she resigned herself to talking to Leigh. Despite her reservations, it was the best course of action, especially since her focus would be clearing Leigh rather than solving the crime. However, even though she was wide awake, she knew most of the world (including her recently dipsomaniacal friend) did not share her appreciation for the peace and quiet of early morning. She wasn't sure Leigh's gratitude for Maddie's investigative assistance would override her perturbation over a crack of dawn fact-finding mission. Since it was too early to go to work and impossible to fall asleep, she used the interim between getting out of bed and a decent hour to contact the outside world in the best way possible—an invigorating, head-clearing run.

Stepping out into the crisp morning air, she felt instantly better. The temperature, chillier than in recent days, still didn't measure up to an average October morning in Chicago, and she allowed herself a moment of joy before succumbing to guilt over her selfish celebration of climate change.

Her lungs burned as the cool air hit them, and as she headed east toward the lake, the calm she usually achieved on a run (even when one or both dogs came along and ground her progress to a halt with distracted sniffing, squirrel chasing, or stick chewing) washed over her. Something about the sound of her steady breaths commingling with the pounding of her shoes on the pavement set her mind at ease and released any tension she felt. She'd seldom found any other experience as liberating.

She exchanged the runner's nod with one of her fellow fitness junkies and considered (as she did so often lately) Leigh's rather grim situation. Though she hated how easily her friend had slipped into habitual inebriation, she could (to some extent) understand it. Like running for Maddie, right now drinking provided a momentary release for Leigh in the form of obliterating consciousness. Not that Maddie didn't appreciate a good upper lip-stiffening cocktail (though she'd seldom relied on booze to erase her worries), but if she was going to help Leigh, she was going to need her to be more lucid and less alcohol-infused.

To that end, she settled on an early-morning visit to circumvent a potentially drunk and unresponsive Leigh. Maddie had no way of knowing how soon after work Leigh started imbibing, but she doubted Leigh would drink early in the morning or jeopardize her career by skipping work to drown her sorrows in the bottom of a bottle. True, she had slipped a little lately (understandably so), but Leigh had always been responsible. She hoped that hadn't changed in recent weeks, but she hurried home just in case. Though she'd almost certainly come face-to-face with a hungover and cranky Leigh, the potential benefits far outweighed the risks.

Haphazard plan firmly in place, she rushed through the boys' morning ritual (effectively dismantling the forgiveness she'd earned just the day before), and promising she'd make it up to them later, raced out the door. But as she stood on Leigh's porch, she doubted her decision. What exactly was she going to ask Leigh? What's your alibi? She was certain the police had already covered that, and assuming Leigh wasn't mistaken about being a suspect, her alibi left something to be desired.

But she had to start somewhere, she thought as she pressed Leigh's doorbell, igniting a torrent of barks from Rufus.

When she opened the door, Leigh looked almost as rough as she had on Saturday. Maddie didn't find Leigh's continued debauchery surprising, but she was concerned that her friend (who had to be at work in just about an hour) hadn't done much more to get ready for her day than roll out of bed—possibly when Maddie hit the doorbell. She hated to delay Leigh further than her obvious hangover had already done, but she had upset her dogs and gone a little out of her way. She might as well get something for her troubles.

"What are you doing here?" Obviously confused, Leigh stood in the doorway scratching her head. She winced at each of Rufus's sharp barks, which thankfully quieted when Maddie stooped to receive his adoring greeting.

"We need to talk. I hope this isn't a bad time." She forced her way inside, feeling zero guilt for her early morning intrusion. If not for the ungodly hour, Dottie would be so proud.

"Actually, I'm running a bit behind this morning. It's been hard to get going." Leigh stayed by the door, probably hoping to abbreviate her visit.

"I'll be quick then." Relieved to smell coffee brewing (at least Leigh had progressed that far in her morning preparations) she followed the delectable scent into the kitchen. Considering what she was volunteering to take on, she didn't think Leigh could begrudge her a little liquid rejuvenation.

"Okay," Leigh sighed and dragged herself into the kitchen after Maddie. "What's going on?"

"I need to know more about Terry and how she died, and right now you're my only source."

"You need to know that now? Why?" Leigh asked, her face scrunched up like she'd just taken a sizable bite out of a lemon.

"I think that will make proving your innocence a lot easier."

Leigh's eyes sprang fully open. "You're going to help me?"

She nodded and sipped from her mug. "What convinced you?"

"My grandmother."

"I love your grandmother."

"She's quite popular these days."

Leigh squinted in confusion again, but she let it pass.

"I figure the easiest way to fix this would be to prove that you couldn't have done it."

"Okay. How do we do that?" Leigh asked as she poured herself a cup of her own coffee.

"We establish your alibi." A flash of panic crossed her face, but Maddie tried to ignore the sense of foreboding it instilled in her. "When did Terry die?"

"It was a couple of Wednesdays ago."

"You can't be more specific?"

She scrunched up her face in thought. "In the afternoon, I think."

"You don't remember the date?" Maddie thought it impossible that such a momentous day wouldn't be seared in her friend's mind. Then again, Leigh had worked overtime lately to wash those memories away.

"Sorry. I'm kind of out of it right now." Leigh shrugged apologetically.

"That's all right." She smiled, sympathetically she hoped. "We'll figure out the exact date later. For now, we can probably assume you were at work on a Wednesday afternoon."

Leigh bowed her head sheepishly, and Maddie braced herself for whatever unpropitious disclosure Leigh was about to make.

"Normally I would be, but I called in sick that day. I wasn't feeling great."

She interpreted that as hung over and tried not to feel discouraged so early on. One minor complication didn't doom the entire investigation.

"You didn't, by chance, visit a doctor, did you? Or any other extremely public place with lots of witnesses and maybe some security cameras?" Leigh shook her head slowly. "I didn't think so." She sighed. This was going to be fun.

CHAPTER EIGHT

Having reluctantly departed from Leigh's not long after arriving (and with little to show for her efforts), Maddie sat in the momentary quiet of the Little Guys office, shaking her head, puzzling over her schedule and wondering how she was going to make this work. She'd secured a pledge from Leigh to meet later that day—a semi-promising development in her mind. The sooner she got started hunting down proof of Leigh's alibi, the sooner she could focus her attention on other matters that occupied her mind, things like Nadia and bowing to Dottie's domestic whims. The downside, of course, was that Leigh had insisted on meeting at a bar, an arrangement that hadn't thrilled Maddie.

"Wouldn't it be better to talk somewhere more private?" she asked, trying to dissuade Leigh. "I think a bar will be kind of, um, boisterous."

"It shouldn't be too bad on a Monday night," Leigh answered dismissively.

She didn't have another ready excuse and didn't believe Leigh wouldn't have an easy answer for any pretense Maddie could dream up. But she couldn't mention her real objection—Leigh's newfound disregard for moderation and her liver. She wanted to talk to sober Leigh, not recent party girl Leigh, which seemed unlikely in such a setting. Nevertheless, she'd agreed, hoping she would have an opportunity (however brief) to get information from Leigh before her indulgence had the desired effect of washing away her memory. Even if that didn't work, she couldn't possibly leave the bar less informed than when she entered.

Her investigation on hold, she settled in to tend to some business in the hour or so before her walkers showed up to start their day. She had a busy day ahead of her—in addition to her regular duties, she and Patrick now had a four o'clock appointment with potential new client Jennifer Wolf and her toy poodle, General Stevery. It seemed like a big name for such a little dog to live up to, and Maddie was torn between hoping his personality matched his name and dreading that particular symbiosis. Packed schedule notwithstanding, she had some personal business to address beforehand. First on the agenda: calling Nadia.

The more she thought about dinner with her possibly former ex, the more she looked forward to it. She didn't know where the evening would lead, though it seemed clear that Nadia wanted to rekindle their brief romance, not that she'd exactly said as much. But even if Maddie misread the situation (always a possibility when Maddie and women mixed), at least she wouldn't have to eat alone.

"What time tonight?" she asked, glad she had caught Nadia before her day got so hectic she couldn't answer the phone. Something about voice mail magnified Maddie's awkwardness by about a million percent.

"Is eight o'clock too late?"

"Not at all," she answered, though she wished that didn't give her doubt quite so much time to run roughshod over her minimal composure.

"Wonderful," Nadia responded. "I wish I could see you sooner, but I've got a crazy schedule today."

"We don't have to do it today," she offered, disappointed at the possible delay.

"Yes, we do. I'm not sure I can wait twelve hours to see you. Don't think I'm going to opt for waiting longer."

"Tonight then." She caught herself beaming at the empty room and scowled. Had she already forgotten the hurt Nadia had caused? Reminding herself not to be so easily swept off her feet, she asked, "Where should we go?"

"Why don't you come to my place?"

"Your place?"

She had expected to end up at a restaurant—possibly a dimly lit, romantic place, but one with plenty of other people and no bedrooms nearby. She had little enough willpower around Nadia as it was. Pairing the persuasive and tantalizing Dr. Sheridan with readily available tools of seduction suddenly felt like the precursor to regret.

"It's not far from my practice, so I'll have a good chance of beating you there, Miss Punctuality. And this way the dogs can come too. Everybody wins."

"Perfect." Maddie, not entirely certain she'd won anything, gulped and felt panic set in.

Almost as soon as she ended her call with Nadia, her phone rang.

"Tell me you're available at five." Harriet, as usual, eschewed the pesky formality of a salutation.

"What's happening at five?"

"You're visiting the future site of Little Guys." Harriet answered more enthusiastically than the prospect of wandering through an empty building warranted.

"You sound awfully confident about this, considering how many future sites I've already seen and rejected."

"And you'll see why at five."

"*If* I'm available."

She bristled at her sister's presumption. Already irritated by her own plentiful acquiescence that morning, she felt obliged to offer at least minimal resistance to her sister. Even so, she felt confident that her overloaded schedule didn't include any appointments between her new client meeting and bar time with Leigh at six.

"Looks like I can make it," she said after consulting her schedule.

And once she'd seen (and most likely vetoed) this place, she could give up the search with a clean conscience. Plus, it would occupy her mind for at least a portion of the time she had dedicated to fanning the flames of her anxiety over dinner with Nadia.

"I'm telling you, Maddie, this is the place," Harriet raved before giving her the address. "You are going to fall in love when you see it."

"We'll see at five," she said and wondered at her sister's optimistic enthusiasm. It was unprecedented, and she suspected, not long for this world.

She considered the familiar address her sister had given her. It was a bit north of her current location but not by much. She walked a few dogs in that area. In fact, she spent a good portion of her day traversing several nearby blocks, but she couldn't picture a shuttered business waiting for her to fall in love with its hidden charms. She didn't even remember seeing any For Sale signs around there. She hated to think she was so oblivious to her surroundings that she'd failed to notice commercial real estate, but no amount of head scratching brought the property in question to mind.

Not that she had an inordinate amount of time to ponder the situation. A short while after hanging up, her phone rang yet again, and she gave up all hope of making headway on any of the projects currently demanding her attention.

"Is this Miss Smithwick?" a female voice inquired, saying the "th" like a "d."

"It is." She grinned at the rare correct pronunciation of her name.

"This is Murphy. We met over the summer."

Her smile grew larger both at the memory of Officer Murphy and (ridiculous though it was) because of the way Murphy described their initial contact. Rather than reminding Maddie of the unfortunate circumstances that had led the charming cop to her door, Murphy had made it sound like a chance and (if her delusion hadn't taken complete control) pleasant encounter. As distractions went, this was one of the better ones.

"I need a cat sitter."

"I'd be happy to help you out with that."

"Great," Murphy said, and to Maddie's hopeful ears, she sounded excited. "How does this work?"

"We need to set up a time to meet you and—what's your cat's name?"

"I have two cats, Stanley and Herbie."

She allowed herself a moment to squeal internally at the adorable old man names. "So, we'll set up a meeting to make sure Stanley and Herbie are comfortable with Eric and to sign the contract and get keys."

"Eric?" For the first time, Murphy sounded hesitant.

"He's my cat guy. Don't worry. Cats love him. I think he rolls around in catnip or dabs tuna behind his ears."

"It's just, well, I thought you would be watching the cats."

"That's certainly possible, but I assure you, Eric is excellent with cats."

"Oh, I'm sure he is. It's not that. It's just that I want you."

She felt her face flush at Murphy's words. She'd already been enjoying the sound of her voice more than she should. Murphy was a potential client after all, and even though Maddie was, technically, still single (at least until eight) and free to swoon over anyone she pleased, it would benefit no one for Maddie to feed a massive crush on a client. She wouldn't act on it, so what was the point? But Murphy had a great voice, and (unprofessional though it was) Maddie hoped the conversation went on far longer than necessary.

"Stanley prefers women," Murphy blurted to her slight disappointment. "Plus, they're my family. I just want the best for them if I can't be here."

"Well then," Maddie, soaring again, answered. "I'd be honored to look after your kids. When are you available to meet?"

"How does tomorrow night around six work?"

"It's a date." She cringed and dropped her head onto her desk as soon as the words left her mouth. She'd been doing so well. "I mean, it's not a date. It's an appointment." Because that's a thing people said. Couldn't someone just kill her now?

"I'll see you then," Murphy said after giving Maddie her address.

"Unless I die of embarrassment first," Maddie muttered and then lifted her head to see several of her employees staring at her.

Her day was off to a great start.

CHAPTER NINE

Given the number of concerns weighing on Maddie's mind, she felt the need to seek advice, and her mind instantly turned to her best friend. Not that Dottie typically served as a source of reason, sound judgment or wise counsel, but sometimes hearing her preposterous take on life offered Maddie clarity (something she had in short supply at the moment). So she texted between her walks with barking connoisseur Baxter Collins and sniffing aficionado Hazel Taylor, then again before her jaunt with the adorably stubborn Bunny Baginski, a big brown mutt who flouted every rule. She squeezed in another text and a call before her walks with unrepentant howler Thora Nguyen and Alphonse the super poodle, respectively. Her attempts to contact Dottie were numerous (and increasingly desperate), but her excessive communication efforts were to no avail. And the longer she went without hearing from Dottie, the more she worried, adding one more item to her list of concerns.

They'd only ever gone this long without communicating during each of Dottie's honeymoons, a realization that conjured a startling question in her mind—had Dottie eloped? Was she off on a tropical island adventure with the financial overlord of some megacorporation? As soon as she finished the thought, she dismissed it. Dottie would never voluntarily pass up the opportunity to be the center of attention. Something else was going on, and eventually Maddie would figure it out.

But for now she had real business to tend to. As she and Patrick walked the few blocks from Little Guys' current location to its alleged new home, the wind picked up speed and strength, impeding their progress and buffeting them with debris and dead leaves. He squinted and braced himself against the assault, and she vowed to show her appreciation through dinner or baked goods (possibly both) in the very near future.

They both stopped short when they approached the address Harriet had given them, though Maddie suspected their collective astoundment had, at its source, very different origins.

"That's your sister?" he asked. Though he spoke softly, she could still hear the infatuation in his voice.

"All my life," she answered and prepared herself to witness his undoing.

Growing up in Harriet's comely shadow had, at times, been as difficult as being Dottie's unremarkable best friend. Where Maddie was short and freckled, Harriet was a comfortable five foot ten and had a model-worthy complexion (with or without the makeup she knew how to apply flawlessly). Unlike Maddie's naturally frizzy and untamable hair, Harriet's long, reddish brown tresses always seemed to behave for her—no matter the humidity—and her large brown eyes missed nothing, especially not her effect on smitten men. When they went out together, she could almost always pinpoint the exact second she faded into the background, becoming scenery rather than a human being. Since this phenomenon mostly excluded her from the notice of men she had no interest in anyway, she didn't usually care, but Patrick's faithlessness (no matter how temporary it might be) stung.

As Harriet approached, he ran his hand through his hair, and Maddie turned her attention to where it would matter—the latest building in Harriet's long string of potential properties.

"A firehouse?" she asked her sister. When she got no response after a lengthy pause, she turned to find that an equally enamored Harriet had completely ignored her sister to introduce herself to Patrick. They stood silently, smiling and nodding, their motionless clasped hands the only evidence of a forgotten handshake.

"Good lord," she sighed and stepped closer. "If you just open the door for me, I can look around on my own while you two make eyes at each other."

"Oh Matilda." Harriet snapped to attention, and finally releasing her hold on Patrick's hand, straightened her already perfect skirt. "Shall we?" she said, inclining her head toward the reason they were there, her focus ostensibly back on business even though she spoke to Patrick rather than Maddie.

"Don't mind me," she grumbled as she followed the pair into the defunct firehouse.

Her first thought once inside was that the place needed work. The floor dipped and buckled in places, and the windows that hadn't been broken had outlived their usefulness. Several walls needed attention beyond what a fresh coat of paint would provide.

"It's a bit of a fixer-upper," Harriet echoed her initial impression.

Only half paying attention to her sister, she nodded and drifted toward the stairs. "So you said earlier."

Before ascending to the second level, she turned slowly, taking in the whole first floor. It was a mess, but she saw the potential. Upstairs there was room for an office and space for any special needs dogs to hang out away from the rowdy, rough-and-tumble play of dogs downstairs. That area was large enough for kennels, a dog wash, and a training area in addition to a space for her employees and customers to move around comfortably. And she felt good in the space. It was filthy and quite possibly falling apart around her, but she felt like she belonged there. It wasn't what she thought she wanted, but now she couldn't see herself anywhere else.

"There's definitely work to be done, but I bet it's not as bad as it seems." Back downstairs, she examined the floor closely and then rose to take it all in again. "I wish Dad was here. I'd like to know what he thinks."

"I can show him the space tonight." She spoke over her shoulder to Maddie before returning her full attention to her next conquest. "Maddie and our father make an amazing team," Harriet told an enraptured Patrick (who had been to Maddie's house and already knew what she and Mr. Smithwick were capable of). "Of course, you don't look like a stranger to manual labor." Harriet tossed a wink at Patrick, but at least she didn't fondle his biceps.

Maddie's eye roll went unnoticed as he blushed, grinned and looked ready to offer to fix something, anything of Harriet's. Before he could start flexing and strutting, Maddie cut him off. "Can I afford this place?"

"It's a little higher than you wanted to go, though I suspect you played it safe with your budget."

She scowled at her sister's perceptive comment but said nothing.

"And I'll cut you a deal on my commission."

"No way. You've already done so much work for me. You deserve to be paid fairly."

"I agree, but you're the reason I'm working with Dottie, and considering the bundle I stand to make on her place, I can lose a little here."

"Don't let her hear you say that."

"I'd think she'd be oddly pleased to be seen as a cash cow."

"Absolutely she would, but if she catches you calling her Dottie instead of Gwendolyn, you won't make a dime."

"Don't worry. I know the rules," Harriet reassured her. "I haven't heard a no yet. Does that mean it's a yes?"

She realized she was nodding as she looked around once more. She could picture herself and her business so clearly in this place. Though the boarded-up windows allowed no light to pass through, she easily imagined how the soft rays of sunlight would stream across her pristine walls and floors as she, her walkers, customers and dogs milled about the wide-open space. It could work and give Little Guys plenty of room to grow.

Though she'd brought him along specifically for his opinion, she didn't even need to consult Patrick.

"If Dad tells me it's not a money pit, it's a yes."

"Yes!" Harriet pumped her fist in a manner that was neither professional nor ladylike, but Maddie understood exactly how she felt.

Now if only the rest of her evening would go this easily.

The end of Maddie's bar-hopping days coincided with her graduation from college, although even before then, she'd been more bookworm than night owl. So despite its status as an independent, lesbian-owned fixture in her neighborhood, she had never set foot in Pi. She didn't look forward to changing that fact. Not only would she be walking into a bar alone, but she would almost certainly have to relive her long history of rejection when she sidled up to whatever ultra-hot, baby-faced eye candy the owners had installed as a top-notch lesbian lure, regardless of her limitations as a bartender. In this instance, her deniable appeal to women, particularly those in the service industry, was grating but probably for the best. A little lubrication before her outing of an undetermined nature with Nadia would be a good thing, but she didn't want to risk too much loss of her inhibitions. They were her friends, and she didn't want to send them off on a booze-fueled vacation.

At first glance, she had no regrets over not supporting this particular local establishment. It seemed little more than a dive. The walls sported the usual collection of beer signage (some in glorious neon) as well as flyers for upcoming events, and the floor had that low-grade persistent stickiness particular to taverns and movie theaters. Except for a small section in the back with pool tables, most of the floor space was taken up by scarred and worn lacquer-coated wooden tables and highboys, all of them occupied. If she didn't know better, she would have thought that Pi had been catering to the lesbians of Rogers Park for fifty years rather than five. In the small blessings department, the absence of a dance floor meant that the music pouring out of the jukebox and reverberating off the walls wasn't that repetitive, unimaginative computer-generated stuff that made her head pound in time with the synthesized beats.

The one standout in the dimly lit and unkempt space was the bar itself. It spanned almost the full length of one wall, its gleaming surface beckoning thirsty patrons like a Siren. Leigh had already found herself a seat at Beverage Central, and wanting to get started (on the lubrication as well as the investigation), Maddie strode up to the bar and settled herself in the empty seat next to Leigh, who, in a pleasantly surprising turn of events, was chasing her beer with water.

"You made it!" Leigh's effusive greeting startled her.

"I told you I would," she said, but Leigh's attention was already elsewhere.

"Kittens!" Leigh called out, and for a moment Maddie worried that her friend had been stricken by the same affliction that fueled Dottie's love of pet names. But in truth, Leigh's outburst had been a summons for the last person Maddie expected to find tending bar in a lesbian establishment.

"Kittens, this is my good friend Maddie. Take care of her."

"What can I get you, love?"

If the British accent hadn't surprised her, the appearance of a stout, bald man (the least kitteny person ever to be saddled with the nickname Kittens, Maddie suspected) did the trick. His stern expression caught her more off guard. It didn't exactly inspire friendly banter, nor did it explain why a lesbian-owned lesbian bar had made him, to an extent, the face of their establishment, but at least she didn't feel inadequate or undeserving of his attention.

Conscious of the need for levelheadedness, she dismissed the part of her that wanted to sample Pi's impressive bourbon offerings and instead ordered a Mudhopper from Skinny Frog, a small, local brewery. She planned to stretch it for the duration of her stay. If the raised eyebrow and gentle nod were any indication, Kittens approved of her choice.

"I hope this one sticks around," he said to Leigh as he placed Maddie's drink in front of her. "She's got better taste than you and your usual company."

"Bite me, Kittens." Leigh added an obscene gesture for his benefit.

"Don't make offers you aren't prepared to follow up on." He winked at Leigh, a jarring display of playfulness that made the exchange all the more surreal.

"I take it you come here a lot," Maddie said to Leigh.

"No, I'm just the only person who's nice to that guy. I'd be even nicer if he'd quit giving me grief about my beer of choice."

"Make better choices, love," he said and dodged the peanut Leigh threw at him as he moved on to another customer.

"Are you sure this is the best place for us to talk?" She looked around the bar, whose business was surprisingly robust for a Monday evening. It seemed like prying ears lurked in every corner. Not that they were discussing classified information, but she doubted she'd want to publicize her own connection to a murder, no matter how tenuous it might be.

"Relax, Maddie. No one here is listening to us. They're too busy searching for their next failed romance."

Leigh's bleak outlook on love notwithstanding, she didn't see how that excluded her friend from the other patrons' attention, but she didn't have the chance to argue.

"Besides, this is where I came the day Terry died. If anyone can vouch for my whereabouts, this is where we'd find them."

Maddie looked around the bar with renewed interest, wondering if her job could be as simple as finding someone in this crowd who remembered seeing Leigh on the day in question. Probably not, but she wouldn't rule it out.

"So tell me about that day, the day Terry died."

"There's not much to tell, Mads. I skipped work because I wasn't feeling great, but I started feeling better around dinnertime. Thought I'd come here."

For a liquid dinner, Maddie suspected. "Did you talk to anyone?"

"Kittens, of course."

"Of course." She made a mental note to visit with Kittens later. "Anyone else?"

Leigh scrunched her face in thought. "There was a brunette, maybe."

Because it would take no effort at all to locate the right brown-haired woman somewhere in the city. "You can't be more specific about the brunette?"

"It was a while ago, and I wasn't the most perceptive I've ever been."

She closed her eyes and gulped her beer in her struggle to quell her frustration. How was she supposed to prove Leigh's innocence when all she had to offer as evidence was Kittens and an unidentifiable brunette? She would have to go about this a different way.

"Tell me about Terry."

"What do you want to know?"

"How about anything? I don't even know this woman's last name."

"Kovacs." Leigh spat out the word and signaled to Kittens for another drink. She'd all but forgotten her water.

"Did anyone else have reason to dislike her?"

"Only anyone who ever met her." Maddie raised her eyebrows in disbelief. "I guess some people actually liked her," Leigh amended. "Lindsey sure did. But a lot of people didn't."

"Do you know who any of those people might be?" She took another too-large swallow of her drink. So much for stretching her one beer.

"Her ex, Lindsey's ex-husband Ray, Terry and Lindsey's neighbors on all sides, at least half of her coworkers—"

"Leigh?" someone squealed at a volume that threatened the well-being of Maddie's eardrums.

Before Maddie had a chance to recover from the auditory assault, a full-figured blonde charged up to the bar and inserted herself between them. Once again Maddie had inadvertently worn her invisibility cloak to a gathering of lesbians.

"What are you doing here?" Blondie pulled a resistant Leigh into a muffled embrace, Leigh's face momentarily lost in the larger woman's décolletage, a fate that, normally, she probably wouldn't have minded. At the moment, however, she floundered for a release from her pillowy internment.

"I'm here with a friend," Leigh said, and Maddie peered around the interloper's substantial form. She offered a thin smile and a wave which Leigh's bosomy buddy promptly ignored. Resigning herself to her fate as woman repellant, Maddie flagged Kittens down and ordered another drink.

"I didn't think I'd see you so soon after...you know. How are you doing?"

So Blondzilla knew about some of Leigh's recent challenges. Maddie wondered what else she knew and if she could help prove Leigh's innocence.

"It's been hard," Leigh answered. The woman stroked Leigh's arm in what was undoubtedly supposed to be a gesture of sympathy, though Leigh looked like it brought her more irritation than comfort. "But my friend here is helping me get through it."

"I know how that goes." The blonde, oblivious to Leigh's hint, threw a conspiratorial shoulder nudge in Leigh's direction. Maddie would have to ask Leigh about that later, if this woman ever decided to give them privacy. "If you need anything, just call. I'll always be there for you, Leigh."

"Thanks, Kat. I appreciate that. Right now I just need to talk to my friend."

"Oh," Kat said and glared at Maddie. At least she'd finally acknowledged her existence. "I see. I just thought, you know, after Lindsey killing herself and all, you wouldn't want to be alone, but I guess you've got that covered. You don't need me."

"Kat," Leigh drew her into a friendly embrace, "don't think I don't need you. I do. Maybe we can talk later this week?"

"I'd like that," a placated Kat said, and after glaring at Maddie once more, threaded her way through the crowd to the back of the bar, where the patrons showed the proper enthusiasm at her arrival. She guessed none of them had opted for a conversation with Kat, or the reception might have been chillier.

Once Kat was out of earshot, she hit Leigh with a Granny Doyle-inspired look of perturbed expectation. "Care to explain?"

"It's a long story," Leigh sighed.

"Then you better talk fast."

Leigh shifted uncomfortably on her barstool, the bowl of peanuts in front of her suddenly commanding her full attention. "Kat and I used to be neighbors, before Lindsey left me."

She considered her neighbors past and present. Not once had she ever hugged one of them, let alone buried her face in any of their chests. Clearly, Leigh had done some editing, but how much?

"When did you start sleeping together?" She waited for a denial, but it didn't come.

"About a month after we got dumped. Kat is Terry's ex."

Maddie choked on her beer, as surprised by that revelation as by her own minor detecting victory.

"We ran into each other here one night. Drinks and commiserating turned into sloppy, drunken comfort sex. We both knew it was a mistake, but..."

"But you've made this mistake more than once."

"Is it so wrong to look for solace from someone who understands what I'm going through?"

"Solace, no, but an exchange of bodily fluids seems like a lot to ask of a neighbor."

"Well, it doesn't matter now because I ended it."

Maddie glanced across the bar to find Kat glaring at them. "Does she know that?"

"Of course." She swallowed the dregs of her beer and flagged Kittens down for a refill. "We're just friends now. We both know it's better that way."

"If you say so," she muttered, but as she looked back at Kat, she wondered if Leigh was right.

CHAPTER TEN

Though her encounter with Leigh ran longer than expected, Maddie thought better of driving to her next appointment, for numerous reasons. One benefit of walking Bart and Goliath to Nadia's house was that it gave Maddie the chance to wear the boys out before they descended upon her home, thus minimizing their potential for damage. As a vet raising a puppy who shared Goliath's DNA, Nadia should understand the importance of leaving nothing chewable (in effect, nothing) within the expansive reach of her canine companions, but Maddie didn't want to risk the chaos an energetic and excited Goliath could bring to Dr. Sheridan and her possessions. She wouldn't put it past him to find some way to demolish an empty room, probably with his tail alone.

But for all his destructive tendencies, he was one of the sweetest dogs she'd ever met. Plus, he had saved her life, pretty much securing his place in her heart and home no matter how many pairs of shoes and sunglasses he rendered unwearable. As if aware of the not entirely favorable chain of thoughts running through her brain, he ambled beside her and nudged her hand with his head, just as though he wanted to remind her of the sweetness that was his saving grace.

"Don't worry, buddy. We're stuck with each other."

Reassured, he trotted ahead to join Bart, who sniffed intently at a desiccated carcass, whether rat or squirrel, Maddie wasn't sure, nor did she want to find out. Fortunately, a firm tug at their leashes and a handful of treats kept her from getting any closer to the dead thing in the form of prying it from one of her dog's jaws.

In addition to giving the dogs a leg up on good behavior, the walk to Nadia's place should have been the perfect remedy not only for her Nadia-centric nervousness and her racing thoughts as she pondered what little information Leigh gave her but also her unfortunate tipsiness thanks to Kittens's attentive and persuasive bartending. That theory, however, was flawed. Though the initial blast of chilly night air gave her the feeling of alertness (if not the actual thing), she minimized its sobering effects once she zipped up her Little Guys hoodie. Somewhat warmer, Maddie immediately began to contemplate the latest development in Leigh's story.

The news that Leigh had slept with Kat, the pushy blonde from the bar, hadn't come as a shocker, but the fact that Kat was Terry's ex and that she and Leigh had spent several nights together in a sort of post-dumped consolation coitus stunned her. Not that Maddie had never made unwise sex decisions in the wake of a broken heart (and could, in fact, be en route to one at that precise moment), but somehow she expected better of Leigh. Even in the midst of the alcohol-fueled foolishness of college, Leigh always made the mature decision.

Of course, Leigh had indulged in the standard revelry of unsupervised semi-adults. She had actually been the instigator of Maddie's first college hangover, but for all the fun she was willing to have with friends, her studies always came first, so she more often ended up mothering the drunkards in her midst. To say it was shocking to see her suddenly so eager to drown her sorrows would be an understatement, and Maddie hoped that once Leigh ceased to be a murder suspect, her newfound love of alcohol would disappear.

Just then, a frigid blast of rain-dappled air pelted Maddie in the face, making her wish she'd thought to put on a jacket or bring an umbrella. She shivered and huddled deeper into her optimistic choice of outerwear, then urged the boys to walk faster. If their increased speed didn't warm her up, at least they'd get to Nadia's hopefully warm house a few minutes sooner.

The boys seemed to enjoy the brisk pace, and as they padded along the leaf-strewn sidewalks, her thoughts turned back to the warring subject matters of Leigh and Nadia. It seemed obvious that proving Leigh's innocence with an unshakeable alibi would be about as easy as convincing Dottie that high heels were the devil's footwear (a war they'd waged for close to a decade). That left Maddie with the daunting task of figuring out who killed Terry, an outcome that seemed as likely as Maddie surviving the rest of her night without developing an ulcer.

As she rounded a corner, the wind and rain picked up speed, whipping around her and penetrating her clothing. Again she regretted that she hadn't worn something more appropriate. If Dottie had been privy to her fashion choice for the evening— jeans, her least wrinkled blouse, running shoes and the sure-to-offend hoodie—she would undoubtedly wish the same thing. Dottie would choke if she knew Maddie had even considered an article of clothing with the word "sweat" in its name as proper attire for potential seduction (which is, of course, the only way Dottie would view Maddie's evening with Nadia).

Maddie still wasn't certain the exact nature of what she was about to walk into, but seduction was off the menu as far as she was concerned, not that that stopped her from fussing with her hair and putting on perfume and makeup before she and the boys left home.

Even though Dottie wasn't around to judge Maddie's choice of "seduction attire," she could easily imagine Dottie's objections: "Are you trying to repel this woman? Or is pity the crux of your allurement tactic, sweets? It's like you're trying to hurt me with bad fashion."

"Because you were my sole consideration when I decided what to wear," Maddie said and frowned. When the boys both turned and tilted their heads at her, she realized she'd spoken aloud. "Great. Now I'm hallucinating conversations with Dottie. It's like the DTs but with criticism."

She sighed and raced the dogs the last few blocks to their destination.

By the time they entered Nadia's blessedly toasty home, she felt battered by Mother Nature. The up-to-then dormant winter weather had asserted itself fully on their brief journey, and Maddie, too cold to monitor her pups' behavior, dropped the boys' leashes and hoped for the best as they made a full circuit of their new environment with a leaping, barking Mabel in tow.

"You didn't wear a coat?" Nadia's concerned expression rapidly overtook the lopsided grin she'd worn when she opened her door.

"I sometimes make poor choices," she chattered. She rubbed her arms with her hands, trying to warm up.

"You're frozen," Nadia stated the obvious. Then after a moment's hesitation, wrapped Maddie in a thawing embrace.

She waited roughly three seconds before sinking into Nadia's softness and reveling in her tight grip. Just for the warmth, she told herself, even as she inhaled the familiar, heady scent of Dr. Nadia Sheridan and suddenly couldn't remember why she'd wanted to keep her distance or what she was mad at Nadia about or how to breathe.

"I'm better now. Thanks." She stepped out of Nadia's grasp, and not knowing exactly how to act around her maybe-date, she turned her attention to Nadia's home.

She hadn't expected extravagance—veterinarians (even those who occasionally performed questionable favors for wealthy clients) didn't reap quite the windfall that their expertise and work warranted—but Nadia's place was surprisingly small and sparse. Aside from a love seat and a coffee table, she had no furniture in her living room. Her bland gray walls (devoid of any decoration) reminded Maddie of concrete. Though she had anticipated a certain amount of puppy-proofed emptiness, this place seemed practically vacant.

She wondered how long Nadia had lived there, but that wasn't the question that came out.

"What did you want to talk about?"

"Wow. Not even any time for small talk. Are you in that much of a hurry?"

"No. I just—this is driving me crazy. *You* are driving me crazy." Unbelievably, Nadia smiled broadly. "Not in a good way."

"Oh." Nadia's face fell.

"I just need to know what's going on. What is this about?"

Nadia moved closer to her, close enough to touch her again, but thankfully, she kept her hands to herself.

"You really haven't figured it out?"

"No, I haven't figured it out, not for lack of insomnia-inducing effort."

"Can we at least get comfortable first?" Nadia reached to help her out of her sweatshirt, but Maddie stepped away from her.

"No," she said, feeling more like a petulant child than a grown woman asserting herself.

"You're really going to make this hard on me."

"No harder than you made things for me."

"Fair enough." Nadia's understanding words were at odds with her pained expression, and damn it, Maddie felt guilty for hurting her feelings.

"Just tell me, Nadia. What did you want to talk about?"

"Us." Nadia gazed at Maddie, her eyes deep, wide, imploring pools of brown, and Maddie shifted uncomfortably.

"There's an us to talk about?" Maddie's voice felt thick in her throat.

"There could be," Nadia said and reached for her hand. "If you give me another chance."

"And why would I do that?" she asked, ignoring the parts of her body that shouted, "Why *wouldn't* you?"

Maddie looked at their entwined fingers, the way their hands seemed to fit together, and she honestly didn't know what to do.

Considering her past successes with women, any relationship she could have had with Nadia likely would have fizzled out by now. She would have let work assume prominence in her life, or she would have begun to find one of Nadia's currently endearing traits grating in record time or, more likely, Nadia would have realized she could do better. So what sense did it make to enter into a relationship that was destined to fail just to face the heartbreak she'd only recently overcome?

"Because I'm sorry." Nadia crashed in on her thoughts.

"You're sorry?"

"I shouldn't have walked away." Maddie tended to agree but managed to keep quiet. "But I was ashamed of what I'd done and afraid that that could hurt you more than it already had. So, I left." Nadia sank onto her love seat, dropping her head into her hands, and Maddie followed her.

"You hurt me to avoid hurting me? You know that makes no sense, right?"

"I do now. And I'm sorry."

"Why?" she asked a perplexed-looking Nadia.

"Why?" she parroted Maddie. "Why am I sorry, or why do I want there to be an us?"

"Start with the second one." She had really been wondering why now and what was the point of pursuing a relationship that had already failed once, but it wasn't like she didn't want to know what potential Nadia saw in them.

"You mean aside from the obvious facts that you're beautiful and intelligent and funny, and you love animals as much as I do and…" Nadia bit her lower lip and one eyebrow quirked up as her gaze swept the length of Maddie's body, "…other areas of compatibility?"

"Yes." Maddie heard the quiver in her own voice. "Aside from those incredibly compelling points, why are you interested in a second chance?"

"Because," Nadia cleared her throat and looked sheepishly at her. "I missed you, and I realized I don't want to be without you."

"You were fine with that two and a half months ago when you walked away after I almost died."

Okay, that was an exaggeration. Certainly, her life had been in peril before Goliath lunged at her assailant. As it was, the worst of her injuries had been a broken arm, some severe burns and (thanks to Nadia) a broken heart.

And why was Maddie putting up such a fight anyway?

"I wasn't fine with it. I hated it. It was the hardest thing I've ever done, and as it turns out, it was one of the stupidest things I've ever done."

"Considering what I know about your past, that's saying a lot."

Nadia blushed and looked away, and Maddie regretted opening her big mouth.

"I needed to figure some things out, like how I ended up making such bad decisions in the past and just how terrible a person I am for caring less about Howard's death than if you would ever forgive me for helping him lie. But the only thing I figured out is that I'm better with you than without you. And the thought of never being with you again, that I voluntarily gave up one of the best things that has ever happened to me—I had to at least try to fix what I broke. I know it's a lot to ask, but Maddie, I haven't stopped thinking about you and regretting how things ended since I walked out your door."

Out of misguided self-preservation, Maddie had been watching Nadia's mouth as she spoke. She had thought eye contact would be too intense, make her too weak and willing to do anything Nadia asked of her. But staring at her soft lips, watching the movements of her mouth had been anything but Maddie's saving grace. Even though she still had reservations, she found herself swept up in Nadia's gravitational pull. She felt herself falling, and she couldn't have said whether she or Nadia initiated the kiss, but once it started, she was done for.

The kiss itself wasn't gentle. Nadia took hungry possession of her, and her hands were in Nadia's hair, pulling her closer. In a move so swift she wasn't aware of it until it was over, Nadia's hands swept the length of Maddie's torso, lightly brushing her small breasts on their path to her waist, before pulling her onto her lap. Nadia raked her fingers across Maddie's thighs and then moved higher, dipping under the hem of Maddie's shirt and teasing the sensitive skin of her abdomen.

She inhaled sharply, breaking the kiss but not their intense eye contact. Nadia favored her with one of her lopsided smiles.

"Can I take that as a yes?"

For an answer, Maddie moved in for another searing kiss. This time she allowed her hands to roam freely over Nadia's voluptuous body, savoring every curve. She bit Nadia's lower lip and pulled away from her to revel in the smoldering look in her eyes. She would probably regret this—no good had ever come from her acting impulsively, but damn, this felt good. That kiss alone would be worth the probable future heartache.

"It's a yes to this," she said and shifted farther back on Nadia's lap. "But not to whatever you're burning in there."

"I forgot about dinner!" After disentangling herself from Maddie, she ran to the kitchen to salvage their meal. Maddie followed the trail of curses and the scent of burning chicken to find a crestfallen Nadia scraping at a blackened mass on the stove. "I think it's a goner."

"There's a lot of that going around tonight," Maddie said as she brushed past a grinning Nadia on her way to save their stomachs.

CHAPTER ELEVEN

Maddie's uncharacteristic bliss—a direct result of her reconciliation (and subsequent late night) with Nadia—lasted almost forty-five minutes into her Tuesday morning before guilt over neglecting her commitment to Leigh took over. Not that she didn't try to hang on to her almost euphoric grogginess, but her exhaustion made her more susceptible to the shifting tides of her emotions. And even though her battle to retain her atypically cheery disposition was a losing one, in this case, she wouldn't trade her easily shifting mood for a good night's sleep. Finally giving in to the remorse-fueled trends of her thinking, she focused on the weird saga of Leigh, Terry, and Lindsey.

The trouble was she didn't know exactly how to proceed. It wasn't like she was a trained professional, and unlike the last time she'd pretended to be a detective, in this instance she didn't know (or care about) the victim or have an in with the possible suspects. If not for Leigh, Maddie would be delightfully unaware of the life and death of Terry Kovacs, and she could spend all of her free time and energy thinking mushy thoughts about Nadia while simultaneously avoiding discussion of her with her friends and family.

But she'd made a promise to her friend (and her grandmother) and couldn't back out now, not even if Leigh turned out to be a hindrance to the very investigation she'd initiated. More troubling than Leigh's unhelpfulness was the threat of her becoming a liability, either through her erratic emotions or through her drunkenness. Even though she could provide access to some of Terry's acquaintances, going through Leigh meant including Leigh, a circumstance Maddie hoped to avoid. She couldn't trust her friend to stay levelheaded enough not to alienate everyone they spoke with. And there was an alarming number of potential suspects.

The complicated romantic entanglements alone gave her too many threads to unravel: Lindsey had been married to Ray before moving on to Leigh and then Terry. Meanwhile, Terry had been with Kat before unleashing her on the general lesbian populace, and though she seemed to have her sights on Leigh, that apparently hadn't slowed her prowling, if the previous night's behavior was any indication. Maddie needed a spreadsheet to keep the relationships in this love tetrahedron straight.

And thanks to slightly more complete information about the victim and a renewed Internet search, she had even more to go on. Not only had she found the exact date of Terry's death to supplant Leigh's hazy memory of events, but she'd also stumbled upon an exceptionally treacly (even for an obituary) death notice. Not that she didn't understand the mawkishness that surrounded death—particularly an unexpected loss—or that she begrudged anyone her grief, but it seemed a bit much to proclaim in a half-page tribute (complete with unflattering photo substantiating Leigh's "hatchet-face" commentary) that, "the light of the world had been extinguished too soon," and, "no one's life would ever be the same" now that Terry was gone.

Setting aside her own visceral response to such an off-putting outpouring of sentimentality, Maddie decided to run through the impressive list of mourners catalogued in a sixty-five-column-inch obituary that must have cost more than a down payment on a luxury vehicle. Though she couldn't be sure anyone listed in the bereavement opus harbored animosity for the victim, those closest to Terry seemed like a good place to start. If nothing else, she could eliminate a large swath of the populace by crossing each of those names off her list of suspects. And if she got lucky, one or more of them might point her in the direction of anyone who disliked Terry. Anyone other than Leigh.

What she soon discovered was the creative force behind the obituary had been optimistic with her expression of the world's all-consuming grief at the loss of Terry Kovacs. While no one she spoke to (under the not entirely believable guise of being a sociology grad student writing her dissertation on sudden death and bereavement) seemed to care enough either way about the deceased to kill her, more of them than not held no warmth or regard for the victim. It seemed "the light of the world" had not truly gone out.

What she did learn was Leigh's unfavorable view of Terry had been more accurate than she would have guessed given the circumstances, and the more tenuous the connection to the deceased, the more willing the subject was to discuss the victim's flaws and speculate about the exact nature of her demise—and the degree to which she "got what she deserved." In addition to the expected conjecture about Terry's ex (as well a startling theory about suicide), she heard from the victim's third cousin that a long-standing feud with Terry's neighbor Esther Snodgrass had culminated in murder. Meanwhile, an aunt hypothesized that a coworker wanted revenge after being passed up for a promotion. Still another distant relative suggested Lindsey's kids had been behind the murder. Surprisingly few people mentioned Leigh, but considering that in two hours of calling, she'd made her way through less than a quarter of the names listed, Maddie opted not to feel hopeful about any developments.

With a few more minutes to spare before she had to head to her first appointment of the day, she scanned the list of names again, wondering if she'd ever get through them all. It occurred to her that one name was noticeably absent from the world's longest death notice—Kat Russell, Terry's (and Leigh's) moodily possessive ex, and a great place to pick up her investigation after work.

She didn't expect Kat to talk to her happily, if at all. Given her surly response at the bar, Maddie wondered if Kat would talk to her unless forced to. But Maddie suspected that, once she'd talked to Terry's ex, she would have a better idea of how to proceed. If anyone would know who hated Terry enough to want her dead, it would be the woman she had been romantically involved with. Or at least that's what Maddie thought should be the case. She knew she could lure her in with the promise of seeing Leigh, but she didn't want Leigh to be a distraction, either through Kat's continued pursuit of Leigh, or through Leigh's hostile contributions to the conversation. Nevertheless, Maddie didn't see how else she would get to talk to Kat. Unless…

"This is probably the worst idea I've ever had," she said to herself as she dialed Dottie's number again.

Not surprisingly, she got no answer, but rather than leave another message, she decided she was done waiting for her friend to get back to her. By the time the afternoon was over, she would know what was going on with Dottie, and the next phase of her investigation would be underway.

"May I help you?"

Maddie jumped a little when she looked up to see a bespectacled, graying brunette carrying a clipboard, wearing a sweater set and staring at her expectantly. She hadn't heard the woman's approach in response to her knock and assumed she was some sort of ninja librarian.

"I'm here to see Dot—um, Gwendolyn Hunter." Somehow she doubted this woman had the liberty to call Dottie by her nickname.

The woman's only response was to consult her clipboard before subjecting Maddie to her dispassionate and unflinching scrutiny.

Maddie didn't think she could be more confused than she felt in that moment. Taking a step back, she reassured herself that she hadn't sauntered up to a look-alike house, but barring her entry into an alternate universe, she stood on Howard's (technically her) front porch. Still, she had no idea who the woman staring her down might be, and she didn't know how to ask without sounding rude. However, the longer the woman stared at her, the less she cared about being rude.

"Do you have an appointment?" the woman finally asked. She had switched her attention to the clipboard in her hands but briefly glanced at Maddie over the tops of her glasses.

"I've never needed one before."

The woman's stern expression didn't budge. Maddie didn't even see her blinking and began to wonder if Dottie had acquired a robot.

"No, I don't have an appointment."

The poster girl for organized efficiency tsked her disapproval then pointed to a plain but functional rocking chair just outside the front door. "Have a seat there. I'll see if Ms. Hunter has a minute in her busy schedule to meet with—are you the plumber or the electrician?"

"I'm the best friend."

Sweater Set took a sweeping glance of Maddie, no doubt cataloguing the disheveled hair, Little Guys hoodie, well-worn jeans and sensible, comfortable shoes.

"Hmm." She nodded almost imperceptibly before gliding swiftly away.

Maddie had no idea if the clipboard queen intended to alert Dottie to her presence, but other than crossing her fingers and hoping for the best, she'd run out of options. Maddie parked herself in the appointed chair and wondered how she had allowed herself to be banished from her own property. It wasn't like she'd been a fixture around the place lately. It still creeped her out a little to be in the space where Howard had been murdered, but she *was* the owner of record. She thought that should entitle her entry of the building. Apparently Dottie's librarian for hire didn't see things the same way.

She considered texting Dottie (again) to gain access to the house, but she had no reason to believe Dottie would answer this text when so many others had been ignored. She was ready to give up on polite docility and barge in when she saw her grandmother heading up the walkway with a container of cookies in hand.

"Granny? What are you doing here?"

Granny looked dumbfounded but recovered quickly. "I'm delivering cookies. What does it look like I'm doing?"

"Since when do you deliver cookies to Dottie?"

"I'm welcoming her to the neighborhood, child, which is more than I can say for her landlord."

"Her landlord has been barred from the premises," she shot back.

"Maybe you should have sprung for a potted plant."

"I'll try that next time," she muttered as Granny thrust the tub of cookies into her hands and headed back down the walkway. A perplexing note on the lid read, "Extra energy for the crew."

"I have to run. Make sure Dottie gets those." Granny scurried away like she'd suddenly remembered she left her oven on.

"You're not staying?" Maddie called after her, but Granny was already halfway down the block. Her grandmother was acting strangely, but before she could even begin to hazard a guess, the front door flew open and Dottie appeared.

"I wasn't expecting you, petite proprietor. You should have told me you were coming."

She found it odd that the queen of dropping in unannounced suddenly had an issue with unexpected visits but let it pass. "I tried to tell you. Check your phone."

Dottie raised an elegant eyebrow but didn't budge from her place in the doorway. Either she had caught her at an inopportune moment, or Dottie was hiding something. She wasn't sure she wanted to find out either way.

"Oh, Carlisle oversees that, ducks. She must have been waiting for a less hectic time before passing along your message."

"Messages. Plural," she corrected, but Dottie breezed past her remark.

"She's a real tiger about my schedule. And so efficient and organized."

"Yeah, I picked up on that."

"I wish I'd found a Carlisle years ago."

"Why is she here?" Maddie asked what she felt was an obvious question, but Dottie didn't always acknowledge the obvious.

"She's my assistant."

"Assistant for what?" She felt more confused than when Carlisle had confronted her earlier.

"For my endeavors," Dottie huffed and folded her arms across her chest.

"Of course." Though she remained clueless about these so-called endeavors, she knew she had to step carefully or risk incurring Dottie's wrath. "Your endeavors. How could I forget?"

Properly placated, Dottie dropped her arms. Maddie craned her neck to see past her, but Dottie shifted to block her view.

"What brings you to the homestead, cupcake?"

"I need your help."

"I can see that," Dottie drawled, her eyes scanning Maddie from head to toe.

"Not with my outfit."

"Let's not delude ourselves, sweet pea." Dottie gestured at her fur-accented jeans with one muddy pawprint on the left thigh. "Unless you're auditioning for a modern interpretation of *Oliver Twist*, I'd say there's room for improvement."

She rolled her eyes but otherwise ignored her assessment. "There's a woman I need to talk to—"

"A special woman?" Dottie perked up immediately, and she wished she'd phrased her statement differently. "Is this part of your plan to win back the reluctant love doctor? Are you going to woo her with jealousy?"

"She's not reluctant."

"So there's been progress? Have you had a sleepover yet?"

She groaned at her mistake. "Why do I tell you things?"

"For the record, you've told me nothing, but you—like so many others—are helpless to resist my charms."

"I'm sure that's it. I need to talk to a friend of a friend, and I think your…charms will be advantageous."

"Why are we talking to this woman?" Dottie asked. "And does the stunning Dr. Feelgood know you're chatting up another lady?"

"I haven't mentioned it to Nadia, but it doesn't matter because this isn't a romantic mission." Never mind that Nadia wouldn't be pleased to learn about Maddie's return to amateur detective work.

"If we aren't addressing your underserved libido, what are we trying to accomplish, pet?"

"We're just sort of casually looking into a murder."

"Who died now?" Dottie swayed in the doorway, but Maddie still couldn't see what her friend might be hiding.

"No one you know. No one I know for that matter."

"I don't know if I should be concerned for your well-being, troubled by your willingness to endanger yourself for someone you have no connection to, terrified by your frequent encounters with the criminal element or pleased at your recognition of my investigative prowess."

"Probably all of the above," she admitted. She was under no delusion that any of this was a good idea, but having promised Leigh, she felt she had to try to find proof of her innocence (or at least reasonable doubt of her guilt), and that started with Kat Russell.

"What's the mission?" Dottie asked, and Maddie was only momentarily taken aback by her willingness to join the insanity.

"Just meet me at this bar at seven." She handed Dottie a matchbook she'd grabbed from Pi the night before. "Drinks are on me."

"I like this assignment already."

"I thought you might." She made one more attempt to see inside the house before giving up. Reluctantly, she passed off Granny's cookies and headed to her next appointment. Whatever Dottie was up to, Maddie knew she would find out eventually.

CHAPTER TWELVE

Nothing about Maddie's encounter with Officer Murphy went as she had anticipated. Despite her years of experience dealing with intensely devoted and often unpredictably quirky pet parents, she'd never experienced (nor expected) a client meeting quite like the one she enjoyed that evening. From the minute she arrived at Murphy's building and (in a somewhat Dottie-esque moment) checked her reflection in the glass of the entryway, lamenting the plain but functional braid that kept her habitually wayward hair mostly in order, nothing happened as she thought it would (or should). Not that she regretted the particular turn of events the evening had taken, at least not entirely. But she found it at least as confusing as it was gratifying. The whole incident left her feeling discomposed (in good and bad ways), a feeling that started as soon as her new client opened her door.

"You're not in your uniform." She cringed as soon as the entirely unnecessary statement left her mouth, but her past encounters with Murphy had left her wildly unprepared for the vision before her.

Murphy's worn, soft-looking jeans couldn't have fit her better if they'd been painted on her trim, fit legs. Her faded red V-neck T-shirt showed off an inviting glimpse of cleavage that Maddie immediately averted her eyes from. Unfortunately for Maddie, Murphy's lean, toned arms—one sporting an impressive (and incredibly sexy) half-sleeve of tattoos—looked just as good, and Maddie was running out of safe places to rest her eyes. Worse still, Murphy smelled amazing, like some strange blend of fresh, clean laundry and jasmine that shouldn't have worked but did, and making her just that much more irresistible, a tiny black kitten perched on her shoulder, playing with her ponytail and purring loudly. Maddie took in the full, glorious picture, thinking that Murphy barely resembled the imposing cop she remembered from their first meeting. And though it shouldn't have been possible, she was even hotter than before.

"I'm not on duty." Murphy laughed good-naturedly and invited Maddie into her home.

Trying to recover, she switched gears. "Is this Stanley or Herbie?"

"Stanley went into hiding the second you hit the buzzer. But Herbie is a big, tough street kitten. He's not afraid of anything. Are you little guy?" Murphy lifted the kitten from her shoulder then rubbed her nose on his as he batted her cheeks with his tiny paws.

Kitten and cop kept at it for several minutes. Meanwhile, Maddie wondered if anyone had ever died of an overdose of cuteness. A long, dreamy sigh escaped from her as she took in the adorable scene, inspiring a knowing, raised-eyebrow glance from Murphy. She immediately felt herself blush from head to toe.

"Can we start over?" She smiled (endearingly, she hoped), and Murphy nodded her assent. Maddie felt certain that her client was trying not to laugh at her. Not that she didn't have plenty of reason to, but at least she was considerate enough not to embarrass Maddie further.

"Hello, Officer Murphy." She stuck out her hand to shake. "It's a pleasure to see you again."

"It's always a pleasure to see you, Miss Smithwick." Murphy grinned and showed no interest in ending the handshake until Herbie leapt from her grasp and skittered out of the room.

"Call me Maddie, please." She hoped Officer Murphy would respond in kind with something she could call her—something other than Officer Murphy or Hot Cop. Instead Murphy offered to take her jacket and disappeared down the hall just as Herbie dashed back in the room and busied himself with chasing a stuffed mouse across the pristine floor.

Trying to relax, Maddie took a deep breath, and that's when she noticed another divine aroma, this one coming from the direction of what she guessed was the kitchen. Her stomach growled, reminding her that she hadn't eaten since breakfast.

"Are you hungry?" Murphy breezed back into the room, and Maddie couldn't help noticing the pink polish on Murphy's toenails—so not what she expected of a cop.

"I'm sorry?" Thanks to the toenail distraction, she missed the question.

"Dinner." Murphy inclined her head toward the heavenly scented kitchen. "I'm starving, so I made way too much food. Would you like some?"

"You don't have to feed me, Officer Murphy." There had to be something better to call this woman. Maddie really wished she knew Murphy's first name. "But if you want to eat before your dinner gets cold, I don't mind waiting." She smiled as her stomach growled again.

"I hate eating alone. Sit." Murphy pointed to a small table just outside a tiny but obviously functional kitchen, and Maddie, reminded of the commanding cop she'd first met, obeyed.

As Murphy moved back and forth between the kitchen and dining nook, Maddie tried hard not to stare, but Murphy, whose compact body moved with graceful economy, didn't make herself easy to ignore. Needing a distraction, Maddie turned her focus to the apartment rather than its occupant.

Murphy's place was definitely small, but what it lacked in space it made up in charm and warmth. Along with a few softly glowing lamps, candles illuminated the space, and she had combated the blandness of the dull, flat beige walls that plagued most apartments with brightly colored accents throughout. A large, comfortable-looking blue couch sat opposite a small television, and tidy, organized bookshelves lined one wall. In a move Maddie found oddly satisfying, she had organized her books according to color, a technique Maddie now considered implementing in her own home. A vase of flowers adorned her coffee table, and a few eye-catching rugs covered the floors in the living room as well as down the hallway that led (Maddie assumed) to the forbidden territory of her bedroom.

Pushing that thought (and its many distracting offshoots) right out of her head, Maddie returned her focus to the living room where, in an acrobatic display worthy of a circus or the Olympic games, a large black and white cat—Stanley, she presumed—had begun grooming himself in earnest on the back of her couch.

The space, neat and tidy as Maddie's home, held more feminine touches than she had expected. Confronting her own preconceived notions (and ashamed of herself for allowing them), she realized she had an idea of a cop's house, and this wasn't it.

In her mind, Murphy's place should have looked more like a bunker or dormitory, something more sparse and militaristic. She had expected to see Murphy's police gear—handcuffs, gun, cop utility belt (which probably had a better name)—sitting out in the open, ready for action. But there was nothing that indicated she spent her days taking down bad guys.

Really what did Maddie expect—every available surface would be festooned with cop paraphernalia?

"Does it pass inspection?"

Murphy's question brought her attention back to her unexpected dinner companion.

"Pardon?"

"My apartment. You've been studying it since you sat down. I'm just wondering if it's up to your standards."

"I'm sorry. This is unfamiliar territory for me. I wasn't expecting—"

"A dinner appointment?" Murphy had the most adorable dimple when she smiled, and Maddie had to look away again or risk feeding her already gargantuan crush on Officer Murphy.

"Can I get you something to drink?" she asked, bringing Maddie's attention back to her.

"Water if you've got it." Maddie grimaced, wishing she could somehow erase her statement. What did she think—that Officer Murphy lived in the only residence in the city without plumbing?

"Plenty of water, or I have stronger options." She held a bottle of wine in one hand, two glasses in the other. That plus the candlelight made Maddie wonder if she wanted to get more from this evening than a cat sitter. As soon as the thought appeared, she dismissed it. On what planet would someone who looked like Murphy either be interested in or have to work at seducing someone like Maddie?

"You may not be on duty, Officer Murphy, but I am."

"Well, when are you off duty?" She smiled again, and Maddie's eyes were riveted to that damn dimple.

"As soon as I'm finished here," she admitted, suddenly wondering why she hadn't hesitated to expose the flimsiness of her excuse—if Murphy wanted, it wouldn't be difficult to work around this obstacle to them sharing a drink.

"So you're saying that once we've wrapped up all of our very important pet-related businessing, you'll be free to have a drink with me."

Maddie tamped down the inner pessimistic optimist that read (most likely incorrectly) her invitation as an advance, reminded her that she no longer had the option of being receptive to flirtation and warned her she was headed for trouble. For all she knew, Murphy wasn't flirting at all, even though it seemed that way. Still, it would be best to say no.

"Yes," Maddie answered. "Once we take care of what I came here for, I'm all yours. I mean, I'm all yours now." She felt the heat of a blush like a solar flare flood her face and dropped her bright red head into her hands. Why did words hate her so much? "I mean, after we tend to business, I'd be happy to have a drink with you."

A grinning Murphy nodded once and disappeared into the kitchen. She returned a moment later with two glasses of wine, which she deposited next to their plates on the small table before breezing into the living room.

"So let's talk about cats," she said as she settled on her couch.

"What about dinner? I thought you were starving."

"It can wait a few minutes." She punctuated her statement with another of those dimple-producing smiles.

Grabbing her bag, she joined Murphy on her couch, inspiring a sullen departure from Stanley, who offered a steady stream of grumbling meows as he stomped out of the room. Maddie perched on the opposite end of the couch from Murphy, hopeful it would allow her to maintain more than just physical distance. "All right, then. Let's talk about cats."

Just then Herbie leapt into Maddie's lap, turned in a circle, laid down and started purring. She stroked his sleek fur and scratched under his chin, then behind his ear, bringing forth an increase in volume.

"You are shameless." Murphy's broad grin was at odds with her criticism. "Aren't cats supposed to be aloof? You could at least wait until I'm gone to replace me."

"It's not his fault," Maddie offered. "Animals can't resist me."

"I don't imagine they can." This time a wink accompanied her easy smile, and there was that dimple again.

Maddie felt herself losing the battle not to blush and turned away. To distract herself from the powerful allure of one Officer Dimples Murphy, she focused on extracting a contract from her bag—delicately so as not to evict the now-sleeping kitten from her lap.

"Tell me what you want," Maddie said. She didn't even need Murphy's reaction to know she hadn't phrased her request in the most innocent way possible.

Worrying what new and fabulous way she would find to humiliate herself before this conversation ended, she decided silence was her best friend and sat expectantly, pen poised and ready to jot down notes, hoping Murphy would have mercy on her and steer the conversation back in the right direction soon.

Through her grin, Murphy explained she'd be gone for the next three days, returning Friday evening.

"Where are you headed?" Maddie asked, though it was none of her business. She hoped Murphy found her nosiness more charming than off-putting.

"Nashville," she answered with no indication of the purpose of her trip or whether she looked forward to it or not.

"Oh," Maddie said and then asked about her preferred schedule for visits.

Over the next ten minutes, Murphy explained her cats' particular needs (including the proper method of playing with the wand toys that Herbie was partial to), showed Maddie where to find food, treats, toys, and the litter box, and signed the contract and handed over her keys. When she placed the keys in Maddie's outstretched hand, their contact again lasted longer than necessary, and she regretted agreeing to dinner or a drink with Murphy.

She attempted to speak around the sudden lump in her throat. "I'll make sure they get all the love and attention they need." She didn't know how long they sat there silently staring at each other, unable to move, the air charged.

"And food," Murphy said, breaking the spell. "Stanley will never forgive you if you forget the food."

"I would never forget the food."

"Speaking of which." She gestured to the table by the kitchen, with its candles and wine and required closeness— easily as intimate a setting as the one she'd shared the night before with Nadia—and she panicked.

"About that," Maddie grasped for a foothold. "Thank you for the offer, Officer Murphy, but I should really get going. It's getting late."

"It's six thirty."

"I have a big day of pet care ahead of me tomorrow, and I'll need to be well rested." She looked deflated but went to get Maddie's coat. "I'll see your boys tomorrow, and I'll let you know how they're doing. Have a good trip."

With that, she was out the door, and as soon as she heard the lock click behind her, she sank against the wall and groaned. "I am in so much trouble."

CHAPTER THIRTEEN

By the time she got a block from Murphy's building, Maddie wanted to find a megalith to crawl under. It wasn't enough that her complete lack of composure got the best of her as soon as Murphy opened the door, but she had to choose that moment to launch herself into Olympic-level mortification. If it wouldn't remind Murphy of what she really hoped she would forget given enough time (or an amnesia-inducing blow to the head), she would call her new client and apologize for her extreme overreaction.

She could just imagine that conversation. "Sorry I fled your apartment, but I thought you were hitting on me, and since I'm insanely attracted to you and apparently have zero willpower or loyalty to my girlfriend of less than twenty-four hours, I couldn't stay. I hope you understand." It would be better to let Murphy think she was just a little quirky. On the plus side, if Murphy actually did like her, Maddie's behavior would be enough to end whatever fleeting attraction might have been there. And if nothing else, at least she'd maintained her long-standing tradition of humiliating herself in the presence of a beautiful woman.

Feeling unduly hopeful that she'd exhausted her aptitude for embarrassing herself, she turned her thoughts to the evening ahead. Considering she would be heading into lesbian central, she probably should have been more worried about her knack for doing and saying the exact wrong thing in the most public way possible, but she felt oddly calm. Not about making any progress in her investigation—on that front she had next to no confidence—but since she wasn't heading to Pi in search of romance, her usual social jitters were absent—a refreshing and unexpected consequence of making up with Nadia.

As if summoned by Maddie's thoughts, the object of her appreciation chose that moment to call. "I was just thinking about you."

"Well that's a good sign," Nadia purred. "Hey, how did it go with your client? I'm not interrupting, am I?" she asked, earning points for remembering anything Maddie said during the snippets of conversation that had interspersed their intense making out the night before.

"It went well." She deftly avoided offering the embarrassing (and somewhat damning) details of her encounter with Murphy. "I just left. I'm heading home to feed the boys." She regretted she couldn't give her boys some much needed spoiling before turning right back around to meet Dottie. She would have to make her frequent absences and sub-par parenting up to them soon.

"It sounds like you've had a good night. Maybe we could make it even better. If you're free, that is."

"Well, I'm heading back out in about twenty minutes, so—"

"For business?" Nadia sounded adorably insecure, an effect Maddie never thought she would ever have on any woman.

"For drinks with Dottie, actually." She probably could have offered a more detailed account of her itinerary for the remainder of the evening, but remembering Nadia's bristly reaction the last time she had engaged in a bit of amateur detective work, she thought better of it. She justified her lie of omission by briefly considering the alternative—the possibility of an argument with Nadia less than a day into their renewed relationship seemed about as appealing as an acid enema.

"Oh." Nadia perked up. "I like Dottie," she said.

She assumed that proclamation came with an implied request for an invitation, which she ignored. As much as she wanted to see Nadia, she didn't want to dance around the potential minefield of her investigation butting heads with her love life.

"She'll be ecstatic to find that out. She loves adoration."

"I could tell her in person. Unless you don't want to see me."

"Of course I want to see you." She gave the only response possible and ground her teeth, hating that she couldn't just look forward to spending complication-free time with Nadia.

But how could she possibly say no? To refuse Nadia's self-invitation would mean lying (which she wasn't good at) and probably hurting her feelings (which she didn't want to do). The best she could hope for was that Nadia would show up after she wrapped up the business that brought her to Pi two nights in a row and that Nadia wouldn't ruin her investigation any more than her investigation would ruin her shot with Nadia. For all she knew the rest of the night would be a bust, so seeing her would guarantee at least one positive outcome from the whole ordeal.

"Great." Nadia sounded relieved, another shock to Maddie. "I've got a couple more appointments, but I can be there by eight."

"Perfect," Maddie said, and she meant it. Assuming Dottie didn't show up later than usual, that just might give Maddie enough time to talk to Kat unsupervised before enjoying an obligation-free night out. Depending on what she learned, she might end up being a bit distracted around Nadia, but she was starting to think this might actually work out for her; however, she drew the line at feeling optimistic about her chances.

Now that she had a reason to attempt to look good (other than staving off criticism from Dottie), Maddie risked upsetting her pups further by devoting some of her brief time at home to primping. She apologized profusely as she fussed with her hair rather than walking them, and she continued her supplication as she repeatedly changed her clothes. Obviously unsatisfied with his truncated time in the yard, Bart pouted in the corner (peppering her contrition with occasional noisy sighs) while she plundered the depths of her closet for something mildly appealing to wear—a challenge for a woman whose wardrobe largely consisted of comfortable, functional clothing.

More forgiving, Goliath curled up on his bed and watched her curiously as she darted back and forth. He barked once after she slipped into a clean pair of jeans and a dark green turtleneck that fit her more snugly than her usual T-shirts and hoodies. Interpreting his vocalization as approval, she thanked him and his still pouting brother with stuffed Kongs and headed out the door with just enough time to walk to Pi before her rendezvous with Dottie, allowing her ample opportunity to talk to Kittens and scope out the scene before Dottie finally made her fashionably late appearance.

Entering the bar, she felt more confident than her hastily concocted plan should have allowed her to be. Remembering Kat's disdain of her and having heard precious little about her from Leigh, she really had no reason to believe Kat would be at the bar two nights in a row or that she could orchestrate a conversation, even with Dottie's aid. Even if she did show up, Maddie couldn't be sure that Leigh wouldn't also be there to ensure failure. So much of this night was unlikely to pan out that Maddie probably should scrap her idea and go back to calling every person Terry had ever met. Her odds of success seemed greater with that approach.

Nevertheless, she charged ahead, overcome with the urge to get this started and learn if she had a chance of finding anything out on her ill-conceived quest for information on Terry's death and Leigh's alibi.

Scanning the premises as she made her way to the bar where Kittens stood impassively surveying the crowd, she rejoiced in her first triumph of the evening. At the other end of the bar, Kat tossed her blond hair about (in what Maddie assumed was a come-hither manner) while chatting with an adorably nerdy young woman in a bow tie and thick black-rimmed glasses. The remainder of the patrons scattered throughout the establishment paid the usual amount of attention to Maddie (which was none) but cast occasional glances at Kat. With Leigh nowhere in sight (and hopefully not because she was tucked away in the bathroom) and the population of the bar looking like it would fall into her trap (once she arrived), she smiled and took a seat at the far corner of the bar.

Now all she needed was for Leigh to stay away from the bar completely, for Dottie to appear before Nadia showed up and for Nadia to arrive after she managed to get some information from Kat. Assuming she hadn't exhausted her lifetime allotment of miracles when she found a flattering outfit *and* wrestled her hair into something close to submission, she just might leave the bar equipped to clear Leigh of murder. She didn't want to consider what would happen if this didn't pan out. She was pinning all her hopes on Kat Russell and whatever information she could share about Terry and (if she got luckier than she'd ever been) Leigh's whereabouts on the day Terry died.

"Two nights in a row. To what do I owe this pleasure?" Kittens asked when he placed a drink in front of her.

"I'm looking for my friend Leigh." In a roundabout way, it was the truth, except for leaving off the part about hoping not to find Leigh in the vicinity of the bar. "Is she here?"

"Not tonight, love. Must be a holiday."

Her heart sank for Leigh at the same time as she celebrated her good fortune. "She's here that often?"

He scrunched his face in thought and gazed at the ceiling. "Four, maybe five nights a week."

She was about to distract him from his work with further questions about Leigh and her whereabouts on the day Terry died when a thirsty patron called him to the other end of the bar. She supposed she'd get to talk to him eventually, though it might be intermittently.

Not three minutes later, Harriet walked in the door and charged up to a stunned Maddie.

"Harriet?" She almost choked on her bourbon. "What are you doing here?"

"I need to talk to you," she said like it was the most obvious thing in the world.

"But why are you *here*?" The last thing she needed was to blow her chance to talk to Kat because she was distracted by her sister.

"Dottie said she was meeting you here tonight, and you didn't answer your phone earlier, so I thought I'd pop in." She scanned the dimly lit room and fluttered her fingers in a charming semi-wave at Kittens. "Why are *you* here? Tell me you haven't resorted to trolling bars to find a girlfriend."

"I'm working on something for a friend."

"Seems dubious." Harriet continued looking around the bar. "Will your friend object to you buying your sister a drink to celebrate?"

"We're celebrating?" Confused didn't even begin to cover what she felt in that moment.

"Why else would I hunt you down at a bar?"

"Because I'm the living example of Murphy's Law." Flustered at that unintentional reminder of her newest client, she felt her face flush. Harriet, who hadn't stopped scanning the bar since their initial contact, finally turned her attention back to Maddie and favored her with a perplexed look. She dismissed it and asked again about her sister's intrusion on her night. "We're celebrating something?"

"Yes." Harriet's eyes widened, and she clapped her hands together, somehow conjuring Kittens. "My sister is buying me the dirtiest martini you can make."

"I've got a knack for making things dirty, love." He winked and set about making Harriet's drink with more panache than if he were in some kind of bartending circus. Maddie dropped her head in resigned disbelief that even cool, detached Kittens had succumbed to the Harriet Effect. Lord help him when Dottie descended.

"You were failing to say about the celebration?" she prodded once Kittens placed Harriet's drink in front of her with a flourish and a smile to which Maddie responded with a strenuous eye roll.

"Dad gave the okay." Harriet beamed and held her glass up expectantly.

"The okay for?"

"The firehouse," she groaned in exasperation. "He said you could talk specifics later, but it looked like a sound investment."

Simultaneously terrified and elated, Maddie jumped off her barstool and hugged her sister. "I can't believe I don't have to look at any more empty buildings."

"You're welcome," Harriet said and immediately scanned the room again.

"Is there something in particular you're looking for?" she asked.

"Is Patrick part of this secret mission for your friend?"

"Subtle, Harriet." No wonder her good news couldn't wait until tomorrow.

"You have to give him my phone number."

"What makes you think he's even interested?" Harriet hit her with an incredulous look over the rim of her glass. "Fine. He's interested. But shouldn't he ask for your number?"

"He's probably just concerned about things with you being awkward."

"A concern you obviously don't share."

"There's nothing to worry about. We're both adults. If things don't work out, we can be mature. What could be the harm?"

Only the destruction of a great guy's self-esteem when Harriet changed her mind. But she kept that thought to herself. She knew Harriet didn't set out to hurt people. She just had no idea how it felt to be the dumpee rather than the perpetual dumper. And it was really none of Maddie's business who Patrick dated. Plus, the attraction was obviously mutual. Who was she to stand in the way?

"Here's his number." She entered Patrick's contact information into her sister's phone. "If you want it, go for it, tiger."

"Really? You don't mind?"

"You're both adults, right? If my sister wants to go out with my kind, thoughtful, sensitive, incredibly big-hearted, favorite employee without whom I'd never survive, who am I to object?"

"You are the best little sister ever."

She accepted the somewhat empty compliment with a wry, "Thanks."

"I'll let you get back to your mysterious project." Harriet grabbed her cocktail and headed off in the direction of the pool tables where a crowd of women was, at minimum, about to be hustled into supplying Harriet with drinks. "And Maddie? Message received."

Maddie contemplated warning Patrick but thought better of it. The less involved she got now, the less she would be dragged into the middle of the morass of Harriet and Patrick's love life. One potential disaster averted (and another one generated), she turned her attention back to the two activities that occupied most of her time—worrying and waiting for Dottie.

CHAPTER FOURTEEN

Without so much as a glance toward the door, Maddie knew the exact moment when Dottie entered the bar. If the not-so-subtle swivel of a score of lesbian heads in her direction hadn't given it away, her friend's propensity for grand entrances surely would have done the trick. In this case, Dottie swept majestically across the scarred and worn floor between the door and the bar. As if she'd orchestrated her entrée (a possibility Maddie wouldn't put past her friend) "Simply Irresistible" started playing on the jukebox the second she stepped through the door, like her personal theme song. Working the room, she peeled off her expensive coat to expose the plunging neckline and elevated hemline of a designer dress, the cost of which surely would have covered Maddie's mortgage for the next three months. Eyes popped around the room, and Maddie smothered a smile at the sheer perfection of the moment. Dottie couldn't have played her part better if Maddie had told her what to do.

Fully aware of her effect on her now rapt audience, Dottie feigned nonchalance as she sashayed to the bar and, after wiping the stool with a handkerchief she extracted from her Chanel bag, perched on the seat next to Maddie.

"Carlisle is parking the car. She'll be in shortly."

"You drove? You live five blocks away."

Dottie glowered at her. "One does not hoof it five blocks in Jimmy Choos." She gestured to her elegant but painful-looking footwear.

"And you brought Carlisle?" Considering the sideways direction the guest list had already taken, Maddie wouldn't be all that surprised to see her grandmother stride up to the bar. (Though it would almost be worth the implosion of her investigation to witness Granny's interactions with Kittens.)

"I couldn't very well leave her at home with her cats, could I?"

"I don't see why not. The woman hates me. Why does she get to horn in on my night?"

"She doesn't hate you, pet. She just hasn't had time to properly appreciate your adorable idiosyncrasies. I'm sure this little outing will do wonders for your standing with Carlisle."

She had little confidence that using Dottie as a lesbian decoy would endear her to Carlisle. "I have my doubts about that." She hadn't yet decided the best way to tell Dottie her role that evening would be as eye candy. Now she wondered if she should even bother.

"True, you aren't traditionally charming, but with a little effort you can win her over. Carlisle is surprisingly open-minded. Except, of course, where her wardrobe is concerned. Not even my considerable fashion campaign has disabused her of her love of sweater sets."

"But it's brave of you to try." She squeezed her shoulder in mock sympathy, though she felt sorrier for poor Carlisle. While she'd borne the brunt of Dottie's disparaging comments for years, she could at least vent her exasperation (with a pointed glare if nothing else). She couldn't imagine silently enduring Dottie's "fashion campaign" as part of her job. Perhaps Maddie and Carlisle had some common ground after all.

Just then, she spotted a priggish, pursed-lipped Carlisle standing just inside the entryway and peering curiously around the bar. Her incongruous presence seemed to make her apprehensive, but once she located Dottie, an air of determination settled on her. At that moment, Maddie noticed a pack of bold and eager women heading Dottie's way (and even though Dottie's flair for grabbing the spotlight was the crux of Maddie's plan, she still bemoaned her own inconspicuousness). As the onslaught of Dottie's devotees approached from two sides, Maddie rose to clear a path, but Dottie halted her departure with a finely manicured hand on her arm.

"Where do you think you're going? I was promised drinks, which you have made no effort to procure."

"I'm going to the now empty side of the bar to talk to someone." Kat, the only person unhappy about Dottie's emergence on the scene, stood alone. She eyed her empty glass and seemed at a loss for what she should do to refill it.

"Not only are you ignoring my thirst, but now you're accusing me of being an inadequate companion?"

"Remember the whole reason we're here?"

"You mean other than tasty adult beverages?" She made no attempt to hide her impatience. "I dimly recall talk of ferreting out the truth from some mystery woman who isn't your stunning girl toy."

"She's standing over there." She suppressed a glower and inclined her head in Kat's direction. "And I need to act now."

"I can't believe you brought me to this hovel to abandon me," Dottie huffed. "And for a trashy bottle blonde who needs to lay off the bronzer. Have you no regard for our epic friendship?"

"I won't be gone long, and you'll have plenty of company, I promise."

"What about Carlisle?"

"I don't know. Maybe ask one of your new friends to buy her a drink."

Dottie's eyes widened at the possibilities. "We'll get a couple of cocktails in her, and she'll loosen up in no time."

Certain that Dottie was more or less in her element, Maddie made her way to the sparsely populated end of the bar to join a dejected Kat whose still-empty glass gave Maddie the perfect conversational inroad.

"I couldn't help but notice you're alone."

"I am now." Kat turned to face her lone admirer. After looking Maddie up and down, she shrugged as if to say she'd take what she could get. Her sorrowful gaze shifted to Dottie holding court with her former throng, and her eyes narrowed, in anger or hatred Maddie wasn't sure.

"I know how it feels."

"Really?" Skepticism dripped from her comment.

"Believe it or not, that's my best friend." Kat did a double take, obviously not believing it. "I've lived in her shadow for years, and it's hard always being runner up—not that you would have much experience being passed over for someone else."

Kat flinched, but Maddie maintained her innocuous, concerned expression. Kat had no reason to think Maddie knew anything about her past, a point Maddie hoped to use to her advantage.

"What do you want?"

"Just to buy you a drink." She signaled to Kittens and slid a twenty his way.

"Thanks." Kat eyed her with suspicion as she accepted the beer Kittens placed in front of her. Based on the change she got back, Kat was no connoisseur of fine beers, but at least she would be a cheap source of information.

"Where's Leigh?" Kat asked.

"I was going to ask you the same thing."

"So you're not with her?"

"Not tonight."

"Are you guys—"

"We're just friends," Maddie clarified, and Kat's posture immediately relaxed.

"I saw you together last night, and I wasn't sure. You know how Leigh is."

"What do you mean?"

"You know, she drinks too much and then ends up with people she shouldn't end up with."

Ignoring for the moment both her impending nausea at the thought of sleeping with one of her friends and the implication that Maddie could be a worse option for Leigh (or anyone on the planet) than Kat, she forged ahead. "Does that happen often?" Kat snorted into her already half-empty beer, a reaction Maddie took to mean yes. "She was never like that in college. I wonder when she changed."

Kat's glare couldn't have said "Are you really this stupid?" any more clearly than if she'd actually spoken the words.

"I know she's been having a hard time because of Lindsey."

"Bitch," Kat spat the word and drained her glass. Maddie signaled to Kittens for another.

"Not a fan?"

"Let's just say Leigh's relationship wasn't the only one Lindsey trashed."

"I'm so sorry," Maddie said. She gave Kat's arm a reassuring squeeze, and wondering if sympathy was the right angle, decided to leave her hand on Kat's arm.

"She was a selfish bitch." Kat shrugged dismissively, as if to suggest she'd gotten over it.

"Still, it hit Leigh pretty hard." She tried to swing the conversation back around to where she wanted it.

"You mean when she died?" Maddie had meant the breakup but didn't see a problem with this slight detour. It wouldn't be too challenging to segue from Lindsey's suicide to Terry's murder. "I can't say I'm sorry she's gone, but what a way to die. And poor Leigh. She's hurting so much right now, but hopefully soon she'll see she's better off."

"In what way?" She tried to keep the judgment from her voice, but it wasn't easy.

"She still thought she stood a chance of getting back together with Lindsey, and she was never going to move on as long as she was in the picture. It's horrible that it had to come to this, of course, but now maybe she'll start seeing her options."

Certain Kat saw herself as one of those options, Maddie shook her head in amazement. She wanted to get away from this callous woman, but she still had questions she hoped Kat could answer. She opened her mouth to steer the conversation back to the information she really wanted, but the words died on her lips thanks to Nadia's sudden presence beside her.

"What's going on here?" Nadia glanced at Maddie's hand on Kat's arm, and seeing how things looked from Nadia's perspective, a wave of unwarranted guilt washed over Maddie.

"You made it." Hoping they could skip past Maddie's perceived betrayal, she stood to kiss Nadia, who dodged her. Rebuffed, she sank back onto her barstool and wondered how she would fix this.

"I thought you were here with Dottie."

"I am. She's right over there." She pointed helpfully in the direction of Dottie's flock. "And as you can see, she's a little bit preoccupied at the moment." But Nadia didn't see. She never averted her angry eyes from Maddie.

"So you just wandered off to grope the first stranger you could find?"

"She wishes I was desperate enough to let her grope me," Kat sneered.

"You'd be lucky if she did." Nadia inexplicably rose to the defense of her allegedly untrustworthy date. Maddie couldn't decide if she should feel more alarmed by her possessive jealousy or pleased by the fact that she'd been vindicated.

"Whatever." Kat rolled her eyes and, grabbing her beer, sauntered off to the back of the bar, leaving Maddie to deal with Nadia's rapidly shifting emotions. She didn't know where to begin. It was little consolation that she didn't have to.

"This is an unexpected side of you." Nadia turned on her once they were alone.

"I could say the same. What just happened?"

"Honestly, I'm not sure." Nadia sank into the seat vacated by Kat and ran her hands through her hair. "It was a crappy day, and I was really looking forward to being with you. Then I got here and saw you with your hands all over that woman—"

"One hand," Maddie corrected. "And it was on her arm—hardly an erogenous zone."

"Why was it there?" The dismay in Nadia's eyes tore at Maddie.

"She was telling me about a rough breakup, and I thought she could use some sympathy."

"So I completely overreacted?"

"Maybe a little." She gave Nadia's hand a gentle squeeze. While she couldn't say she considered jealousy the most appealing character trait, she found Nadia's earlier display oddly flattering. Nevertheless, she decided never to tell Nadia about her almost dinner with Murphy.

"I'm sorry. It's just—I just got you back. I don't want to lose you again."

"I don't want that either," Maddie said and moved in for the kiss she didn't get earlier.

She knew they should talk more—about Nadia's perplexing possessiveness and all the secrets Maddie kept. She knew ignoring their issues would only make them harder to deal with when they returned (and she had no doubt they would), but something about Nadia banished everything but physical need. Forgetting common sense and her own more modest nature, she grabbed Nadia's shirtfront and pulled her in for a deeper kiss. If her whimper was any indication, she didn't object to this forceful side of Maddie. In fact, she seemed ready to devour her, and Maddie was ready to let her.

"Maddie, you can't just go around kissing people in bars."

"Oh god." Maddie buried her face in her hands. Meanwhile, Harriet, apparently finished with pool and free martinis and flirtatious lesbians, loomed over the recently oblivious couple.

"Not even if it's her girlfriend?" Nadia asked, more playful than hostile.

"When did you get a girlfriend?"

"Last night," Maddie admitted.

"Why didn't you tell me?"

"For this exact reason," she muttered but had no time to say anything further.

"Nadia, dear." Dottie joined the multitude of onlookers, deepening the blush that engulfed Maddie's entire head. This was probably why she never dated. "So good to see you again."

"You're Nadia? *The* Nadia?" Harriet jumped back in but gave a flustered Nadia no time to respond. "This explains the extreme moping. Are you back for real or just long enough to make my sister sad again?"

"This is your sister?" Nadia asked.

Maddie dropped her head onto the bar. "Somebody get me a drink."

"I'd love one myself, but Carlisle has hijacked the bartender."

She lifted her head long enough to glance down the bar where a hyperattentive Kittens poured a glass of Maddie's favorite bourbon for a demurely smiling Carlisle.

"Perfect," she groaned again and surrendered to the inevitable chaos of her worlds colliding—without the soothing effects of alcohol.

CHAPTER FIFTEEN

"Harriet told me she met your lady friend."

Granny's call interrupted Maddie's total lack of progress in Leigh's case. Considering that all of her effort the night before had gotten her absolutely nowhere, she had renewed her efforts to contact Terry's friends and family—no small task given that her only source of information was names listed in an obituary that rivaled *The Odyssey* in length. Then she had to hunt down individual contact information (and really, the Internet could only get her so far), hope she found the right Michael Jones or Mary Smith in a sea of Michael Joneses and Mary Smiths, and finally convince these people to talk to her. It was an arduous (and in most cases fruitless) task, one she would be more than happy to wash her hands of.

Hearing from her grandmother would have been a welcome distraction had the conversation not started on a touchy subject about which Granny sounded so prickly. Though Maddie did not want to dissect her tenuous love life with Granny Doyle, she suspected she had little choice in the matter and less hope of redirecting the conversation. Once Granny seized something, she rarely let go. Still, she wanted to try to soothe her grandmother and downplay this discussion at the same time.

"Purely by accident," Maddie offered in an attempt to appease Granny.

"What's that supposed to mean? Are you ashamed of her or us?" Granny snapped, and Maddie wished she'd thought her comment through. Clearly she had upset her grandmother through no fault of her own. Had it been up to her, Harriet and Nadia still wouldn't have met. No matter, an upset Granny was not how she wanted to start her day. "I should think you'd want her to meet your family if she matters to you."

Maddie bit her tongue. Now that her dander was up, Granny would take almost anything she said the wrong way. She had no chance of winning.

"Of course I want her to meet you." Preferably after she and Nadia had more time to sort out last night's misunderstanding and following the strenuous efforts to prepare her for the onslaught that could be her family (the minutest glimpse of which she'd already gotten thanks to Harriet).

"Then I'll expect you for dinner."

"Wait. What?" She couldn't believe she'd walked into that.

"You heard me, child."

"I heard you, but it's kind of short notice." And not at all what she had in mind for a third date.

"What does she have going that she can't take time to eat?"

"Granny, Nadia works long hours. Sometimes she doesn't get home until after eight o'clock. That's too late for dinner."

"Then bring her for dessert."

She should have known a pesky thing like Nadia's availability wouldn't stand in Granny's way. "I'll see if she can make it, but I'm not promising anything."

"Just tell me what kind of pie she likes, and I'll expect you at eight fifteen."

Exasperated, Maddie hung up the phone. Though she knew she should return to her futile efforts at detective work before her walkers showed up for the day, she felt she needed to warn

Nadia as soon as possible, giving her the rest of the day to invent a believable excuse and reschedule with Granny, several weeks in the future if possible.

"I hope you like pie," she said when Nadia answered her phone.

"You're making me a pie?" Nadia was understandably confused.

"Even better, my grandmother is making you a pie, which we are expected to enjoy with her tonight. Unless you don't want to. I can find some excuse."

"And disappoint your grandmother? I wouldn't dream of it."

"You don't want me to try to get out of it?"

"Well, I could be wrong, but I'm guessing your grandmother is as, um, strong-willed as her granddaughter, so it won't be easy to change her mind."

"No, it won't."

"And I would like to meet her. She is partially responsible for us dating."

"In much the same way clocks are responsible for the passing of time." She felt flabbergasted by the turn this conversation had taken. Of all the ways she thought Nadia might react, eager acceptance had not been an option. "You're really all right with this?"

"I really am. I've never dated a woman with such an invested family before."

"They can be a bit much," she replied apologetically.

"I like it. It's nice they're so accepting. I'm more accustomed to people wondering what the neighbors will think, so this is kind of nice in a mildly terrifying way."

"You are something else," she said, her thoughts already turning over Nadia's comment as she ended the call.

Thanks to Nadia's apparently rocky dating history, Maddie realized she'd neglected an easier path to information about Terry and kicked herself for not thinking of it sooner. Flipping through her notes, she found the name of Terry and Lindsey's neighbor, the one she'd heard had not been a fan of Terry. If living in one of the more sociable areas of the city had taught her anything, it was that neighbors knew one another and talked. Unhappy neighbors talked more. Her recent association with Lester Parrish was testament to that. It was time for her to pay a visit to Esther Snodgrass.

Though she'd considered her options throughout the day (even bouncing ideas off the animals in her care, who as it turned out, had no advice on human interactions), she wasn't sure how she'd manage to talk to Esther. While she knew what building the woman lived in, her home could be any of the hundreds of units in that high-rise, and it wasn't like she could go knocking on every door until she found the right one. Beyond that, other than her name and her distaste for a couple of dead women, she knew nothing about her. How could she possibly schmooze her way into this woman's world? Not that she wouldn't try. The attempt seemed preferable to making a thousand cold calls to strangers. But she doubted she would make it past the first obstacle in her path: the doormen at these high rises, who had historically never found it difficult to resist her total lack of charm. If she thought for a second Dottie was available and not a little peeved with her over the previous night's failed mission, she would recruit her gregarious friend for this smooth-talking operation. For now, she would hold off on any further damage to her friendship.

In the gap between her walk with Tabs Stewart and her visit with the feline Murphys (her final stop of the day), she took a small detour to the building where Lindsey had died and where Esther Snodgrass still lived. Fingers crossed, she hoped she would get more for her trouble than a bit of exercise. She cruised past the building once, still trying to decide the best approach to the doorman and Mrs. Snodgrass. In a perfect world, Esther would have a dog she could offer to walk, giving her a foot in the door. And if Esther was anything like her neighbors, once she was engaged in conversation, it wouldn't be too hard to get Esther to talk about her neighbors.

But for all she knew Esther hated animals and didn't care much for chitchat either. If that was the case, she would have to be more direct and hope that Esther answered her questions, assuming she could even get in to see her, which was a rather large assumption. She probably would have been better off calling Mrs. Snodgrass, but since she was already at her building, she thought she might as well try to finagle a face-to-face conversation.

Turning back around, she dismissed her nerves, determined to make the best of the situation. So focused was she on her internal pep talk that she failed to notice the person walking toward her until she was right on him. Her apology died on her lips as she stared up into the irritated gaze of Detective Fitzwilliam. As usual he looked about as happy as if he'd spent the last day and a half digesting a cactus.

"Miss Smithwick." He used the same incorrect pronunciation of her name he'd insisted on since their initial encounter. "Just out for a walk, or are you trying to complicate my life again?"

"Neither, actually. I'm hoping to meet a potential new client in the building." She offered a thinly stretched version of the truth and felt no guilt about it. If her machinations somehow managed to net her information that cleared Leigh (and possibly even pointed to the real killer), she was actually doing Fitzwilliam a favor.

"How nice for you," he drawled, his disinterest palpable. "I hope the dogs will keep you busy enough to stay out of police work. The last thing I need is a helpful citizen getting in the way."

"Not to worry, Detective Fitzwilliam. I wouldn't dream of interfering."

"Again," he added, and she wrestled with the choice commentary that lurked within her. The only thing that would get her was unwanted scrutiny from him.

"Right. Again," she agreed.

"Keep it that way, Miss Smithwick."

She ground her teeth at his habitual abuse of her name. Was it really that difficult to say "Smiddick"? She didn't think so. She'd been doing it since childhood.

"Now if you'll excuse me, I have legitimate detective work to tend to." He turned to go, missing her indignant expression, but before he got far, a tiny, bespectacled, silver-haired woman in a blue polyester dress came scuttling out the door, calling his name and waving frantically. In one hand she carried a plastic food container.

"Mr. Fitzwilliam!" Maddie exulted in Fitzwilliam's flinch at the "mister." "You forgot your coffee cake."

"Thank you, Mrs. Snodgrass." He looked about as happy to accept it as he would a hug from a boa constrictor. He took the proffered container and continued on his way.

She felt no surprise that he couldn't muster any happiness about receiving baked goods from a sweet old lady. He probably spent his entire December tripping mall Santa Clauses. But his habitual irascibility aside, she celebrated the uncommon luck that had planted Esther Snodgrass in her path, no subterfuge required.

"Excuse me." She approached the older woman. "Are you Esther Snodgrass?"

"Yes dear." Esther, apparently pleased at being recognized, beamed and clapped her now empty, age-spotted hands together. "Can I help you?"

"My name is Matilda Smithwick. I was hoping you had a minute to talk."

Esther looked instantly flustered, as if she had asked her to choose between oxygen and food. "*Jeopardy* is about to start. Will this take long?"

"I promise to be quick, Mrs. Snodgrass."

"What is this about, dear?"

Instantly deciding the road to information was paved with deceit, she asked, "Do you have any pets?"

Her eyes lit up, and Maddie (feeling only momentarily guilty) knew she'd made the right call. "Thelma and Louise are my babies," Esther gushed. "Oh, I wish I could show you some pictures."

"Better yet, you could introduce us," Maddie suggested, simultaneously hoping that Esther Snodgrass was and was not gullible enough to invite a complete stranger into her home on the string-thin connection of a professed interest in animals.

"They would love that," Esther raved. "Are you sure you don't mind coming up?"

"Not at all," Maddie said, falling into step behind the adorably trusting Mrs. Snodgrass.

CHAPTER SIXTEEN

Maddie's first impression of Esther's home was that it was in dire need of a renovation. The space, not much more than a studio, was crammed with ornate (some might say tacky) décor, including several vases of varying sizes and matching lamps on either side of a tufted, floral-print couch that had been hermetically sealed in clear plastic to preserve (Maddie assumed) its elegance. The lamps' output barely put a dent in the gloom created by heavy maroon drapes covering the windows. Nevertheless, Maddie's vision snagged on the golden silk tassels dangling from the valance of each window as well as from the lampshades. An imposing, intricately-carved coffee table (burdened by a wealth of doilies strewn across its dark surface) occupied the middle of the blue shag carpet. And though she had never felt claustrophobic before, Esther's wallpaper—a cream background obscured by a profusion of peonies—gave Maddie the sense the room was closing in on her. The whole experience was like stepping inside a miniature time capsule.

Stockpiling static electricity as she shuffled toward her avocado green kitchen, Esther cooed lovingly at two tiny, yapping balls of ruddy fluff. Needing to focus on something other than her garish yet mesmerizing interior design choices, Maddie squatted to greet the perpetually barking Thelma and Louise. The dogs yipped and spun furiously as she doted on them. She didn't know what kind of dogs they were, but if she had to guess, she would say someone had managed to breed Persian cats with Pomeranians.

"Would you care for some tea, dear?" Esther's reedy voice barely reached Maddie over the noise of the dogs and Esther's flat-screen television, the one concession to modernity she appeared to have made.

"You don't need to go to any trouble for me, Mrs. Snodgrass."

"It's no trouble at all." The sharp whistle of a teakettle added to the commotion of her tiny home. "The water was still warm from my visit with Mr. Fitzwilliam."

"Does Mr. Fitzwilliam stop by often?" she asked, relishing the minor revenge of calling him "mister" even though he wasn't around to hear it. "Is he a friend of yours?"

"Heavens no, Matilda. He's a policeman. A detective," she announced proudly, like she was in some way responsible for his career path.

"A detective?" She feigned astonishment. "I hope you aren't in trouble."

"Not me. My neighbors. I probably shouldn't say anything." She lowered her voice to a conspiratorial whisper. "He's investigating a murder."

Maddie supplied the appropriate surprised gasp (hopeful that it would spur Esther on to sharing more confidences). Her counterfeit alarm soon turned genuine as she watched Esther totter into the room carrying a silver tray laden with an ostentatious tea set and two slabs of coffee cake on delicate filigree plates, all of it atop the requisite bed of doilies. Esther executed a complicated dance around the attention-seeking Thelma and Louise, and Maddie (alternating between awe and concern) wondered if Esther would respond to an offer of help with the same independent irritation as Granny Doyle.

Unaware she'd been holding her breath, she exhaled once Esther's cargo had landed safely on the coffee table, and the threat of disaster had passed.

"Both of my next-door neighbors have died in the last month," Esther continued her illicit tale. "Under suspicious circumstances." They sat on the grandiose sofa at the same time, producing a thunderous crackling from the plastic cover.

"How awful that must have been for you." Maddie worried she was overdoing it a little, but Esther didn't seem to notice.

"I don't like to think there's a killer on the loose, but Mr. Fitzwilliam will catch whoever is responsible. He's very smart." Esther scooted one of the plates in her direction. "I made it myself," she informed a smiling Maddie.

She took a bite of the coffee cake and instantly regretted it. Forcing herself to swallow the glob of sawdust (guessing by the texture), she attempted to wash the overwhelming taste of salt from her mouth with a swig of weak, scalding tea. No wonder Fitzwilliam had seemed so disappointed at receiving the gift of Esther's baked goods.

She spoke once she'd recovered from the assault on her taste buds. "What a tragedy to lose friends so abruptly."

"Oh, they weren't my friends, dear."

"No?"

"I'm afraid we didn't get along very well."

"Why is that?" She shifted in her seat, yielding another clamorous report from beneath her. She hated to consider the horrors of visiting Esther on a sweltering summer day.

"It wasn't because they were lesbians, if that's what you think."

Maddie choked on her second sip of tea and gave up hope of ever ridding her burned mouth of the lingering taste of Esther's confectionary offerings. "Of course not."

"Because I have no problem with you gays."

Never sure how to greet such proclamations, she offered a tentative, "Thank you," and wondered briefly what about her had set off Esther's surprising gaydar.

"It's just that they weren't very nice people."

"In what way?"

"I baked them cupcakes when they first moved in, and they never thanked me or returned the favor." For which Maddie thought Esther should be eternally grateful.

"Was there anything else?"

"My goodness, yes. Visitors coming and going at all hours. Their children were unruly and disrespectful. No wonder, considering their role models. They had drunken arguments, even with that nice man Ray. He was Lindsey's ex-husband, and he wanted to raise the children himself, give them some discipline."

"For people you didn't get along with, you know a lot about them."

"Thin walls, dear." She gestured over her shoulder at what must have been the adjoining wall to Lindsey and Terry's home. "And they had the nerve to complain about Thelma and Louise barking. I know they get a little excited every now and then, but they aren't maniacs like those awful women said in their complaint."

"They filed a complaint?"

"They were trying to get us kicked out." Her voice rose in her indignation. "I've lived here for forty years. Where would I go?"

Maddie clucked her tongue in sympathy but didn't dare suggest the sacrilege of choosing any of the thousands of other available living spaces in the city.

"But then they died and the problems all went away. Mind you, I'm not happy that my next-door neighbors were killed, but it did work out for me and the girls." She shrugged and sipped her tea, apparently oblivious to the fact that she'd just revealed a motive for killing her neighbor. Though Maddie found her blasé attitude about murder somewhat troubling, her other comment deserved more attention in the moment.

"They were both killed?"

"Not exactly," Esther admitted. "Lindsey took her own life, but I wonder..."

Maddie waited half an eon for her to finish her statement but then gave up hope that she would ever pick up where she left off. "What do you wonder, Mrs. Snodgrass?"

"I heard Lindsey talking with someone just before she died, and I do wonder if that person maybe said something that sent Lindsey over the edge."

Maddie cringed at the unfortunate pun. "Who was it? Do you know?"

Though there wasn't automatically a connection between Lindsey's final conversation and Terry's death, Maddie hoped this bit of gossip would at least give her a lead to follow—something other than Terry's obituary. She swore she would choke down an entire cake of Esther's making if she helped her prove Leigh's innocence.

"Oh no, dear. It was time for my walk with the girls, so I left. When we came back, the police were here, and I guess Lindsey was dead." Maddie slumped in her seat.

"So you have no idea who it might have been?"

"It could have been anyone, I suppose. Ray or Deborah or maybe one of those other women who came over all the time."

"Who is Deborah?"

"One of our door people. She flirted with Lindsey regularly, right in front of Terry even. Terry didn't care for that of course, but Deborah kept on flirting, and Lindsey ate it up. Not a nice girl." Esther sipped her tea again and then paused, her cup halfway to the table, "Pardon my asking, dear, but why are you so interested in all of this?"

Maddie took that as her cue to leave. "Well, it's a fascinating story, don't you think? And I was enjoying your company so much, Mrs. Snodgrass. I rarely get to sit and chat with people, but it looks like *Jeopardy!* is starting." She rose noisily and pointed to the television. "I should leave you to enjoy it. Thank you so much for the tea and the coffee cake. It was incredible."

"But Matilda, we never discussed what it was you wanted to talk about."

"Another time, maybe." She made her way to the door, Thelma and Louise a barking, whirling dervish in her wake.

"I'd like that very much, dear. Come by any time."

"I really hope that's not necessary, for so many reasons," she said to the empty hallway before hurrying to her next appointment.

An hour into her scheduled thirty-minute visit with Stanley and Herbie, Maddie realized she would never make it back to the office in time to collect keys from her walkers and close up shop. Given the choice between upsetting the cats in her care and relying on her second-in-command, she opted for asking Patrick to tend to the end of day business in her absence, a request he met with a typically enthusiastic, "Will do, boss!"

Though Officer Murphy had requested (and paid for) significantly less of Maddie's time, she didn't mind the delay. The reason for her extended stay—a rare display of affection from Stanley, who (according to Murphy) had perfected the art of feline detachment—made it almost impossible to leave. If the large cat sprawled across her lap drooling and purring wasn't enough to inspire her to tarry, the unexpected thunderstorm and her total lack of preparedness for it made lingering in Murphy's home an irresistible option.

Having tended to her fair share of misanthropic cats, she was stunned when, halfway through their appointment, Stanley came out of hiding, hopped up on the couch where she sat playing with Herbie's feather toy and settled on her lap. Certain this was a case of mistaken identity, she cautiously touched the top of Stanley's head. Instead of swatting her hand away, hissing or finding some other way to make her pay for his error, Stanley immediately began purring and drooling. He even grabbed her hand when she attempted to stop petting him. How could she do anything but sit there, stroking Stanley with one hand while entertaining Herbie with the other? Eventually Herbie, tired of killing feathers on a stick, joined his big brother on her lap, and they refused to move for close to an hour. With little to occupy her mind as two cats slumbered on top of her, she soon replayed her interview with Esther Snodgrass.

It seemed somehow wrong to suspect an elderly woman of murder, like thinking that Granny Doyle could ever be guilty of more than being occasionally pushy or cranky. But Esther certainly had motive. Considering the nature of the crime, it wouldn't be difficult for her to pull it off. True, she was a terrible baker, but it was possible she had feigned incompetence just to throw the police off (though that didn't explain why she'd forced Maddie to choke down her arid brick of salt masquerading as dessert). As evidenced by Maddie's current train of thought, it wasn't much of a red herring. Beyond that, the brownies that killed Terry didn't have to taste good. They just had to be deadly. She didn't know how Esther would have gotten Leigh's recipe or why she would have reason to know about Terry's peanut allergy. However, given her talents at eavesdropping, neither was impossible.

More intriguing was Esther's claim that Lindsey hadn't been alone when she killed herself. Assuming an old woman's ability to hear through walls and above the cacophony of her television and the steady output of Thelma and Louise could be relied upon, that meant someone was with Lindsey when she died, which meant maybe it wasn't Lindsey who had taken her life. If that was the case, Maddie wondered how likely it was that two members of the same household were murdered by different people in a two-week span of time. It seemed highly doubtful, which most likely meant that whoever killed Terry also killed Lindsey, a questionable conclusion that didn't look good for Leigh. Though she believed Leigh would never kill anyone, especially not the woman she loved, and there was no doubt in Maddie's mind that Leigh, inexplicably, still loved Lindsey, she doubted that Detective Fitzwilliam would share the same certainty about her friend.

Since he may have already arrived at the same startling conclusion thanks to his earlier chat with Esther, Maddie needed to work fast.

CHAPTER SEVENTEEN

No way could Maddie out-detect a veteran of police work like Fitzwilliam (as he loved to remind her), especially considering his sizable head start, but for Leigh's sake she had to do something. For that she needed a plan, which meant she needed clarity, more than she could gain from sitting in a near stranger's house, petting her cats and continuously reviewing the events of her afternoon. Having already successfully extracted her phone from her pocket without disturbing either dozing feline, she reached out to one of the least likely sources of clarity available to her.

"I'm not sure I thanked you for your help last night." Although she hadn't known if she'd get Dottie rather than voice mail or the ever-attentive Carlisle, Maddie had decided that, no matter what, supplication would be her best opening.

"And you never did buy me a drink. Are you calling now to atone for your gross abuse of my good nature or to make more empty promises?"

"It's not my fault your surprise guest bewitched the bartender into uselessness."

"Don't remind me of that fiasco, peaches. Carlisle has been bordering on chipper all day. It's disturbing. I can't believe you did this to me."

Dottie's long-suffering sigh penetrated the air for several seconds, but rather than pointing out, again, her sole responsibility for introducing Carlisle to Kittens, Maddie attempted to get the conversation back on track. "Well, I appreciate your help, and I promise to make the drink up to you."

"Please tell me you managed to ferret out some information, or better yet, that you solved the crime. I couldn't bear it if my great sacrifice proved unprofitable."

"The only thing I ferreted out was extreme frustration. I left the bar with more questions than answers, I'm afraid." Though she supposed she had, in a roundabout way, netted some information from their excursion. It was through Harriet's chance encounter with Nadia and her subsequent conversations with Granny and Nadia that she ended up in Esther Snodgrass's florid living room, so in a sense, the evening hadn't been a complete waste of time and energy. Still, it hadn't gotten her nearly as far as she hoped it would.

"If need be, I suppose I could be persuaded to return to that charming neighborhood oasis in our continued search for the truth. I told some of the girls to keep an eye out for me," a pronouncement no doubt influenced by the generosity of Dottie's new friends. "Do you think any of them can afford a trophy wife?"

"I think that's an avenue best left unexplored." She hated to think of the possible damage caused by Dottie dabbling in lesbianism.

"Which makes it all the more appealing to me. What time should I meet you there?"

"I'll have to pass on bar-based truth seeking tonight," she answered, a jolt of nerves surging through her as she considered how much she would rather accompany Dottie to a lesbian bar in search of a murderer than expose Nadia to Granny Doyle in the infancy of their relationship. Undoubtedly, she'd need a drink before the night ended, possibly before it even began.

"A murderer is on the loose, pet. What do you have going on this evening that's more pressing than the hunt for clues? A little physical therapy with the love doctor, perhaps?"

"That's highly doubtful," she muttered before filling Dottie in on Granny's expert finagling of a meeting with Nadia. "I may never have sex again."

"I could come along and run interference for you."

She imagined that would go about as well as using butane to douse an inferno. "Thanks, but I think I'll just risk letting Granny run Nadia off with a well-intentioned interrogation and some aggressive doting."

"Fine," Dottie sighed again. "But I expect a full report."

"Of course," she said, though she had no intention of reliving whatever interpersonal horrors awaited her at Granny's. It would be quicker to agree and move on than to argue with Dottie. "Anyway, after last night I'm rethinking my whole approach to helping Leigh." As surprisingly enjoyable as Pi and Kittens were, both of her bar expeditions had thus far bordered on counterproductive. Her only other lead at this point was the phone book of Terry's obituary. She'd rather elope with a serial killer than return to that never-ending list of names.

"What's the new plan?"

"Instead of hunting for the real killer, I'm going to try to prove that a suicide wasn't really a suicide."

"So now you're inventing crimes."

"I'm not inventing anything." At least not on her own, but she might too readily be spinning the hearsay of an old woman into solid evidence.

"What on earth makes you think that a suicide is anything other than self-slaughter?"

"A possibly murderous little old bird told me." Herbie's little head popped up at the sound of the word "bird," and he ambled off to the window, possibly in hopes that her utterance could conjure up some enticing prey for his amusement. Stanley barely flinched.

"Intriguing and appalling at the same time. How do you plan to uncover this ultra-devious angel of death?"

"I'm not sure yet, but I think it starts with a man named Ray."

"I'm in," Dottie bellowed.

"In for what? I just told you I have no plan."

"You'll cook something up, beef cheeks, and when you do, I assume you'll need me to beguile this Ray person for you. I do have considerably more experience exploiting male weakness."

Maddie hadn't gotten that far in her machinations, but Dottie raised an excellent point. "That's actually a great idea."

"Don't sound so surprised, ducks. I happen to be brilliant."

"I never doubted that," Maddie said before promising to find Ray for the next phase of the investigation.

Almost nonexistent plan in place, Maddie felt marginally more proactive, but she still questioned the wisdom of her revised course. What if she wasted time hunting down the killer that never was while Fitzwilliam continued amassing circumstantial evidence against Leigh? She needed input from someone a little farther removed from flights of fancy than Dottie. Her legs falling asleep from roughly twenty pounds of cat holding them in one position for so long, she shifted slightly, rousing an irritated Stanley. And as she watched the perturbed feline sauntering off to his own side of the couch (grumbling all the while), she realized she had the perfect candidate.

"Your cat pinned me down for over an hour," she wrote. It seemed like a good opening, but she hesitated before sending the text. Though she would be delivering on her promise to update Murphy on her kitties, she could also end up doing more damage than good if Murphy took offense to a little opportunistic brain picking on Maddie's part.

Never in her life had she expected to become someone who would exploit a relationship with a client (and someone she genuinely liked), yet there she was considering just that. On top of abusing her position, she also might be handing the affable cop one more reason to think less of her. She could be putting her integrity at stake and risking damage to her business (and the chance of a friendship with Officer Murphy) but might not get anything in return. Ultimately, though, the chance that she could prevent Leigh from spending her life in prison for a crime she didn't commit overrode Maddie's desire to make a good impression on Officer Murphy. She hit Send.

I can't believe you stayed that long. Murphy answered immediately, making Maddie wonder just how much Murphy was enjoying her vacation.

Well, he was sleeping so peacefully. I didn't want to disturb him. Plus, it was raining, and I didn't have an umbrella. Being a cat bed seemed like the better option.

It almost always is. What do I owe you for all that extra time?

Nothing at all. I just thought you'd like to know how well we're all getting along.

No surprise there. Herbie is a love bug. That's actually how he got his name.

Tabling for the moment that adorable glimpse of the softer side of Officer Murphy, she replied with her own surprising development. *Not Herbie. Stanley.*

Are you sure you're at the right house?

Unless I somehow stumbled into an alternate dimension.

That's a distinct possibility. Stanley doesn't like anybody. He doesn't really even like me.

Maddie seriously doubted that last part. Grumpy though he could be, Stanley seemed far too wise to dislike someone as thoroughly likeable as Murphy.

I'm kind of like Snow White, so don't take it too hard.

Is that your way of telling me you live with seven men? A winky face emoji accompanied her question, reminding Maddie all too powerfully of the free-flowing, dimple-accentuating, in-person winks of Officer Murphy.

They're messy, but it does help with living expenses, Maddie answered.

She hated to sacrifice the playful mood, but she needed to get to the point and let Murphy get back to whatever had taken her to Nashville. Crossing her fingers that she wasn't about to ruin everything, she went for it. *Have you ever heard of a suicide that wasn't a suicide?*

She stared at Herbie chasing the raindrops trailing down the window and waited for a response.

Is this a riddle? Murphy answered after a pregnant pause.

Not a riddle. I need your professional opinion. Almost as an afterthought, she added, *For a friend.* Maddie's phone rang almost instantly, and for a moment she stared at it stupidly, wondering what was happening.

"Should I be worried about you?" Murphy sounded stern and concerned at the same time, and Maddie kicked herself for nonchalantly dropping a loaded word like "suicide" in something so casual as a text.

"Not at all. I'm fine, and I swear this is not a cry for help. I'm sorry if I scared you. I shouldn't have bothered you on your vacation."

"Tell me what's going on."

"I'm so sorry. Please just forget it. I really don't want to trouble you."

"It's a bit late for that," Murphy said, but she sounded more amused than upset. "What happened?"

Having little choice but to see the mess she'd made through to the end, she did her best to explain without making herself look worse. "My friend's ex killed herself a few days ago, but it was so sudden and unexpected—"

"That your friend wants to believe it was murder rather than suicide."

"Something like that." The fewer details Murphy had, the more blameless Maddie appeared.

"Tell your friend that most suicides are exactly that."

"Most?" She grasped at the straw of hope offered by Murphy's statement. It wasn't a ringing endorsement of the investigation Murphy knew nothing about, but it was an indication that she might not be totally off base. "Meaning some aren't?"

"That's not going to bring your friend any peace of mind, especially if the police aren't investigating it." She again questioned whether Fitzwilliam had any intention of exploring the slender possibility that Lindsey's death might be a homicide or if he even knew that chance existed.

"I guess it's stupid to think the police have time to look into every death in the city, no matter how odd it seems."

"It's not stupid to want to understand what happened, and it's natural to wish things were different." Murphy's sympathetic voice held no traces of pity or judgment, and she imagined what a reassuring presence the capable cop must be when disaster struck. "I'm sorry your friend is going through this."

"Thank you, Officer Murphy. I'm sorry to have intruded on your vacation."

"I can think of worse intrusions," Murphy said softly, leaving Maddie with the slightly unmoored feeling she was beginning to associate with the companionable police officer.

Satisfied that it wasn't completely preposterous to think Lindsey might not have taken her own life (though not at all satisfied that she wasn't racing off in the wrong direction), she decided to take the risk of making a giant mistake. She just hoped the gamble was worth Leigh's life.

CHAPTER EIGHTEEN

Maddie knew she should capitalize on the minimal progress (or possible backslide) she'd made in Leigh's case. Her nagging doubts that she was racing in the opposite direction of the truth, plus the looming specter of Fitzwilliam's misguided pursuit of Leigh, told her she had no time to waste, and she had every intention of calling Leigh to learn what she could about the next target of her snooping—Lindsey's ex-husband, Ray. But when she finally got home, Bart and Goliath met her at her door, their sad eyes begging for attention. Knowing she'd be leaving them alone again later that night, she couldn't bring herself to rely on a quick visit to the yard to meet their needs. The boys were her family, and time with them was anything but a waste, so she leashed them up, and tails wagging, they headed out the door.

As they wound their way through the neighborhood streets, Bart and Goliath competing to startle rabbits and squirrels along their route, her doubts about what would probably be the second most awkward date in her history took over. What if Granny disliked Nadia? As an intelligent, articulate, friendly, animal-loving business owner, Nadia possessed many of the qualities Granny admired in potential suitors for her granddaughters, but that didn't guarantee her blessing. Not that Maddie would allow her grandmother's partiality to dictate her romantic entanglements, but historically speaking, when Granny disapproved of a person, that person usually ended up proving her an exceptional judge of character. Plus, Maddie didn't look forward to the added complication of juggling her loyalties to her girlfriend and her grandmother. Having done that once already (with little to show for it but regret for not listening to Granny sooner), she wasn't eager to reenter the stressful world of keeping her girlfriend away from her grandmother.

Assuming, of course, that Nadia remained her girlfriend after tonight. Among the countless potential calamities inherent to mixing the strong personalities of Granny Doyle and Nadia Sheridan was the chance (remote but not impossible) that Nadia wouldn't like Granny—an unforgiveable offense and grounds for immediate breakup. But even if everyone got along and behaved (an outcome that seemed as likely as Dottie wearing sweatpants in public), Maddie could easily imagine at least a hundred other things that might go wrong, not least among them Granny's health. Though she hadn't had another troublesome episode with her blood pressure since the one that had landed her in the hospital a few months earlier, Granny put as much stock in doctors and medicine as she would a vegetarian's recipe for meatloaf. Her reluctance to follow doctor's orders plus the stress of hosting the possible demise of Maddie's love life might put her in the emergency room before the night ended.

She knew she was being ridiculous but couldn't help spinning worst-case scenarios as the dogs sniffed and strolled their way through a large chunk of East Rogers Park. By the time the boys padded into the house an hour later and plopped, tired but happy, onto the kitchen floor, she had considered just about every possible calamity that might befall her that evening and needed a distraction from her own mind. Resisting the palliative call of alcohol (and its potential to cause more problems than it solved), she sighed and grabbed her phone. She might as well turn her mental commotion into something productive.

"What do you know about Lindsey's ex-husband?" she asked once Leigh picked up.

"You mean Ray?"

"Does she have another ex-husband I'm unaware of?"

"Right." Leigh laughed a little uncomfortably. "He's a decent guy. We were never close, but we got along when we had to."

"Does that mean you fought when no one else was around?"

"It wasn't like that. We just avoided each other as much as possible, and when we couldn't, we played nice. For the kids."

"So, he didn't hate you or have a grudge against you?"

"Well, his wife left him to be with me, so I don't think I was his favorite person. But he never threatened me or anything."

Stunned to learn that Leigh had broken up Lindsey's marriage, Maddie reconsidered Ray's possible role in the murder. People had killed for less compelling reasons than being cuckolded, but it seemed implausible he would wait over six years to act on his anger. And why would he kill Terry but not Leigh? While he might be framing Leigh for murdering the woman who continued the steady tradition of breaking up Lindsey's partnerships, Maddie felt he was either innocent or terrible at revenge. Still, she wanted to speak with him.

"Do you know how I can contact him?"

"What do you want to talk to him about?"

"The murder you asked me to investigate." She couldn't help her impatient tone.

"You think he did it?"

"I think I need more information, and he might have it."

"You're not going to be obvious about it, are you? He's got a temper, and I don't want you making him angry."

"I know a thing or two about subtlety." She huffed in defiance of her limited gifts with subterfuge. She filed away the information about Ray, hoping she wouldn't bear witness to his short fuse.

After a minor pause, Leigh rattled off a number. "That's his business phone, but it's the only number I have for him."

"What's his business?" She didn't see a connection between Ray's profession and the likelihood that he was a murderer, but she was curious.

"He's a house painter," Leigh answered. "Or at least he was the last time I talked to him. I hope that helps."

"It does. It definitely helps," she said absentmindedly, the germ of an idea forming in her mind. "Boys," she announced to the snoozing and entirely uninterested canines sprawled across her floor, "I think I have a plan."

Stepping over her dogs' supine forms, she headed toward her bedroom to ponder the specifics while she prepared for her date.

"Are you sure you want to do this?" Maddie stopped abruptly on Granny Doyle's front porch and seized Nadia's arm. The all-too-fleeting distraction of murder and investigative strategizing had done little to abate her nervousness, which flared up now that she was face-to-face with Granny's door. "Because it's not too late to back out."

"It's five after eight. It's completely too late to back out. And yes, I'm sure I want to do this." Nadia took her hand from her arm and gave it a gentle squeeze. "Unless your grandmother can't bake. I take dessert seriously, and I don't want to have to lie to one of my elders to spare her feelings."

Nadia's ever-perfect chestnut hair fluttered in the chill wind that nipped at them, and her reddened nose and cheeks managed to accentuate her beauty, like she was in a Christmas ad for some gloriously elegant brand of vodka or a wildly expensive piece of jewelry—not at all like someone who would be on Maddie's arm, heading into Granny Doyle's house for pie and polite interrogation.

"You aren't nervous at all?" she asked.

"It's pie with your grandmother. Should I be?"

"Yes. You should be terrified."

"Why? Is she mean?" For the briefest of moments, she looked appropriately alarmed.

"She's the Stalin of grandmothers. It's what I love best about her."

"In that case, it sounds like we're in for a really fun night." Her expression relaxed into her habitual, bewitching grin, and she pulled Maddie close. "What's going on with you?"

"What do you mean?"

"Ever since you invited me to your grandmother's you've been trying to change my mind about going. It's almost like you don't want to introduce me to your family."

"I'm nervous about it."

"Because you don't think they'll like me?" She leaned against the porch railing, apparently settling in for a longer conversation than Maddie had meant to start. "Obviously they heard about what happened over the summer, that I broke your heart."

"Really, you just bruised it a little."

"Still, I'm guessing they weren't too happy with me."

"Thank you, Harriet," Maddie muttered and shook her head.

"Harriet was just being a big sister. I've got one of those, so I get it. And I know I screwed up, not just with you. There's a chance your family will always hold a grudge. That doesn't mean I can't try to win them over. But that's not going to happen if you never let me meet them. So what's going on in that gorgeous head of yours? What are you so worried about?"

She sighed. She wished she'd kept her mouth shut and just settled for the inevitable awkwardness inside her grandmother's house rather than introducing more of it into her evening. "I like you a lot," she confessed. Given any other option, she would have withheld that admission for as long as possible.

"What a tragedy. How do you plan to cope with such a hardship?"

"I'm starting to like you less, you know." But she couldn't stay irritated when Nadia smiled her lopsided smile and kissed her hand. "My family, lovable and well-meaning as they are, has no idea where the line between supportive and terrifyingly overprotective lies. So on the rare occasion when I find someone who will go on more than one date with me, they insist on meeting her and scare her off in under an hour. In case you were remotely curious as to why I'm single—"

"Past tense," Nadia corrected.

"Right. Why I *was* single has a lot to do with my family being way too invested in my love life."

"What monsters."

"Whose side are you on here?"

"Yours, but I'm still having trouble understanding what's so horrible about a supportive family."

"It's not horrible. It's just overwhelming at times. I love them, but sometimes I wonder why I couldn't have been a ward of the state."

"For what it's worth, I don't scare easily."

"That theory will be tested." She bit her thumbnail.

"You're adorable when you're distraught."

She glowered at Nadia but said nothing.

"And for the record, I think maybe you might be just a little bit crazy. I would kill for a grandmother, or a mother, or anyone in my life to take such an interest in who I'm dating, beyond trying to convince me that it should be a man."

"You say that now."

"And I'll say it again when you wonder why you've never met my parents." Nadia took Maddie's hands again. "It's going to be fine, you know."

"If we survive, I'll remind you that you said that. And that I tried to give you an out."

"I don't want an out." Nadia stared into her eyes and cupped her face. "The last thing I want is an out."

Forgetting that she stood a few feet from her grandmother's front door, she leaned in and kissed Nadia with a fierceness wholly inappropriate for Granny Doyle's front porch.

"That's not fair." Nadia held her at arms' length, and she smiled innocently. "You can't kiss me like that and then expect me to go charm your grandmother. I am so not in grandmother mode right now."

"Believe me, my first choice in this moment is not quality time with Granny." She stole another bruising kiss. "Just hang on to that for the next hour."

"An hour? You're killing me. Who takes an hour to eat dessert? I can be done in five minutes."

"Hey, if you promise not to bail on me because of my family, I promise to make it up to you."

"You drive a hard bargain." She winked and moved in for one more kiss when a sudden light splashed across the porch, illuminating them like a searchlight in a prison yard.

"Are you two lovebirds ever coming inside or are you going to spend the night necking on my front porch?"

She dropped her head, praying that Granny had seen little and heard less (but doubtful she could ever be that fortunate). Her face inflamed with the extreme mortification that might now be a permanent condition, she made the introductions. "Nadia, this is Granny Doyle."

"So I gathered," Nadia whispered and then smiled her irresistible smile and shook Granny's hand. "It's a pleasure to meet you, Mrs. Doyle."

"Call me Granny. Everyone does." She stepped aside to let them enter. "Come on in and take off your coats. Matilda, hang those up for me and then join us in the dining room."

"But," she sputtered for a moment trying to find a reason to keep Nadia with her. Granny worked fast, and she didn't want to learn what damage she could do in the two minutes it would take to obey her grandmother's request.

"Don't have a fit, child." Granny dismissed her distress. "Nadia doesn't look fragile. She'll survive a few minutes alone with your old grandmother. Now get hustling with those coats before I find something else to keep you busy."

Wasting no time, she thrust the coats into Granny's closet, not even caring when her jacket slipped off the hanger. Granny's impeccable floors posed no threat, and this was no time to start worrying about wrinkles. Instead, she needed to focus on damage control, but the second she took in the scene in her grandmother's dining room, she realized she was already too late for that. There at the table Maddie's parents smiled politely as they flanked her date, like hyenas ready for the kill.

She couldn't believe she hadn't seen this coming. In all her alarm over what the night would hold, not once had she considered an ambush by her parents, though it really shouldn't have been a surprise. In fact, it should have been the first item on Maddie's catalog of worry. Had she not been so naïve, she could have planned accordingly. She would have warned Nadia that her father looked like the love child of a biker and a lumberjack but was essentially harmless, especially if she could find some way to work tools, construction, or housing into a conversation with him. The perfect counterpoint to her blue-collar husband, Mrs. Smithwick seldom wore anything that could be considered casual (or comfortable in Maddie's opinion), but her buttoned-up appearance belied her affable, cordial demeanor, and she hated when others misread her appearance as an indication of conservatism or dreariness.

She could have given Nadia all the tools she would need to survive a full-on family assault, but she'd been so focused on the Granny-Nadia dynamic that she'd neglected the Maureen-Colm angle. Nestled between Mr. and Mrs. Smithwick, Nadia looked more amused than aggrieved by this plot twist, but that did little to alleviate Maddie's dread. Assuming Nadia didn't run away after the rest of this nightmare unfolded, Maddie vowed to spend the remainder of the week apologizing to her for allowing Granny to waylay them both. Meanwhile, she had her family to deal with.

"What? June and Harriet couldn't make it?" she asked, hoping her traitorous family picked up on her extreme displeasure at being ambushed.

"They send their love," Granny said before ushering her granddaughter to the table.

Taking her seat across from Nadia, she mouthed an apology. Nadia winked and offered a reassuring grin before turning her attention back to Mrs. Smithwick just in time for the probing to begin.

"We heard you're a doctor." Unlike some mothers, Maureen Smithwick wasn't usually enthralled by the idea of her daughter dating a doctor, so Maddie found her opening statement mildly puzzling.

"A veterinarian," Nadia clarified.

"That's the best kind," Granny chimed in.

Starting with the guest of honor, Granny served up hearty slices of her spiced bourbon apple pie (Maddie's favorite and the one small consolation of the entire encounter). A scoop of ice cream complemented each still-warm-from-the-oven slice, and Maddie watched the look of pure bliss spread across Nadia's face as she enjoyed her first taste of mouthwatering, flaky-crusted euphoria.

"Now," Granny commanded Nadia's attention, "tell us, what do your folks do?"

And they were off. Before Nadia had a chance to take a second bite of her dessert, she had answered the verbal equivalent of a ten-page questionnaire. Taking turns, Maddie's parents and grandmother touched on all the vital aspects of Nadia's life: her roots, parents, upbringing, education, why she moved to Chicago, what made her start her own practice and so on.

While Mr. Smithwick quizzed Nadia about the soundness of her home, Mrs. Smithwick ascertained the stability of her career. How big was her practice? Was she looking to expand? What were the opportunities for growth? Not to be outdone, Granny fired off questions that Maddie hadn't even had the nerve to ask.

"What are your thoughts on marriage?"

Maddie choked on her drink and suppressed the urge to crawl under the nearest boulder, but Nadia seemed unfazed.

"It would be nice to be married someday," she said. "When the time is right."

Granny's perfunctory nod of approval didn't slow her bombardment in the least. "And what about children? How many do you want?"

"Granny," Maddie hissed. "That's kind of personal."

"And how do you expect me to get to know Nadia if I can't ask personal questions? I'm not a mind reader, child."

"I like children," Nadia offered diplomatically. "But for now, I think the four-legged kind is about what I can handle."

Maddie braced herself for whatever might come next, but she eventually realized she needn't have worried. Throughout the grilling, Nadia retained her laid-back, unperturbed attitude (a stark contrast to Maddie's anxiety). She seemed so patient and serene, like it was normal for her to be probed over pie. Maddie marveled as Nadia joked with Maddie's family and outmaneuvered Granny Doyle's push for great-grandchildren. Not that she should have expected anything less. Nadia had, after all, charmed her way back into Maddie's life without much of a fight. Still, she watched in wonder as Nadia deftly handled each question lobbed her way.

Her eyes danced when she laughed at Granny's blunt commentary, and Maddie just about lost her composure when Nadia's tongue darted out to grab an errant crumb from her full lips. Maddie checked her watch, hopeful it wasn't too soon to make their excuses and leave. She had a hellish family outing to make up to her verbally dexterous girlfriend, and she was prepared to start that moment.

"Are we keeping you, Matilda?" Granny's raised eyebrow told her she'd be in for a scolding later, when they didn't have company.

"No, Granny," she answered meekly and tried not to squirm in her seat.

"Glad to hear it." Granny started to serve up seconds when Nadia stopped her.

"Actually, Mrs. Doyle, I've got to be in surgery early tomorrow, so as much as I'd like to stay, I think we should call it a night." She frowned apologetically before thanking Granny and offering to help clean up.

It was almost like she had a script for enchanting Granny (a most effective one based on Granny's decidedly un-Granny behavior). Instead of taking the usual three years to say goodbye, Granny rushed them out the door. She offered zero commentary to a flabbergasted Maddie and hardly gave her the opportunity to say goodnight to her parents before shooing them out into the cold night air.

"You weren't exaggerating," Nadia said once they were on the sidewalk and safely out of Granny Doyle's earshot.

Still speechless, Maddie grabbed Nadia and kissed her hard, something she'd wanted to do for the past twenty minutes. "It's a shame you have to get up early."

"That was a lie." Nadia barely breathed the words before her lips were on Maddie's again. The whole world disappeared as she roughly pulled Maddie closer, her mouth opening to explore Maddie. "Come home with me," she said when she finally broke the kiss.

"God, do I want to," Maddie said, her words a hungry whisper. "But the boys."

"And I have Mabel." She dropped her head in frustration.

"Too bad the dogs aren't better at self-care. Or all in the same place."

"They could be." She grinned a little wickedly. "Mabel and I can be at your door in twenty minutes."

Maddie kissed her again. "Try to make it fifteen."

CHAPTER NINETEEN

Maddie couldn't decide if she wanted time to move slower or faster as she rushed to take care of her dogs before Nadia and Mabel arrived. Physically, she was about ready to burst and wasn't sure she could wait even five minutes to get her hands on Nadia, but emotionally she was as close to ready as Dottie to the poverty line. She had no reason to believe that more time alone with her thoughts would result in anything resembling assurance, but like waiting to have her teeth drilled, a delay seemed like her ally.

While she and Nadia hadn't neglected the physical side of their fleeting relationship (allowing her to blow past her initial shyness in the bedroom), almost three months apart had fortified her standard first-time jitters. What if their chemistry had disappeared in the interim? What if Nadia regretted pursuing her? What if she lost interest after seeing her naked? Even though she remembered Nadia had seemed far from disappointed after her accidental bath time preview, Maddie felt zero confidence that her skinny, freckled, flat-chested self could hold the interest of a woman like Nadia for long.

Before her thoughts spun too much farther out of control, the doorbell rang, inciting the dogs into a barking, tail-wagging frenzy. As they pranced about the living room, eager to greet (not protect her from) whoever might be on the other side of the door, she considered offering a prayer for her sex life but worried such supplication from a lapsed Catholic would be doubly inappropriate. Her hand trembled as she turned the knob. The door opened in what felt like slow motion, and there stood Nadia.

She somehow looked better than she had twenty minutes earlier. The strong breeze had tousled her hair, leaving her looking windblown and wild. Her heightened color and that damn lopsided grin made her almost irresistible. At her side Mabel danced impatiently in place, and Maddie moved to let them in.

"Hi," she said shyly. She leaned against the door and watched Nadia struggle to keep Mabel heeling in the face of two freely roaming and eager to play dogs. Maddie understood the importance of enforcing the rules consistently in puppy training (if Nadia demanded good behavior only some of the time, Mabel might decide to misbehave all of the time). Still, she wished Nadia would just unclip Mabel's leash and let the dogs entertain themselves so they could do the same.

An eternity later, Nadia finally released Mabel to frolic with Bart and Goliath. After taking a moment to ensure everyone still got along, Nadia took Maddie in her arms. "That was the longest twenty minutes ever," she said, and then her lips were on Maddie's.

The kiss was all hunger, all need, and as their tongues volleyed, their hands roamed. Nadia had pinned her to the door, but now she spun her around and started inching toward the back of the house.

Nadia's coat hit the floor, and Maddie didn't know which of them had removed it. She kissed the hollow at the base of her throat, drinking in her incredible aroma. Next, Maddie's shirt landed on the coffee table as they stumbled through the living room, never once breaking contact. Nadia's top and bra came off somewhere in the hallway, but Maddie hardly had time to appreciate her bare skin before Nadia growled and lifted her. Her legs automatically wrapped around Nadia's waist, and they both groaned when Nadia caressed her backside.

They collided with a wall as they kissed their way to Maddie's bedroom. Since Nadia's hands were otherwise occupied, she removed her own bra and dropped it somewhere along their path. It was the only truly sexy undergarment she owned, and for half a second she worried about it ending up as a chew toy for a curious puppy. But then Nadia's tongue was on her nipple, and her focus shifted completely to the woman whose strong arms held her.

When Nadia laid her on the bed, she reached for her, but Nadia stood just out of reach. Her gaze swept over her, a glance she felt as potently as Nadia's fingers moving across her chest and down her stomach.

"So beautiful," she whispered, her voice a reverent hush, her expression barely discernable in the dim glow of moonlight peeking through the window.

Maddie felt a rare surge of boldness, and grabbing Nadia by the button fly of her jeans, she pulled her in for a searing kiss. "Show me."

Nadia moved above her, kissing her neck and mouth. Her hands massaged Maddie's small, responsive breasts, eliciting a moan from Maddie. Before she realized what was happening, her jeans and panties had been discarded, and she lay naked beneath a hungry Nadia. Her eyes flashed, and another moan escaped as Nadia returned her attention to Maddie's breasts.

As Nadia's mouth stirred Maddie higher, her hand slipped lower, skimming Maddie's tight stomach and trailing along her thigh, first from her hip to her knee and then back up the sensitive skin of her inner thigh. Maddie squirmed under her, trying to maneuver her need to Nadia's hand, but Nadia continued teasing her for several minutes. When she finally gave Maddie what she wanted, Maddie cried out at the first touch of Nadia's fingers to her aching center.

Nadia's eyes locked on hers, her gaze unwavering as she watched the pleasure on Maddie's face. They moved together, Maddie inching closer to the edge, the only sounds their breathing and Maddie's occasional mewling moans as the waves of pleasure she felt intensified. Finally, she cried out and pressed herself firmly against Nadia. Hands in her hair, she pulled her in for a deep, thorough kiss.

Not knowing where she found the strength after the orgasm that had ripped through her, Maddie flipped Nadia onto her back, intent on finally having her way with her.

"These have to come off." She tugged at Nadia's pants. "Now."

"I like this aggressive side of you," Nadia said and shifted to make her task easier. Maddie enjoyed both the wicked smile Nadia flashed and the obvious evidence of Nadia's desire as she stripped her naked.

Her eyes roamed Nadia's voluptuous body, drinking in every glorious, gorgeous curve from head to toe. She tamped down the desire to dive right in to the spot that most demanded attention. Instead she lingered on Nadia's full breasts, savoring what she longed to touch earlier.

Nadia's soft "Mmmm" sent a chill down Maddie's spine and threatened to capsize her already weak willpower, but she tarried on Nadia's breasts a moment longer before giving in and traveling down her lush body. Settling between Nadia's legs, she tasted her, tentatively at first and then with the full force of her desire. Nadia moaned and writhed beneath her, her hands grasping at the sheets and then Maddie's hair. Too soon, she groaned and wrenched herself away from Maddie.

"Come here. I need to touch you." Nadia pulled Maddie to her and kissed her roughly.

Their bodies intertwined, Maddie marveled that neither of them was satisfied. She pressed her thigh between Nadia's legs and thrilled at her sharp intake of breath. Then suddenly everything stopped.

Mabel's sharp bark pierced the air, triggering her canine companions. Nadia froze, and Maddie lifted her head. Time stretched as she strained to hear anything over the cacophony of three startled dogs competing to fill the air with noise. Maddie had no clue what had set Mabel off or what to do about this unknown threat until she heard a familiar voice, and the source of the current turmoil in her home became painfully clear.

"Petunia?" Dottie called. "I've come to strategize. Where are you?"

"Please let this be an extremely vivid waking nightmare," Maddie whined and fell back on the pillow. Nadia, meanwhile, raised herself up on her elbows, realization dawning.

"Didn't you lock the door?" she asked, as if a locked door would ever slow Dottie down.

"She has a key," Maddie whispered.

"Maybe next time you should hang a sock on the doorknob." Nadia looked at Maddie, panic in her eyes. "If we stay quiet, will she go away?"

"You aren't in bed already, are you, sugar?" Dottie's voice sounded dangerously close. "Only infants and the elderly retire before eleven."

"Not a chance."

She offered Nadia her thousandth apologetic look of the evening and, in the few seconds remaining before Dottie burst through the door, moved to minimize their impending exposure. She managed to untangle the sheet and pull it up to their knees before the bedroom door flew open, and all three formerly banished canines plus Dottie's dog Anastasia charged in to begin their thorough exploration of what they'd been barred from. Goliath and Mabel sniffed and circled the bed, their frenzied tails whipping everything in their path, while Bart claimed his spot on the bed, nestling himself between Maddie and Nadia and effectively preventing them from pulling the sheet from beneath his immobile form.

"Well, well, well." Dottie smirked and leaned against the doorframe. "Nadia, I didn't realize I'd get to see quite so much of you now that you're back in Maddie's life."

Grabbing a T-shirt from her dresser and hastily pulling it over her head, Maddie pushed Dottie out the door and into the hall. "Is there something you need?"

"A cold shower." Dottie fanned herself.

"So, what? You just popped in to sabotage my sex life?"

"Don't be so dramatic, pumpkin." Maddie crossed her arms and glared at Dottie, waiting for whatever explanation her friend had to offer for her latest unexpected visit. "We have an espionage date."

"Tomorrow. Why are you here now?"

"For scheming purposes. We can't rush in without a plan. The perp will make us in no time flat."

"And the trail of clothing to the bedroom didn't tip you off to the fact that I was busy?"

"I thought maybe the housekeeper had taken the day off."

"Dottie, *I'm* the housekeeper."

"You don't sound appropriately grateful for my help. Perhaps I should let you deal with this on your own."

"It's just that now really isn't the best time."

"So I saw." Dottie wiggled her finely sculpted eyebrows, but rather than taking Maddie's elephantine hint to leave, she headed for her friend's well-stocked liquor cabinet.

"I'll call you in the morning, Dottie." Maddie considered removing the booze from Dottie's hands but thought better of it—she valued her limbs.

"I'm swamped in the morning, ducks."

She sincerely doubted Dottie would be busy with anything other than beauty rest, but she didn't argue. That would only inspire more resistance from Dottie.

"How about I figure out a plan and fill you in tomorrow?"

"Plan for what?"

She spun around to find Nadia standing in the doorway looking undeniably sexy in nothing but a plaid button-down shirt she'd borrowed from Maddie's closet. Maddie wasn't sure whether Nadia naturally felt confident enough to stroll around half-naked, or if she'd simply decided to roll with the already established exhibitionism of the evening, but she knew she had to get Dottie out of there fast.

Unfortunately, she didn't see a way around this conversation. This wasn't how she wanted Nadia to find out about her extracurricular activities. She dreaded Nadia's reaction, but she refused to lie to her outright. Her best hope was to soften the truth by dancing around it.

"We're meeting a guy tomorrow to discuss some issues."

"That's nice and vague," Dottie drawled as she poured her martini.

"I was thinking the same thing," Nadia said, and Maddie glared at an oblivious Dottie. "You're not planning some big surprise, are you? Because I think it's way too early for a proposal."

"Definitely not a proposal." She wholeheartedly agreed with Nadia on the prematurity of such a move (though she absently wondered if that would go over better than the news she was about to reveal). "It's actually something I'm working on for my friend, Leigh."

"What's going on, Maddie?"

"You see, Leigh, my friend who I just mentioned, she's one of my oldest friends, and she's in kind of a bind with the police, so the thing is—"

"She's investigating a murder," Dottie cut to the chase. "Was that so hard?" she asked an aghast Maddie.

"Again?" Nadia seemed surprised but not angry, and at this point Maddie would claim any victory, no matter how small.

"Sort of." She shrugged her answer.

"Why didn't you tell me?"

"I thought you'd be upset." She shrugged again.

"As opposed to what I am now because you lied to me?"

"Only because you found out," Dottie interjected, earning a double glare from Maddie and Nadia.

"I didn't lie."

"Well, I don't think you can say you were honest with me." Nadia crossed her arms over her chest, closing herself off.

"Are you upset that I'm investigating a murder or that I didn't tell you?"

"A little of both, I guess." Nadia sank into one of Maddie's kitchen chairs. "I don't want you to be afraid to be honest with me, and I don't like the idea of you hiding things from me. But I really hate the thought of you endangering yourself. Again."

"There's no danger." She sat next to Nadia and took her hand.

"Isn't that what you said last time? You promised me you would be careful, and then you walked through a murderer's front door and basically asked to be bushwhacked."

"That's not going to happen again."

"How can you be sure?"

"So far the biggest threat I've faced is to my digestive system." Nadia looked understandably puzzled as she reflected on her enlightening but indigestion-inducing visit with Esther Snodgrass, but she just frowned and moved on. "I've made a few dozen phone calls and talked to a little old lady. Tomorrow I'm going to meet a man—"

"A strange man who might have killed someone."

"But I won't be alone. And I'll send you all of the information I have on him in case something happens."

"That will be a great comfort to me when a jogger finds your mangled body on the side of the road."

"Good point, Nadia." Dottie, of course, found no flaws in Nadia's overestimation of the peril they faced. "Smart and sexy. I understand why Maddie is so captivated by your considerable assets." She raised her almost-empty glass in a toast.

"And that's your bodyguard." Nadia gestured at Dottie, who munched on an olive (possibly her only sustenance that day) as she poured herself a second drink.

She sighed. "She's more formidable than she appears."

"I don't like it."

"So I gathered."

"Is there even the remotest possibility I can talk you out of doing this?"

"Let me know if you figure out a way to change her mind." Dottie settled at the table across from them. "I could use some help convincing her not to wear T-shirts and cargo pants."

Maddie rolled her eyes but kept her focus on her girlfriend. "I made a promise to a friend. I can't let her down."

Nadia bit her lip, apparently lost in thought. She stayed silent for a lifetime, allowing Maddie's uncertainty ample opportunity to take over. Just as she decided she would be single as soon as Nadia figured out the best way to break up with her, Nadia broke in on her thoughts.

"Then let me help you."

"What?" She didn't know if emotional whiplash was a real thing but felt like she was experiencing it in that moment. "I thought you hated this."

"I don't hate that you care about your friends and want to help. Or that you're intelligent enough to solve crimes. I just wish it didn't include the risk of grievous bodily injury." She lowered her voice and leaned close to her. "I'm particularly fond of your body, and I don't want anyone to lay a finger on you." Nadia gently stroked her face. "Anyone other than me, that is."

Maddie kissed her softly, losing herself until Dottie cleared her throat.

"So, where do we start?" Nadia asked.

Dottie waved a toothpick and said, "You might want to start by putting on some pants."

CHAPTER TWENTY

It only took Maddie thirty minutes to explain everything she'd learned since treading back into the murky waters of crime solving (a task she could have completed in less than half that time if not for the need to navigate multiple "helpful" interruptions from Dottie). Discussing the case with Nadia proved beneficial. Not only was she (like most people over the age of five) more inclined to logic than Dottie, but her fresh perspective also helped Maddie reassess certain aspects of the case, starting with her gift for racking up enough potentially guilty parties to fill a stadium.

"You have a thousand suspects." Nadia rubbed her eyes after poring over the pages of Maddie's handwritten notes.

Atop the lengthy inventory of potential killers sat the volatile ex-husband Ray, somewhat oblivious wronged neighbor Esther, unpleasant scorned lover Kat and, if she was being realistic, Leigh. Though she hated including her friend, she'd uncovered zero evidence of her innocence.

"And that's not even the complete list," she admitted. She still had to find a way to finagle information from the door people at Terry and Lindsey's building, and she hated to consider how many more names would be added if she ever slogged all the way through the phone book of Terry's obituary.

"Apparently Terry wasn't beloved," Dottie said after a brief, disdainful glance at the papers in front of Nadia.

"There must be some way to narrow this down," Nadia groaned.

"I'm open to suggestions," Maddie sighed. "But for now, I'm still trying to find anyone who knew Terry and didn't want to kill her."

"Seems like you'd have better luck finding elegant footwear in your closet." Dottie punctuated her comment with a healthy swallow of her cocktail.

"But doesn't the killer have to be someone who knew both Terry and Leigh?" Nadia's brow furrowed in her concentration. "Or do you really think Terry's cousin Lou randomly fed her the allergen-laced brownies your friend is known for?"

"It's possible there's no connection between Leigh and the killer. The brownies might just be a coincidence."

Maddie considered how readily Leigh passed out the recipe for her magical heart-healing, soul-soothing brownies. She'd even offered it freely at the numerous bake sales for school and scouts and the million other youth groups that had benefitted from her confectionary genius. Her charitable baking had lifted more than one after-school program from the brink of failure, a feat Maddie doubted Leigh's replacement had replicated.

Suddenly her heart ached with sadness over Leigh's terrible loss. She'd loved those kids from the beginning and taken on the role of parent without hesitation. Though Maddie had never met Terry, based on the widespread disdain for her, she questioned the likelihood that substitute Leigh had been half the parent Leigh had been. Had Terry ever worked a full day only to come home and bake for a school fundraiser or rush to a soccer game so the kids had unflagging support in all their endeavors? It was possible, of course, but somehow Maddie felt justified in harshly judging the maternal qualities of the dead stranger who'd wrecked her friend's home and life.

Leigh had been a good parent, one the kids (and Lindsey) were lucky to have. Maddie felt heartsick at the pointless loss that whole family had faced, and her determination to help Leigh surged. Not only would she learn the truth and ensure Leigh wasn't charged with a murder she didn't commit (no matter how justified), but she also intended to find some way to reconcile Leigh and her kids.

"But doesn't that seem like a lot of effort to go through if your only goal is a corpse?" Nadia broke in on Maddie's contemplation. "A gunshot would accomplish the same thing."

"Or garroting with piano wire," Dottie interjected, a macabre gleam in her eye as she polished off her drink.

"So you think the killer wanted Terry dead and Leigh to look guilty?"

"Maybe. Even if the killer wanted Terry's death to be agonizing, some unrefined peanut oil slipped into just about anything would have had the same effect. The brownies seem like a deliberate choice."

"Good lord, she's even hotter when she's brainy," Dottie interrupted her mixology to coo Nadia's praises.

"Tell me about it." She bit her lower lip and for the millionth time wished Dottie hadn't chosen that night to start being proactive.

"Really?" Nadia favored her with a suggestive look. "Because I could rattle off a mess of medical terms right now if that's your thing."

"Simmer down, ladies. Much as I appreciate the aphrodisiacal effects of science talk, we still have work to do," Dottie called from the kitchen counter where she poured a fresh batch of nuclear cocktails, this time offering up her concoction to her coconspirators.

"Right." She couldn't believe Dottie was the one keeping them on track rather than galloping off on a whirlwind tour of tangents and digressions. "Murder, painful death, friend in trouble. I'm focusing."

"So how do we know who on your exhaustive list of suspects had ties to both women?"

"Leigh would be our best source of information." Maddie checked the time, sighing at the realization that, though Leigh should be fast asleep, she would more likely be nose deep in a bottle. Either way, it would be pointless to reach out just then. "I'll call her tomorrow."

Though the thought of making even one more phone call filled her with dread, if it saved her the effort of making an additional forty cold calls, she would happily pick up the phone, especially since this route carried the added bonus of not doubling her list of suspects just to try to narrow it down again. She almost wished she'd fessed up to Nadia from the outset of the investigation. She might have avoided the frustration of chatting up half of Chicago in an effort to learn anything about Terry's death.

"Does that mean my services are no longer needed tomorrow?" Dottie pouted at the potential lost opportunity to dazzle and manipulate.

"No. We still need to talk to Ray."

"Who's Ray?" Nadia asked.

"Our current best suspect," Maddie said before explaining the sordid details of Lindsey's past entanglements.

"Lindsey sounds like a delight," Dottie said, her expression a clear indication of her distaste. Coming from a thrice-divorced, unrepentant gold-digger, such judgment of Lindsey's morals seemed extra harsh (though no less apt).

"Agreed," Maddie said.

"And Ray probably wasn't happy with Lindsey either," Nadia nodded slowly, the pieces seeming to fall into place for her. "So your faked suicide theory still holds up. But how do we get information from him?"

"I can only surmise your experience with men is as circumscribed as Matilda's, or you'd be aware of the paralyzing effect that breasts can have on the male brain." Dottie gestured to her spectacular cleavage to emphasize her importance to the investigation. To Nadia's credit, she barely acknowledged

Dottie's surgically enhanced bosom. "I've never met a man who wouldn't give me what I want."

"I have no doubt that's true, but I think you need more than cleavage in your arsenal." Dottie looked wounded, and Nadia clarified. "Unless you're hoping to randomly cross paths with Ray and mesmerize him with your boobs, you'll need some plan to get him in the same space as your, um, assets."

"According to Leigh, he's a painter."

"You think I should commission him to do my portrait." Dottie seemed inordinately pleased with the idea of immortalizing herself on canvas.

"Not an artist," Maddie clarified, feeling a momentary pang at causing her crestfallen expression. "He owns a house painting business, so I thought we could lure him to your place for a consultation."

"Impossible," Dottie snapped before softening her tone. "I'm not ready for paint yet."

Maddie had no idea what prep work Dottie thought her vacant condominium required before it could be painted but decided not to pursue that line of questioning.

"He doesn't need to know that, Dottie. We just need a plausible story to get him to your condo."

"Oh," Dottie stretched the word into several syllables, her relief disproportionate to Maddie's statement. "In that case, of course we can meet at the condo."

"Absolutely not," Nadia interjected and hit the table with her fist, startling the dogs.

"Ooo. She's forceful," Dottie purred over the chorus of barks and yaps.

Maddie would have been amused had she not been so irritated by Nadia's controlling tone.

"I didn't realize that a handful of dates in three months' time gave you veto power over my life."

"It doesn't," Nadia began.

"But the sex might," Dottie offered her opinion, earning yet another glare from the other women.

"I just think it might not be advisable to invite a potential murderer into either of your homes. Maybe you should aim for something more public."

"Like what? Starbucks? I'm sure he'll realize I'm not looking to spruce up the corporate giant's coffee shop on the corner."

"Or maybe my office?" Nadia suggested, the trace of sarcasm in her voice earning her no forgiveness from Maddie.

"Won't you be using your office?"

"I have four exam rooms. I can keep one open for you if you tell me what time to expect you."

She considered this, grudgingly accepting that it could work (though not as well as her plan, she was sure). Before she could concede Nadia's point, Dottie jumped in.

"What's the lighting like in your offices, Nadia? Tell me you don't use fluorescent bulbs. Even my radiance fades under the harsh glare of industrial lights, and that will torpedo the entire plan."

"No fluorescent lights, I promise."

"Then I approve." Dottie set her once again empty glass on the table and rose (surprisingly steadily) to her feet and called Anastasia to her. On her way out the door, she said over her shoulder, "Let Carlisle know what time tomorrow, puss. I trust I don't need to remind you, nothing before noon."

Maddie thought she'd let go of her anger when they went to bed, but she woke up (just five short hours later) feeling irritated, so much so that despite her weariness, she still forced herself out of bed for her morning run—an activity much more likely to improve her mood than additional sleep. None of the dogs stirred as she quietly dressed for the chilly morning temperatures.

For that matter, neither did Nadia, who (not surprisingly) looked stunning even as she slept. The sheet only partially covered her, allowing her the mouth-watering view of Nadia's full chest rising and falling slowly with the deep, even breathing of slumber. Her hair fanned across the pillow, and one arm was flung to the side, while the other rested above her head. She still couldn't believe such a gorgeous woman had ended up in her bed. She should have been reluctant to leave her, and if not for the irascibility that gnawed at her, she would have crawled back under the covers until the alarm urged them both awake. But she had too much to think about, especially the brunette sound asleep in her bed.

Invigorated by the first blast of cool morning air against her face, she shivered and looked east to where the sky was just starting to lighten as the day inched toward sunrise. She headed toward the lake, and as her feet fell into a steady rhythm, she allowed her thoughts to wander over the source of her sour mood that morning—Nadia's domineering proclamation the night before.

She thought she might be unnecessarily peevish. Her edict had more likely sprung from tenderness than tyranny, but Maddie couldn't seem to shake the ominous feeling in her gut. She'd been down this road before, and at the time she'd been so young and desperate to please the only woman who'd ever returned her affections, she'd willingly given in to all of her girlfriend's demands. With no frame of reference, she had assumed that was what love was. It had taken far too many months (and a stern talking to from Granny) to open her eyes to the truth of her relationship. She had vowed never to be controlled again, and warranted or not, she saw Nadia's sharp decree (not to mention her earlier flash of possessiveness) as warning signs.

The more she considered it, the angrier she became, and though her rage provided excellent fuel for her run as evidenced by the speed with which she reached her four-mile turnaround, she knew she would have to stop running eventually. Among other things, she had a full schedule even without a possible double homicide to solve.

She was still irritated when she returned home to find a yawning Nadia moving about her kitchen. She wore the same shirt she'd borrowed the night before (a shirt that did little to restrain her full breasts), and anger be damned, she took in the alluring view of Nadia's long bare legs when she crossed the room on her way to the coffeemaker to pour two cups of coffee.

She was in dire need of caffeine, but Nadia's thoughtfulness didn't mitigate her aggravation any more than her effortlessly sexy appearance did. And the intimate smile that spread across her face didn't make Maddie want to relinquish her anger and head for the bedroom. Not at all.

"I can't believe you went for a run."

"Should I have asked for permission first?"

Nadia, who had been moving toward Maddie, now took a step back. "You're upset."

"What gave it away?" She grabbed a banana and halfway through peeling it wished she'd picked a less comedic fruit.

"Is this about last night?"

She said nothing but glared at her over her breakfast, wondering if her likely resemblance to a chimpanzee diminished the impact of her anger.

"Baby, I just wanted to keep you safe. Remember the whole reason I said I'd help you?"

She remembered. She wished she had earlier, before she spent a morning feeding her distemper. Still, she wasn't ready to completely dismiss her feelings.

"Is it so terrible to have someone looking out for you?"

"No," Maddie admitted testily, her defenses still up.

"Then why are you so upset with me?"

"You were so…lord and mastery about it. I'm not your child or your possession, Nadia."

"I know that, but I'm not going to stay quiet when I think you might be in danger. I care about you, Maddie, and I know I'm repeating myself here, but I don't want you to get hurt."

Her expression radiated concern. Her furrowed brow and stormy eyes looked so different from her habitual easygoing air, and her lips were drawn in a thin, straight line. Maddie knew she had a point. The only thing Nadia had done was voice her concern more abruptly than Maddie cared for. But wasn't that mostly a good thing? That was, after all, what a girlfriend should do, wasn't it? She couldn't very well stay angry at Nadia for caring about her.

"You're right. I'm sorry."

"I'm sorry too. I didn't mean to be—what did you say? Lord and mastery?" Maddie cringed at her word choice and nodded. "Does this mean you'll meet Ray at my office?" Nadia moved closer, her expression pleading, and Maddie again nodded her agreement. "Thank you. And how nice is it that I'll get to see you in the middle of the day? Just try not to look too gorgeous."

"You say that like it's a challenge."

She pulled Maddie in for a lingering kiss, one that Maddie hated to end.

"For you, it's probably impossible."

CHAPTER TWENTY-ONE

Maddie's day proved no easier after she headed to work. Two of her walkers called in sick, leaving her and Patrick scrambling to tend to all of their animals without compromising their high standards of pet care. Of course three of Maddie's charges chose that day to test the limits of her patience. Sophie, a basset-chihuahua mix, got two blocks from home, sat down and refused to move for nearly ten minutes. Maddie ended up carrying her to her preferred patch of grass just to make sure she got some relief on their outing, but that was still better than Janice, the wiry-haired mutt who not only ate poop on a regular basis but that day decided to roll around in it, necessitating a bath Maddie had no time to administer but couldn't neglect.

Then there were Murphy's cats, who continued to defy her description of them at every turn. The moment Maddie opened the door, allegedly lazy and aloof Stanley darted into the hallway. When she retrieved him, his brother launched into the hall in his place, sparking a five-minute game of Chase the Cat, featuring the alternating antics of both of Murphy's suddenly high-energy felines. By the time she got them both in the apartment with the door safely shut behind them, she wanted to call in sick on her life. But even though they signaled the end of the pet care portion of her day, she still had to face a potential killer and, as it turned out, step into the emotional tsunami of her sister's love life.

"Have you heard from Harriet lately?" Patrick asked as they tended to their close-of-day routine. She suspected his tone was supposed to be nonchalant, as if she had no clue he had the hots for her sister. She didn't even have the energy to roll her eyes.

"Not since Tuesday night. Why?"

"I'm just thinking about Little Guys. I'm concerned about our space here. We outgrew it weeks ago, and we keep getting bigger, so we need to do something soon. If the firehouse doesn't work out, we should go back out looking for a new place to call home. I mean, we owe it to our clients and ourselves to scour the city for the best space possible, don't you think?"

"How magnanimous of you." Maddie didn't even try to hide her sarcasm or the fact that she knew his interest lay elsewhere. "She put the offer in yesterday. I haven't heard anything since then."

"What if it falls through? Shouldn't we keep searching, just in case?"

"I thought I'd take a cue from you and be optimistic about this one. I think it will work out fine."

"Oh. Good. That's good." Maddie couldn't remember ever hearing anything that sounded farther from good than her typically unflappable assistant in that moment.

"Was there something else?"

"Wh-what else would I, uh, want to know?" She had never witnessed a nervous Patrick. It was adorably heartbreaking.

"Maybe if she asked about you."

"Did she?" He looked like a kid on Christmas, enthusiastic and full of expectation.

"Not as such." She watched his eager expression fall flat. "She did tell me to give you her number."

"Really? Can I have it?"

"No," she said and watched his excitement dim once more.

"Because she's your sister and it might affect our working relationship?"

"That's a good reason, but no. It's because I gave her your number instead."

"Is she going to call me? Wait, she's had my number since Tuesday? Why hasn't she already called me?"

"Maybe because she's busy trying to secure that new headquarters you're so concerned about," she said, but her comment was lost on him.

He seemed to have shifted into an emotional tailspin, the likes of which she could have been proud of. She watched as he paced and muttered to himself, the furrow in his brow increasing with every step he took, and she wondered how she would pull her normally laid-back, stoic assistant back to steadier footing.

Suddenly he spun around wide-eyed and asked, "Is this going to be a problem, boss?"

"Your love life is your business as long as it doesn't affect my business."

"Thanks, boss. You're the best."

And in just the sort of blurring of personal and professional lines she feared, he hugged her before floating off on his own incredibly buoyant mood, leaving her to hope her sister would appreciate him as much as she did. However, she had no time to dwell on what she hoped would be Harriet's least tumultuous entanglement to date because she still had to review her walkers' notes for the day before locking up and hustling over to what she hoped would be her last interrogation.

Twenty minutes later, she dashed into Nadia's practice feeling doubly out of sorts. Not only was it odd to visit a vet's office with no appointment, no pet and no professional need to see the doctor, but she had arrived only ten minutes before her scheduled meeting with Ray. Even more distressing—Dottie, whose habitual lax approach to timeliness should have delayed her arrival for at least ten more minutes, sat waiting for her, an unsmiling Carlisle at her side. While Maddie appreciated Carlisle's unquestionable influence on Dottie's unprecedented punctuality, she saw no other benefit to the phlegmatic assistant's presence and planned to say as much.

She stopped abruptly, causing a collision with Franklin, Nadia's vet tech nephew, who shared his aunt's compassion for animals as well as her taste in women. He had eagerly volunteered to act as her escort for the thirty-foot walk to the tiny exam room where she hoped to get a break in this case, but he had spent the brief duration of their walk cracking his knuckles, clearing his throat and scratching nervously at his ill-shaven chin. Now he hovered at her shoulder, apparently unable to end their magical time together.

"Can we talk?" She glared at Dottie, hoping to convey the need for a Carlisle-free zone.

"What do you need, Miss Smithwick? I'll get you anything." Franklin looked so hopeful and pleased to be of service that she let his mispronunciation of her name slide.

"Thank you, Franklin. That's sweet of you, but I actually need to speak to my friend for a moment. Privately." She laid her hand on his forearm and watched his eyes widen. "But I'll call you if I need anything." She couldn't help herself. She winked at him. His entire head turned red, and he looked almost ready to swoon. She'd forgotten her inexplicable effect on Franklin but had to admit it was fun being the cause of such a reaction rather than the one always having it.

"I do believe that boy is smitten with you." Dottie stood at her elbow watching the flushed and enchanted vet tech back down the hallway.

"Runs in the family, I guess," she muttered. Once they were alone with a door between them and the ubiquitous Carlisle, she hissed, "What is she doing here?"

"She's my assistant. She's assisting me," Dottie huffed as if it was the most logical thing in the world for her to have an assistant and for that assistant to be present for almost every aspect of her life. "I didn't realize it was invitation only. Or can we only expand our investigative circle to include your girlfriend?"

Maddie sighed in frustration. It wasn't like she had sought Nadia's help, and she wouldn't even have it now if not for Dottie bringing their mild vigilantism to Nadia's attention, a point Dottie was sure to ignore.

"Fine. She can stay. How will Carlisle be assisting us today?"

"She's a whiz with shorthand, so her notetaking skills will be invaluable."

"I appreciate your total lack of confidence in my ability to remember the important parts of one conversation."

"She's also my understudy, should Ray prove impervious to my considerable charms."

"*Carlisle?*" She peered through the cutout window at what Dottie deemed a more viable alternate than herself. Carlisle wore a long skirt and her habitual sweater set, this one in a blue so dark it looked black. In deference to the gloomy forecast, she balanced an umbrella on her lap as she pored over the contents of her ever-present clipboard, reading over the tops of her glasses rather than removing them. "You expect her to have a better chance of bewitching Ray than I would?"

"Remember the bartender, starfish? Carlisle has a proven track record with males whereas you have hardly any track record to speak of."

"What about Franklin? He likes me."

"And you make a darling couple, but beyond one atypically starstruck young man, what kind of attention do you generally garner from the unfair sex?" She thrust out her jaw but said nothing. "If not for your lackluster approach to fashion and your aversion to worthwhile grooming, you'd be invaluable in this endeavor. You're certainly attractive enough to capture a man's attention, but you scarcely have the aptitude for flirtation when the other party interests you. What hope do you have when seductive subterfuge is called for?"

"I can flirt," she huffed.

"Firecakes, can you honestly say you have a chance of beguiling this man? You don't like sports enough to create a connection with our mark, and assuming he's more or less as average as the average male, you'll need that or boobs to make an impression."

"So *Carlisle* is your plan B? She looks like a middle-aged Mary Poppins."

"As opposed to your homage to GI Jane?" Dottie scowled at her drab olive cargo pants and sweater.

"Let's just get this over with," she sighed and trudged back into the room to wait for Ray. "We're doomed if you need either of us."

The tiny room felt cramped before Ray Warner bustled in—right on time Maddie noted with satisfaction. Though she knew punctuality didn't preclude murderous tendencies, she still appreciated his promptness. His appearance, however, was somewhat unexpected. While she had expected some disparity between Leigh and the man she cuckolded, he couldn't have been more her opposite than Maddie's casual attire was to Dottie's designer wardrobe.

He stood an inch or two shorter than the unquestionably short Maddie. With the extra weight he carried, he looked like a ruddy, blond Oompa-Loompa, a stark contrast to tall, slender and usually tan Leigh. Their personalities appeared to be diametrically opposed as well, and Maddie found herself puzzling over the likelihood that Lindsey could be attracted to both laid-back, quietly attentive Leigh and Ray, who acted like a puppy eager for treats.

"You're looking to repaint the whole place?" he asked, one leg bouncing rapidly as he scanned his surroundings.

Maddie could almost see the dollar signs in his eyes as he contemplated the fee for painting four exam rooms and a spacious lobby, not to mention the expansive behind-the-scenes area. She felt a twinge of guilt at abusing the aspirations of a fellow small business owner. Then again, if he was guilty of murder, he deserved much more than dashed fiscal hopes as punishment.

"Not exactly, Raymond." Dottie crossed her legs, drawing his eyes to her shapely calves. "I'm in the throes of a remodel, and I'm interviewing artistes."

"For your home?"

Dottie's cover story was new to Maddie. They'd agreed to tell him exactly what he assumed was the reason he'd been called to a veterinary clinic—that the clinic needed to be painted. She managed not to let her bewilderment show, but he seemed understandably thrown by this twist.

"I don't think I can give you a fair estimate without seeing the space."

"I've never found estimates particularly interesting." Dottie brushed his concern aside. "I'm more partial to personal connections. I can't work with someone I'm not drawn to." She grinned and placed a hand on her chest, highlighting her cleavage (to great effect, Maddie noted).

"You just want to get to know me?" Dottie nodded and batted her eyelashes. Ray blushed deeply and then looked at Maddie like she was the dreary chaperone on an otherwise hot date. "What are you here for?"

"She's my interior designer. Such a flair for colors and textures." Maddie wondered how much it pained Dottie to spin that tale. "The evidence of her wardrobe notwithstanding."

"And you?" He lifted his eyebrows questioningly at Carlisle.

"She's my assistant, my right-hand, my Girl Friday. I can't very well conduct such an important interview without my team, can I?"

"I guess not." He looked doubtful. "But why are we meeting at a vet's office?"

Maddie could tell he was trying not to offend his eccentric potential client, but considering the perplexing situation, it was a fair question.

"I just adore animals, Raymond. I find their presence so comforting, so soothing," she said as a dog in the next room filled the air with pitiful cries that slid into a plaintive yowl. "Don't you?"

He looked about as soothed as if he'd consumed a gallon of espresso in under ten minutes, but he wisely agreed. "Do you have pets?" he asked, and Maddie wondered if his palpable nerves sprang from the bizarre nature of their interaction or the fear of having to work around the equally strange menagerie he must have feared encountering in Dottie's home.

"My borzoi Anastasia is my world."

"Borzoi? Is that a dog?"

"Russian wolfhound," Carlisle explained succinctly. She barely glanced at Ray, focused as she was on her superfluous note taking. "Show worthy."

"And you, Raymond?" Dottie asked. "Any animal companions at the Warner abode?"

"No. My daughter is allergic." He looked appropriately repentant for his failing. If nothing else, he was a quick study in Dottie.

"A daughter. Does that mean there's a Mrs. Ray?"

"There used to be. She died."

Maddie found it odd that he offered Lindsey's death rather than their divorce as the explanation for her absence. Did he think it was more respectable, more sympathetic perhaps to be a widower rather than a divorcé? Or did he still harbor feelings for her that made her death easier to acknowledge than the end of their marriage? If that was the case, were those feelings intense enough to inspire murder? Or were they grounds for believing in his innocence? Hopefully Dottie would bring them around to some answers without tipping him off to the true nature of their discussion.

"That must be difficult for you."

"Well, we've been divorced for a while, but yeah, it's rough."

"So you still cared for her?" Maddie asked, hoping to get them on track before Nadia's office closed for the day.

"We didn't split up because of me." He frowned before continuing. "My kids are hurting pretty bad right now. I think we're still in shock."

Though she could be mistaken, Ray seemed like a man in genuine pain. Grief didn't equal innocence, of course, but she couldn't easily dismiss his obvious sorrow over his ex-wife's death.

"When did she die?" Dottie sounded innocent and concerned, not at all like she was angling for a confession.

"Saturday."

"And you're back at work already?"

"I still have to pay the bills." He bristled at her question, and that flash of ill temper gave Maddie pause.

"Say no more, Raymond. I understand completely." As if Dottie had worried about finances since she'd landed the first of her loaded husbands. "May I ask, how she died?"

"Why do you want to know?"

"I merely wondered if it was sudden or if you'd had time to plan ahead, coordinating childcare and the like. I'm curious, of course, because of the potential impact on your ability to devote yourself to the restoration of my space."

"Oh." He seemed to accept her pale excuse. "It was unexpected. She, uh, she," he cleared his throat. "It was suicide."

"Why?" She sounded both shocked and sympathetic, an apparently winning combination for Ray.

"I wish I knew."

"She gave you no indication?" She was appropriately aghast.

"I guess her partner's murder might have had something to do with it." He suddenly found the pet health posters adorning Nadia's walls of great interest.

"So much loss," she tsked. "Your children must be beside themselves with grief."

"Not for their bitch stepmother. We all would have been better off if she'd died sooner."

"You didn't kill her, did you?"

Maddie's mouth dropped open at the same time Ray sprang from his chair so forcefully it teetered on its back legs for an agonizing moment before righting itself with a clatter. Several veins popped out on his face and neck, but Dottie didn't flinch in the face of his rage.

"What?" he barked. "Why are you asking so many questions about my dead wife?"

"Ex-wife," Maddie chimed in and instantly wished she hadn't.

He flashed his anger-filled gaze on her, then lunged toward her. Maddie, who had nowhere to go in the tiny room, braced herself for whatever was about to hit her. But before she felt the impact of his rage, the door behind him opened, and his progress was halted by a firm hand on his shoulder. Nadia, who must have heard the commotion, spun him away from Maddie, catching a beefy fist to the face for her trouble. She tumbled backward, the cut beneath her already-swelling eye dripping blood. Enraged and appalled, Maddie leapt onto his back.

He yelled and spun around wildly in his fury, but she clung to him, alternately terrified of being flung into a wall and of increased violence without the minimal resistance she offered. The room whizzed past in a blur as he gyrated wildly and her efforts to subdue him failed utterly. She closed her eyes for a moment to quell her nausea, and when she opened them, a dark, indistinct form crossed her field of vision. Then they tumbled to the ground, and she looked up to find Carlisle standing above him, her umbrella hooked around his ankle and a triumphant look on her face.

"Ninja Mary Poppins," Maddie muttered in the second before he shoved her away. He flailed his arms and sputtered angrily in his efforts to right himself, but Carlisle shoved him back to the floor with the pointed end of her umbrella as Maddie dodged another of his fists and slid over to Nadia, who sat holding her eye.

"Honey, what did he do to you?" She cradled her face and suppressed the urge to kick Ray where he'd feel it for days. Carlisle had him under control, and it wouldn't help anything to rile him up again.

"See why I was worried about you?" Nadia looked dazed but smiled weakly.

"I'm so sorry he hit you."

"I was aiming for you," Ray snarled, and Carlisle poked him again with her umbrella.

"You just moved to the top of the suspect list, pal." Dottie glared down at him, and Maddie didn't have the heart to remind her that he had occupied that position even before he tried to turn their interview into a UFC event.

The door flew open again and Franklin wedged himself into the overfull room. "Should I call the police, Dr. Sheridan?" He held the phone in his hand, ready to save the day.

"I'd rather have an ice pack," she said, and Franklin disappeared again.

"Can I have one too?" Ray called after him.

"No," Dottie said, and Carlisle poked him again.

"Are you sure you don't want to press charges? He did assault you." And Maddie would feel safer with a jail cell between them and the tempestuous Ray Warner.

"I'd rather not draw any more attention to this incident than we already have, and I don't want my clients asking questions."

"Sweetie, you look like you have intimate knowledge of the first rule of Fight Club," Dottie said. "There will be questions."

"Wonderful." She rose and brushed off her pants, and with trembling hands took the ice pack Franklin handed her.

"Let me up, you bitch," Ray growled and swatted at Carlisle's umbrella.

"Lower your voice, Mr. Warner, or I will call the police."

"Sorry," he muttered. "About your eye too. I didn't mean to hit you."

"Oddly enough, that doesn't make it hurt any less." Nadia knelt next to him. "I hope you'll talk to these women without giving them any more trouble. I get cranky when I don't feel my best, and I'd hate to have to take that out on you." He nodded solemnly. "Good. Now if you'll excuse me, I have an arthritic pit bull to tend to."

She didn't make eye contact before she left the room. Maddie didn't want to let her leave, not when she was injured and possibly angry, but she doubted she could do anything in that moment to make things better. She watched her walk away with a mix of affection, admiration, and regret and decided that, if possible, she would make it up to her later.

"What am I supposed to talk to you about?" he asked. "It obviously isn't paint."

"Murder." Since Dottie had already employed the direct approach, Maddie didn't see any reason for further subterfuge. "And your role in it."

"I didn't touch that dyke," he snarled from his place on the floor.

"Considering your recent outburst and the conclusion you've jumped to about which victim we're talking about, your assertion of innocence means almost nothing, Raymond. Regardless, you'll have to be more specific as our current investigation, at last count, included five dykes."

"Technically four dykes and a bisexual," Maddie said, not at all sure why she felt the need to clarify Lindsey's status.

"One of whom you struck down in your attempt to assault another. So which lady-loving lady are you claiming not to have touched?"

"Terry. I had plenty of reason to hate her, but I swear I never hurt her."

"Aside from suing for full custody of your kids," Maddie pointed out.

He regarded her curiously. "How do you know that? Who the hell are you?"

"We have a mutual acquaintance. Leigh Mathews."

"I should have known." He let out a small, bitter laugh. "Terry probably thought I did her a favor." He seemed calmer, enough for Carlisle to release her hold on him, though she still regarded him with a wary eye. "She didn't care for my kids. She thought they were brats. Not that I expect you to believe me any more than that detective did, but that's why I wanted full custody, not to hurt Lindsey or that ugly bitch. It was to protect my kids from Terry." He laughed again. "Much as I hate to admit it, they were better off when Lindsey first turned queer with Leigh." Carlisle jabbed him again and he yelped. "You want to know who offed Terry? Talk to their neighbor."

"You expect us to believe that sweet little old lady had anything to do with this?"

"All I know is Lindsey hated her. She wanted to move because the old lady was always butting into everybody's business and making her life hell. According to Lindsey, she caused too much trouble."

"She's a gossip with noisy dogs and zero culinary skills. How much trouble could she cause?" Maddie asked.

"Maybe enough to add to the city's already impressive body count," Dottie said.

"I guess I need to talk to Esther again." Maddie sighed. "God, I hope she doesn't bake."

CHAPTER TWENTY-TWO

At a loss for how to proceed, Maddie took a detour to Leigh's house after the calamitous interview with Ray. She needed clarity now more than ever, and though she'd meant to call her earlier, like every other part of her day, that hadn't worked out. Now that Ray had thrown her inquiry into turmoil, she hoped even more earnestly that Leigh could set her currently directionless snooping on a less volatile trajectory.

She knew, of course, she shouldn't blindly accept the word of a stranger, especially one as temperamental as Ray. While she wanted to believe in his claims of innocence (if for no other reason than to eliminate at least one suspect), his role in the murders was still unclear. At the very least, it seemed he still loved Lindsey too much to hurt her (not physically anyway), and despite the total lack of evidence to back her up, she felt certain there was a connection between Terry's murder and Lindsey's alleged suicide. If she was right in surmising that he didn't kill Lindsey, then she believed someone else must also be responsible for Terry's death.

But Esther? The idea seemed preposterous. Though her familiarity with Esther was on only slightly less shaky ground than her acquaintance with Ray, she couldn't believe the old woman was guilty of anything more serious than crimes against flavor. The fact that she had no more evidence for that outlook than her intuitive supposition of Ray's innocence meant she needed proof. And that meant a visit to the source of most of the current turmoil in her life.

Operating on yet another baseless theory (apparently the cornerstone of her investigative process), she hoped to establish Esther's innocence by proving she had no connection to Leigh. That process should take no more than a couple minutes, leaving her ample time to tend to her pups, call Nadia to apologize again for the injury she had peripherally caused and (depending on the efficacy of the apology) prepare some magical dinner that would inspire her girlfriend's forgiveness. Though she wasn't at all certain what foods best said, "Thanks for voluntarily taking the punch that was meant for me," she felt confident that a home-cooked meal had decent odds of inspiring leniency in the culinary-challenged Nadia. With any luck, she'd be in bed by ten, hopefully with company who didn't shed or leave pools of slobber on the blankets.

Leigh, however, clearly misunderstood Maddie's goals for the evening.

"You *knew* Esther?" she asked a third time, certain Leigh had misheard the question. They'd already run through her suspect manifest and ruled out most of the people on it, but Esther was a sticking point.

"We weren't boon companions, but yes, I spent some time with her."

"Esther Snodgrass," she clarified on the off chance that Leigh's social circle included multiple Esthers.

Leigh nodded. "That's the one."

"I don't believe this." She flopped onto the couch behind her.

"Why would I make that up?"

"Because nothing in my life can go smoothly," she muttered. Hoping theirs was little more than a passing acquaintance, hardly the foundation for a murderous plot, she opted for more information. "Explain this to me."

"I ran into her in the hall one day."

"In what hall?" she asked, sure her friend didn't mean the hallway Esther shared with Leigh's ex, a hallway Leigh had no reason to be in.

Leigh offered a remorseful look, and Maddie prepared herself for the worst. "I was leaving Lindsey's place."

"When was this?"

"Maybe two months ago? It was right after she married Terry."

"And you were there why? You thought it might be tacky to offer your best wishes via text message?"

"I wanted to talk to her. I needed to understand what Terry gave her that she didn't get from me."

"Oh, Leigh." Her heart broke once again for her friend. Certainly she had wandered down the same treacherous mental path numerous times, but even at her most desperate and lovelorn, she never actually pursued the painful truth from one of her exes. It was excruciating enough to know she wasn't desirable. Why go chasing after a catalog of her flaws?

"Don't look at me like that, Maddie. It was a mistake. I know that, but I just needed to see her, to know she was all right."

"And?"

"I'm not sure. She didn't seem unhappy, but I could tell she was tense. She'd started smoking again. I knew as soon as we—" Leigh stopped abruptly, her eyes wide, and Maddie guessed she hadn't been on the verge of confessing anything virtuous.

"As soon as you what? Kissed your married ex in the home she shared with her spouse?" She raised her eyebrows and waited for Leigh to continue the tale of terrible decision making.

"Made out, really. If Terry hadn't come home early, I don't know what else we might have done." Leigh looked away, pain and shame etched on her face. "Esther was in the hall when

Terry threw me out. She took pity on me and invited me in for tea and cookies."

"As if you hadn't suffered enough." She cringed at the cruelty of Esther's baking as the sole comfort after an undoubtedly harsh encounter.

"Her cookies tasted like raw sewage, but she was so sweet and kind. I liked spending time with her, and I still wanted to be close to Lindsey, so…"

"What did you do?" Confident she'd reached her limit of bombshells in one sitting, she wished she could block whatever Leigh was about to tell her.

"I offered to teach her to bake."

"It didn't work."

"Well, we only had one lesson."

"Please tell me you started with soufflés." Leigh shook her head, and her heart sank, realization dawning. "Pies? Tarts? Anything other than your brownies?"

"It seemed like an easy jumping off point."

"Oh, this is not good."

"What's the problem with trying to help a little old lady?"

"Leigh, you taught her how to make the murder weapon."

She fell heavily onto the couch next to Maddie. "I need a drink."

"I came here to eliminate Esther as a suspect, not to build a case against her."

"You really think Esther might have killed Terry?"

"And Lindsey," Maddie said and explained her theory about Lindsey's suicide not being suicide at all.

"And you believe Esther could have killed them both? She's a thousand years old and not exactly the pinnacle of fitness."

"Neither murder required brute strength. You said yourself that anyone can tamper with an EpiPen."

"How would she know about Terry's allergies and her injector?"

"Thin walls and Olympic-level eavesdropping." She sighed and buried her face in her hands. This was not the plot twist she'd been hoping for.

"But why would she call Lindsey's suicide into question if she murdered her? Wouldn't she want people to believe Lindsey took her own life?"

"What risk was there in telling me? I was just a sympathetic stranger with an iron stomach. She couldn't know I was investigating Terry's murder or that I suspected her of anything."

"It still seems like an unnecessary risk."

"Maybe she's deranged. How else do you explain weaponizing baked goods?"

"So what does this mean?"

"It means I'm going to have to pay Esther another visit." She groaned and offered her digestive system a preemptive apology.

Still moderately (and inexplicably) optimistic about a pleasant end to her evening, she called Nadia after leaving Leigh's, but she got no answer. Under normal circumstances, she would have left a message and waited (not entirely patiently) for a return call. But after the events that had transpired that afternoon, she disregarded the probability that Nadia was with a patient and instead assumed she was angry and ignoring her. Not that she didn't have reason to be upset—an unwarranted slug to the face could ruffle even the saintliest of saints. But ample justification for her anger did nothing to ease Maddie's mind.

Neither did a walk with her boys (her typical go-to for peace of mind). It didn't help that, rather than having time alone with her thoughts and her dogs, she got the mobile equivalent of a block party. All along their winding route, they encountered excessively chatty neighbors who felt the need to discuss in depth such profound topics as the abrupt change in the weather and the rapid passage of time signaled by the approach of Halloween. Like she was trapped inside the world's least entertaining video game, each time she escaped from one, another appeared.

By the time they evaded Deirdre Dietz (the neighborhood's reigning busybody champion and unfortunately, one of Bart's favorite people from whom to solicit attention), Maddie wanted to explore the possibility of becoming an eccentric recluse, but she still had a murderer to catch and, if her romantic history was any indication, a relationship to eulogize. In a vain attempt to keep her mind off the smoldering wreckage of her brief commitment to Nadia, she focused on the equally daunting prospect of solving a double murder before the weekend. She got no further than breaking out her In Case of Emergency bourbon (the bottle of Widow Jane Ten Year her oldest sister had bestowed upon her as a housewarming present) when her doorbell rang.

Mabel trotted in as soon as Maddie opened the door and, after pausing for the requisite attention from her dumbfounded host, headed directly to the tail-wagging duo who waited in the middle of the room. Though Maddie loved how quickly Mabel had grown comfortable in her home and with her boys, she wondered as she watched the dogs' impetuous romping if she should rearrange her furniture to accommodate the pups but, turning to Nadia, questioned if that would be necessary.

"I wasn't sure I'd see you tonight," she said as Nadia followed her dog into Maddie's home.

"Why not? I'm the one with the bad eye." She pointed to her bruised and swollen face and attempted a wink.

"I thought maybe you were mad at me." Maddie closed the door and leaned wearily against it.

"Why would I be mad at you?"

"For this." She pointed to Nadia's bruise but didn't make eye contact.

"Ray did this, not you."

"But—"

"But nothing. I got involved so I could keep you out of trouble, remember? And I've witnessed the aftermath of one of your investigations. I knew the risks."

She shrugged her nonchalant acceptance of being punched, as if a black eye was just something to be expected, like bad hair days for Maddie. But Maddie couldn't so easily shake her guilt. Still not making eye contact, she took Nadia's hand and moved toward the kitchen, her progress impeded somewhat by the vigorous canine wrestling match taking place directly in her path.

"I was about to make dinner. Can you eat?"

"I've never had trouble in the past."

"I meant because of that." She gestured at Nadia's injury again. "Did he hurt your jaw too?"

"I'm not sure. We may have to test it out." Nadia pulled her close. Her good eye scanned Maddie's face, settling on her lips.

She leaned toward her. "I don't want to hurt you." She caressed the tender area around Nadia's eye.

"Unless you have some incredibly kinky moves in your arsenal, I think my face will be safe in your hands."

"We'll hold off on the kink until you heal." She blushed as soon as the words left her mouth, and (in a pathetic attempt to circumvent some of her embarrassment), she changed the subject immediately. "I talked to Leigh, and we're down to a handful of suspects who know both Leigh and Terry." For the millionth time Maddie contemplated which of her current suspects was the most likely to have committed murder: Ray, Kat, Esther, or Leigh?

"A handful is better than a thousand, but I didn't have to get punched in the face for that insight."

"I promise I will make this up to you."

"What did you have in mind?"

"Anything you want," she answered, then wondered if she'd just given Nadia too much leeway.

"You know, we've never really had a chance to be a regular, boring couple without someone's murder in the background. Maybe, if you set your investigation aside, just for a night, we could try that."

She searched Nadia's face for some clue she was trying to maneuver her away from the investigation completely, but Nadia looked shyly hopeful rather than demanding, like she didn't want to ask for too much. Considering what she'd been through that day, how could Maddie deny her completely reasonable request for one night free from the tumult of crime solving?

"I think boring, regular couples like to have dinner together."

"And discuss mundane topics like work and the news."

"They might even take the dogs for a walk and go to bed early."

"Why haven't we tried this before?" Nadia said.

"We must be slow learners." Maddie closed the meager distance between them, confirming their agreement with a soft, lingering kiss that threatened to nullify their dinner plans.

Nadia backed her up against the kitchen counter, and her hands moved beneath Maddie's sweater, her fingers grazing the soft skin of her abdomen before skimming up her back. Just as she reached the clasp of her bra, the front door opened, setting off the dogs and instantly killing the mood.

"We really need to get you sturdier locks." Nadia sighed and rested her forehead against Maddie's as they waited to learn who had interrupted them this time.

"Dottie told me everything," Granny called from the other room.

"That's a terrifying prospect," Maddie muttered.

"So much for our boring night," Nadia grumbled as they both turned their attention to their visitor.

Easily sidestepping the pack of eager dogs jostling for attention from the newcomer, she bustled into the kitchen and deposited a plate of her no-raisin oatmeal cookies on the counter. Freed of her confectionary burden, she immediately set to making dinner for the three of them.

"What did she say?" Nadia asked, her attention half on Granny, half on the goodies she'd provided.

Meanwhile Maddie, relieved of her chef duties, switched to bartending—wine for Nadia, a Manhattan for Granny and for her the drink she'd needed even before her string of surprise guests had started trickling in.

"That Maddie had landed herself in another perilous predicament and needed backup. What else did she need to say?"

"Only about a thousand other things," she said and handed Granny her drink.

Granny removed the plastic wrap from the plate of cookies and nudged them closer to Nadia. "You look like you could have used these ten minutes ago."

Nadia took one bite and moaned appreciatively, but when Maddie reached for a cookie, Granny swatted her hand away.

"What about my 'perilous predicament'? Don't I deserve a cookie?"

"Not until you tell me what you did to get your girlfriend banged up like she went a round with Jersey Joe Walcott."

"Why do you assume this is my fault?" Her exasperation shriveled in the face of Granny's knowing glance. "It's only partially my fault."

"It's not her fault at all." Nadia jumped to her defense before snagging another cookie from the plate that only she could reach.

"You're sweet to defend her, Nadia, but if I know my granddaughter, this has to be the byproduct of her stubbornness or her indiscretion."

"It's the byproduct of the murder investigation you pushed me into."

"And how's that progressing?" Granny switched conversational gears effortlessly, conveniently ignoring any responsibility for Nadia's current state.

"You never told me what happened with Ray after I left." Nadia paused in her cookie consumption long enough to second Granny's blame-shifting inquiry. "Please let this story have a guilty ending."

"I'm not sure," she answered honestly.

Certainly Ray was an angry man, possibly even angry enough to kill someone, but his was a temper that flared up in the moment then fizzled out. The thought of him planning an elaborate revenge scheme rather than lashing out immediately seemed far-fetched. Beyond that, how would he have tampered with Terry's EpiPen? She would have to verify his story, but if his relationship with Terry was as contentious as he claimed, Maddie doubted he would have been allowed in his ex's home aside from brief visits to pick up and drop off his kids. That wouldn't allow him much time to access the autoinjector. Nor could he have popped in with brownies. Even if he didn't seem about as likely to bake as to march in the pride parade, what possible reason would Terry have to welcome him and his lethal dessert into her home unless the kids were with him? And she doubted even the world's worst father would bring his children along for murder.

Though Maddie supposed he could have left the brownies with the door person, that still didn't answer how Ray could have accessed Terry's EpiPen, but it also meant she couldn't completely eliminate him as a suspect.

"He's definitely a hothead, which Leigh told me."

"And you couldn't have given me a heads-up?"

She frowned apologetically. "I expected raised voices not fisticuffs." She sipped her drink and reflected on her eventful day.

"So we're back where we were last night."

"Not exactly. I'm not sure what his word is worth, but he suggested that Terry and Lindsey's neighbor might not be the harmless little old lady I thought she was."

"Last time you talked to her, all you got was some possibly misleading information."

"Don't forget indigestion." She shuddered at the memory of Esther's offending coffee cake.

"So how do you expect to get more out of her this time?"

"Aside from enduring another stellar example of how not to bake, I have no plan."

"I can take a crack at her," Granny said and served up the honey lemon chicken stir fry she'd made as effortlessly as if she'd poured a bowl of cereal. "We probably have one or two things in common, especially if she has a strong-willed granddaughter with a dangerous independent streak."

"I appreciate the offer, Granny, insulting as it was, but I don't want anyone else endangering themselves for this."

"What danger? I already know not to eat her baked goods. And if you think I can't handle an old fussbudget, you've obviously never been to my house on pinochle night. I speak elderly. I stand a better chance than you of getting this old bird to tell us what we want to know."

"Not to gang up on you, but your grandmother has a point." Nadia picked up another cookie and nibbled at it.

"Pretty and smart. You need to hang on to this one, Matilda." Granny topped off Nadia's glass of wine.

"Have I told you how much I like your grandmother?"

"Thank you, child."

Maddie's eyes narrowed to slits as she stared at the pair teaming up against her, but she refrained from succumbing to their digression. "You know, I've had some practice in getting information from an old woman." She looked pointedly at her grandmother, hoping at the last second that Granny didn't take offense to being called old.

"But only about as much success as a perforated condom," Granny cackled. "How often do you get me to talk about things I don't want to talk about?"

"You're an exceptional case," Maddie growled, but she knew her grandmother was right.

"Which means I'll be exceptional at this task." Maddie opened her mouth to argue, but Granny wouldn't hear it. "What time should we meet?"

"You tell me," she sighed. "When are old ladies most likely to confess to homicide?" She resigned herself to the inevitable chaos of mixing Granny Doyle and a murder investigation, knowing inherently that it wouldn't go well.

CHAPTER TWENTY-THREE

Despite waking up ten minutes before the buzz of her alarm (thanks in part to an enthusiastic tongue bath from Goliath), Maddie started her day with the oddest sense of hope. True, she had yet to learn if she'd acquired new headquarters for Little Guys or if she'd be forced to feign interest in commercial real estate until she died. She still had two unsolved murders hanging over her head, her best friend seemed to have replaced her with the prosaic role model for efficiency, and her favorite employee was on the verge of heartbreak and misery at the hands of her sister, a mushroom cloud of agony that would surely engulf her too. But no matter how much she considered the upheaval of her current life, that unfamiliar ball of hope continued to sit there, drawing her attention to its unwarranted presence and preventing her from wallowing in the misery she was more accustomed to. Maybe it had something to do with the exquisite woman currently sharing her bed.

She shifted slightly, both to evade Goliath's steady slurping of the lower half of her face and to admire Nadia. She lay perfect, naked and alarmingly beautiful—even with the souvenir of her brief meeting with Ray—snuggling against Maddie's side. Her breaths came steadily, and even in the peaceful repose of slumber, a hint of that lopsided, mischievous grin lingered on her face. Maddie didn't think she'd ever seen anything so beautiful, and though she'd never considered herself the kind of woman to be swayed into romance-based complacency, she'd also never conceived of a world wherein a woman like Nadia would even consider ending up in her bed.

But, as a not-so-gentle nudge from Bart reminded her, there was more to life than having a girlfriend. No matter how much she liked this particular girlfriend, she'd get no closer to solving a murder and returning her life to somewhere in the proximity of normal (or as close as her life ever came to that particular designation) by watching Nadia sleep.

Mabel apparently agreed. As soon as she tried to sit up, the gangly pup launched herself onto the bed, one giant paw with the force of all seventy-five pounds of her behind it landing squarely on her chest. Apparently not satisfied that her startled response was enough to rouse her human companion, Mabel added her surprisingly deep bark to the mix.

"I'm up. I'm up." As if by command, Nadia sprang to life and lunged for the door, ready to tend to her dog's needs.

"Are you going to take the dogs out?"

"Yeah, Mabel's still working on her bathroom skills, so when she tells me it's time to go, it's time to go."

"You might want to put some clothes on. Unless you want to feed the crush Mr. Butzbaum already has on you." She grinned at the thought of her old (but apparently still frisky) neighbor's reaction to Nadia playing with Mabel au naturel.

Nadia frowned adorably at her own nudity. "You may have a point. Any idea where my clothes ended up last night?"

"Kitchen maybe?" Maddie squinted then smirked, remembering exactly how their night had unfolded once Granny made her welcome departure. "That's where we were when Granny left."

"You know," Nadia said as she stepped in the hall briefly before returning with her pants (which Nadia had kept on much longer than anticipated). "World's greatest cookies aside, your grandmother ruined our date night."

"I think we recovered nicely." Maddie stood to begin the search for her own clothing.

"True, but I want a whole night, without a family-imposed intermission." Nadia stepped into her jeans but remained topless as Mabel danced around their feet, frantic either for attention or the bathroom. "Tonight."

"I'll clear my schedule," she agreed, hopeful her outing with Granny that afternoon would make this a nonissue.

"We should probably go to my place. I don't want to find out who else is likely to barge through your front door at inopportune moments."

"Good thinking." Maddie sealed their agreement with a kiss, one that was cut regrettably short by the limitations of a growing puppy's bladder.

Even in the face of that unpropitious start to her day, her rosy outlook held (and even blossomed). She didn't know how she would accomplish it, but she determined to solve Terry's murder before her date with Nadia. She realized she shouldn't tailor her schedule around her love life (particularly in matters of literal life and death), but she didn't see how she would ever give Nadia her full attention if half her mind was pondering murder. And she wanted to know what it would be like to date Nadia without the distraction of a mystery getting in their way. On top of that, it would be nice to return to boring, normal life where she didn't have to worry that her extracurricular activities would put her at risk of angering local law enforcement. Who knew she would ever look back fondly on the days when her biggest excitement involved folding her socks?

Though she and Granny weren't ambushing Esther until late that afternoon, that didn't mean Maddie had to sit idly waiting for the case to solve itself. She didn't have an inordinate amount of time to put toward finding the real killer, but if she got lucky, she could prevent a repeat engagement with Esther— an outcome both she and her stomach would happily accept, yet one she feared was as likely as Goliath suddenly disregarding his independent nature and deciding to listen to any of her commands. Really, how did she expect to catch the murderer if she didn't talk to one of her main suspects? It wasn't like a person who plotted agonizing, allergy-based assassinations would be considerate enough to march up to her and confess. She sighed, resigning herself to the sensory overload that a visit to Esther entailed, but even that terrible realization did little to disrupt her positive equilibrium.

Her mood faltered slightly near the end of her day when a concerned (and selectively observant) citizen confronted her as she walked Zeus the Yorkie.

"You have to clean that up," the bespectacled busybody called from across the street, her thoroughly disgusted expression a precursor to what Maddie suspected would be an unwelcome and undeserved harangue.

Had she not been wearing a shirt with her company's name and logo emblazoned across it, she might not have suppressed the urge to fling the fruits of Zeus's labors at her. But certain as she was that this waste product watchdog would acquire crystal clear vision, zeroing in on the Little Guys logo from across the street, she bit her tongue and kept her focus on Zeus and his output. True, she may have opened her eco-friendly waste bag with a bit more flourish than usual, but she otherwise refused to acknowledge the woman's existence.

She had only one more stop after Zeus—her final visit with Murphy's cats, which would be blessedly free from unnecessary critique or redundant advice. That thought (plus her critic's shrill cry of fear at Zeus's yap of disapproval) lifted her spirits once again.

"Good boy, Zeus," she whispered as they made their way past the now jittery complainer.

"Your mom will be home tonight, boys. I know it goes against your brooding cat nature, but try not to be too aloof when she gets here." She talked to Stanley and Herbie as she filled their bowls for the last time.

One-sided conversations with her charges were nothing new for her. It probably wasn't an exaggeration to say she spent more time chatting with dogs and cats than with other humans, a circumstance Dottie would no doubt find horrifying and entirely believable. For Maddie, though, talking to her animals was one of the perks of the job. She found solutions to most of her problems when she shared them with the dogs and cats she cared for. She lived in her head, and airing her woes to the sympathetic ears of her animal friends was often just what she needed. Though they never offered advice or suggested any course of action, they also never chastised, mocked or lectured her, a refreshing change from most of the majority of her human interactions. So she thought nothing of her current idle feline banter, at least not until she heard the click of the lock in Murphy's front door.

She stopped midsentence and creeping toward Murphy's utensil holder, reached for anything she could use as a weapon. Armed and uneasy but unwilling to let the cats come to any harm on her watch, she tiptoed toward the living room, terrified to confront the intruder. Herbie, meanwhile, charged ahead, eager to greet any violent criminal who might be lurking in the next room, noiselessly ransacking Murphy's home. Not wanting the friendly kitten to suffer at the hands of a ruthless malefactor, she hurried after him, weapon at the ready. Just as she reached the entryway, arm raised to defend herself, she heard a delighted cooing of Herbie's name and looked up to see Officer Murphy (criminally alluring in worn jeans and a black leather jacket) cuddling her cat.

"You scared me."

"Apparently." Murphy eyed her with amusement. "A potato masher? That's your weapon of choice?"

"I just grabbed what was handy."

"In my kitchen where the knives live?"

"Maybe I was going for the element of surprise," she offered weakly.

"Mission accomplished." Murphy smiled, her dimple appearing to make her that much more captivating, not that she needed any help in that department.

"So," Maddie fumbled with the potato masher as she tried to focus on anything other than the tantalizing Officer Murphy. "You're back early." Murphy stepped close enough to take the utensil from her suddenly weak grasp. "Aren't you?"

"A little early. Traffic wasn't bad."

Of course she looked radiant after a road trip, whereas Maddie barely managed the brief walk from her bathroom to her living room without negating all her efforts on the esthetic front.

Looking for something to do (other than stare into Murphy's brown eyes), she crouched to pet Stanley, who'd been rubbing his plump body against her calves almost since Murphy came through the door, as if to show her how little he was interested in his recently negligent mother.

"You must be tired from your trip, and the cats missed you, so I'll get out of your way."

"Clearly they've been pining for me." She gestured to Maddie's feet where both cats were now busy purring and rubbing their faces on her shoes. "And we never had that dinner you agreed to. You should stay."

Murphy hit her with another dimple-enhanced grin, and she felt all the air leave the room. She swallowed hard. "I'd love to, but—"

"You have somewhere else you need to be." She nodded, not trusting her voice. "Another time then."

She nodded again and inched toward the door, grateful and sorry to hear the ringing of Murphy's phone, pulling her attention from Maddie, who both needed and dreaded relief from her intense gaze.

"I should take this." Murphy apologized to her for the interruption (probably some cop emergency, Maddie guessed, instantly excusing her) and then frowned at her phone before answering.

Wondering if Murphy was dismissing her or if she should stay to provide an in-person report on the cats, Maddie lingered by the door awkwardly glancing around the room. As she hesitated, she couldn't help but overhear Murphy's half of the conversation and felt bad about listening in, but it wasn't like

Murphy tried to move to a less occupied area of her home. And (at least initially) the conversation didn't seem to be private in nature.

"I am free tonight. I just got back," she told the caller. "I'll be there at six." Murphy sounded happy about seeing whoever was on the other end of the call (probably some supermodel in need of companionship, not that Maddie cared). "Anything for you, babe."

"I'll just let myself out then," she muttered to the cats and slipped out the door, chastising herself for the eavesdropping she regretted every second of.

It wasn't until she stepped outside and took a deep breath of fresh, crisp air that she felt herself regaining her poise (to the extent that she ever could claim to have poise) and shook her head to clear it of pervasive thoughts of Officer Dimples Murphy.

"Now, if I can just survive Granny Doyle, P.I., I can call it a day," she said to no one in particular as she made her way toward her grandmother's house.

CHAPTER TWENTY-FOUR

Maddie found Granny Doyle sitting on her front porch, ready to go. In deference to the mild temperatures, she wore a light sweater but no jacket. Wisps of her hair that had escaped from its habitual braid fluttered in the gentle breeze, and now and again she tucked a fluttering strand behind her ear. She wore the gym shoes Maddie had given her for her birthday, a clear sign she was eager for their adventure, and a container of some baked goodness sat on the table beside her.

"Cutting it kind of close, aren't you?" Granny said by way of greeting. She rose and began gathering her things.

Maddie checked her watch to confirm that her exchange with Murphy hadn't put her too far behind schedule. "Granny, I'm ten minutes early."

"And I was expecting you five minutes ago. You tend to show up early, you know." She barreled down her stairs, and after pausing to offer her granddaughter a brief but warm greeting, she continued down the sidewalk at a brisk pace. "And given your fondness for extreme punctuality, I don't think you can blame me for worrying that you'd forgotten our plan."

"You're that eager to visit an old lady with bad taste and possibly worse morals?"

"You're that reluctant to spend time with your grandmother?"

"Maybe I don't want to share you with anyone," Maddie said and offered to carry the pie Granny insisted on taking to Esther's house.

To Maddie this seemed like an unnecessary risk—the sight of confections would undoubtedly inspire Esther to unveil her own miserable culinary offerings for their "enjoyment," leading to some potentially unpleasant results. Still hopeful about eschewing sustenance of any sort at Esther's, she tapped the lid of the pie container and ventured a question.

"You know you're just going to inspire her to share, don't you?"

"She was going to do that anyway, so I brought this as a palate cleanser."

"That's actually a great idea."

"Don't act surprised, child. You didn't think your brilliance came out of thin air, did you?"

"There's brilliant, and then there's devious. I could never hope to be so deviously brilliant."

"Nonsense. I just know how to read people. Like you." Granny studied her as they strode purposefully toward Sheridan Road. "What's got you so cheery? Is it that girlfriend of yours?"

"What do you think of her?" she asked to deflect the question. Not that she didn't want to discuss Nadia or the very real possibility that her love life was, in fact (and in defiance of the dire romantic precedent she'd established over the years), the source of her atypical joyfulness. Mostly she wanted to enjoy the feeling while it lasted, and knowing her luck, that wouldn't be long.

"Don't think I don't know what you're doing, young lady. I invented that move," Granny countered, their habitual game of conversational chess picking up at the stalemate where they always left it.

"Can't I be interested in your opinion of the person I'm seeing? What you think of Nadia will impact me as long as she sticks around, so if you don't like her, the next couple week[s] could be hard to get through."

"She seems a whole lot more taken with you than that, child."

"She does, doesn't she?" Maddie couldn't help the grin that spread across her face, even though she knew Granny would pounce on it.

"I guess I've got my answer."

"But I don't," she countered.

"It's early for me to say anything," Granny answered cautiously.

"That's never stopped you in the past."

"I'm older and wiser now."

Maddie stared at her expectantly but prudently said nothing to contradict her.

"You know, you've never been this concerned with what I think of your girlfriends in the past. Why the sudden interest in my opinion?" Granny studied her face carefully. "Are you in love with Nadia?"

"Pfft." She dismissed her question with a fluttering wave of her hand. "It's too soon for me to fall in love."

"Now, I'm not a worldly, accomplished woman like you. I married the third man I ever dated, stayed married for thirty-five years and haven't the slightest interest in anyone other than your grandfather, but in my limited experience, I don't recall ever learning of a timeframe for loving someone. You either do or you don't. Of course, some folks are too thick-headed to realize it for a while. Takes 'em even longer to admit it, but that's why god created pushy grandmothers."

"He broke the mold with you."

"Which means you better get to talking."

She weighed her odds of outlasting her in a contest of wills and decided to surrender immediately. The end result would be the same, but she could bypass most of the frustration that came with trying to keep anything from her.

"I like her a lot, probably more than I should after a collective two weeks of dating."

"But?"

"But what if I confuse strong like for love? And what if I settle for what I have now and never get more? Or what if I hold out for more that never comes? Isn't it naïve to expect that everyone gets a happy ending? Shouldn't I just be satisfied that anyone wants to spend time with me at all?"

"Slow down, child," Granny admonished. "You're so concerned about crossing the finish line you're willing to skip the race. Maybe you should enjoy where you're at and give yourself room to feel what you feel about Nadia."

"Is that what you did with Grandpa?"

They turned up the walkway to Esther's building.

"There was no need to. I think I loved your grandfather from the moment I saw him."

"Oh," she sighed, touched by her grandmother's story but saddened by her own shortcomings in that area.

"'Course it took some time for me to recognize that and break off my engagement to your almost-grandfather."

"What?" Momentarily in shock, Maddie stopped short just before the entrance to the building.

"Are we here already?" Granny breezed past her stupefied granddaughter and stepped into the revolving door.

"You aren't getting out of this so easily," she called after her but fell silent when she caught the stern gaze of the doorwoman.

"Is Esther Snodgrass in?" Granny asked sweetly, and just like that evaded another discussion of her personal life.

"Matilda, what a pleasant surprise." Esther stood in her doorway, beaming as Maddie and Granny made their way down the hall. "I'm so glad you came back. And you brought a guest. Come in, come in."

Over the babel of Thelma and Louise's solicitous greeting, Maddie introduced the old women, who seemed to have little more than advancing years in common. Almost immediately upon entering, Granny reared back, her expression one of petrified amazement. Maddie could almost hear her thoughts as she took in the whole of Esther's garish living space. Even on her second time around, Maddie found it jarring, but Esther (obviously inured to the poor taste with which she surrounded herself) merely shuffled forward, chattering about putting on a kettle for a fresh pot of tea and dancing around her moving furry obstacle course.

"I'll skip the tea if you have anything stronger," Granny called to her, earning a glare from Maddie. Though alcohol might make the experience more agreeable, she doubted Esther would have anything less revolting than dandelion wine to offer, and she didn't want to run the risk of drinks with Esther turning her off booze forever.

"Now that you mention it, it's a bit late in the day for tea, and this is such a special occasion. Other than that nice Mr. Fitzwilliam, I so rarely get visitors. An aperitif would be a wonderful way to celebrate. I think I have some spirits my Leonard left."

Esther hauled out a rickety stepladder and positioned it haphazardly in front of the avocado green refrigerator. Before she could set foot on the bottom step, Maddie rushed to her side.

"Let me get that for you," she said, mounting the steps and praying those wouldn't be her last words.

Relieved of her daredevil bartending duties, Esther began arranging cupcakes on a doily-laden plate. Maddie prayed that Granny's pie would earn a spot on the tray Esther was preparing, but after a second glance at the cupcakes, she renounced all hopes of an indigestion-free evening.

To her surprise, the cabinet above Esther's refrigerator held not only what she suspected was the ancient prototype for modern crockpots, but also an impressive selection of alcohol. As she rummaged through the bottles of vodka, gin, scotch, cooking sherry, whiskey and (to her disgusted amazement) Malort, Granny commenced her interrogation.

"Goodness, Esther, you must have been here a long time."

She admired Granny's tactful method of commenting on Esther's impressive accumulation of clutter.

"Forty years."

She looked up from her improvised mixology to see Esther beaming proudly.

"You must like it." Granny glanced around again, her expression clearly conveying her amazement that anyone could be happy in a space like Esther's. "How are your neighbors?"

"Wonderful. Everyone here is so nice."

Maddie wondered if Esther had forgotten that she shared the story of her nightmare neighbors, but she decided not to ask until Granny got wherever she was going with her line of questioning.

"How lucky you are. I've always been hit or miss with my neighbors. The one to the right will be a blessing, but to my left it's scoundrels and layabouts. I'd love to have your good fortune with neighbors."

As far as Maddie knew, Granny had had more trouble with hangnails than she ever had with any of her neighbors, but she wasn't about to point that out.

"Well, it's fine now, but there was some trouble earlier."

"What kind of trouble?" Granny asked and crumbled her cupcake on her plate, creating the convincing appearance of having eaten it.

"Oh, just little things. Noise and unfriendly behavior in the halls. I don't think either one of those women next door even knew how to smile."

"Unpleasant to be sure, but considering what else is out there, I don't know that I'd be happy they left." Granny smiled and tasted the drink Maddie offered her, apparently unfazed by her granddaughter's heavy-handedness with alcohol.

"They didn't leave. I mean, not like you think."

"What other way to leave is there, Esther?"

"In body bags." She sipped demurely from her cocktail, her eyes widening in concern as Maddie choked on her own beverage. "But my new neighbors are wonderful. They love Thelma and Louise, and they don't mind that I have a key to their place."

"You have a key to their place?" Every time she tried to eliminate Esther as a suspect, she found more evidence to suggest she was some kind of well-intentioned, elderly serial killer.

"Yes, dear." Esther returned her focus to her drink, apparen unaware of the bomb she'd just dropped.

Granny raised her eyebrows in a question, the universal signal for more information.

Maddie, infinitely less patient than her grandmother, couldn't wait for Esther to take the hint. "Why do you have their key?"

"I've always had a key."

"But, why?"

"The owners of that unit live in Florida. They wanted someone close by they could trust to have access, in case there was any trouble."

"So you had a key when your previous neighbors lived there." Maddie gulped her drink, wishing she hadn't bothered to mix anything with the booze.

"Of course, though, they hated it. They asked Lucille—she's one of the owners—to take my key back."

"Did you give it back?" Granny asked.

"No. I promised Lucille I'd only use it if we found ourselves in a predicament, and then they died."

Esther smiled again and placed a second cupcake on Maddie's plate. Meanwhile, Maddie wondered just what sort of predicament would inspire Esther to use her all-access pass to Terry and Lindsey's home.

"That is not how that meeting was supposed to go," Maddie sighed as she and Granny made their way home in the waning light.

"What do you mean? I thought we were trying to catch a killer."

"We are, but I was really hoping it wasn't Esther."

"It isn't her, child."

"Were you in a different conversation than I was? Because she basically admitted she had motive and means to kill both the victims. Every time I turn around, she looks more likely to be the murderer."

"Well, turn the other way because Esther is innocent."

"I hope you're right, Granny."

"Mark my words, the only thing that woman has killed is my appetite."

"I need slightly more in the evidence department than just your word."

"And you'll find it, but it won't be by looking at Esther Snodgrass. I'm more likely to commit murder than she is."

Maddie wanted to believe in her grandmother's homicide sixth sense—it would certainly make finding the killer a breeze. But she wasn't convinced, and in truth she had as much to go on with Esther as with any other suspect. She wondered if she'd ever catch a break in this ridiculous, mind-boggling case, and considering how long she'd been working to get to a minimally less populated field of suspects than she'd started with, she figured she would be collecting Social Security before she ever found out who killed Terry and Lindsey.

She should probably quit before she got herself in trouble. Aside from helping her friend, what was she getting from this investigation anyway? It wasn't like she knew the victims and would find some peace of mind by discovering who killed them. No, the only reason she had invested any energy in this puzzling case at all was because of Leigh, and since the police still hadn't arrested her, maybe she was already in the clear.

"Who's that on your porch?" Granny asked, breaking in on Maddie's thoughts.

She hadn't noticed anything out of the ordinary until Granny's question snapped her out of her reverie. But as she studied the silhouette at her front door, she discerned two people huddled close together. What they were doing at her door, she had no idea.

"Harriet?" Granny called when they got closer. "What are you doing on your sister's porch? And who's that with you?"

"Granny?" Harriet cried out, obviously taken aback by the appearance of their grandmother.

Meanwhile, Maddie recognized the other figure on her porch. "Patrick? What are you doing here? With my sister?" She thought she'd made her desire to be uninvolved abundantly clear, but there they stood, holding hands, fresh from a canoodling session on her front steps.

"We were headed to dinner, but Harriet got a call."

"And she had to take it here? I can think of at least thirt other places in this neighborhood alone that have better phone reception than my front porch." She breezed past the crowd at her entryway and opened her door, assuming she'd get an explanation eventually.

"What's this about dinner, Harriet?" Granny chimed in. "Who's this you're camped out on Maddie's porch with?"

"Granny, you already know Patrick."

"I know the nice young man who works for my granddaughter. I'm not sure why he's spending time with my other granddaughter on his boss's front steps."

"I'm pretty sure they were on a date," Maddie announced as she led the way to her liquor cabinet for a much-needed drink.

"Is that so?" Granny eyed Patrick more carefully, and his posture instantly improved under her scrutiny.

"It could be serious. You should probably have them over for dinner." Harriet glared at her, but Maddie ignored the venomous look, enjoying a rare opportunity to torment her older sister.

"Indeed. I'll see you tomorrow, won't I, young man?" Granny posed her question in such a way that Patrick understood the only acceptable answer was "yes."

"Does that work for you, Maddie?"

"Me? Why do you want me there?" She was shocked by her grandmother's question, but a smirking Harriet found it all too amusing.

"I want to have you and your lady friend over for dinner. Might as well feed everybody at once."

"Safety in numbers," Harriet whispered in her ear, but she ignored that sage advice.

"You already had us for dinner."

"I had you for dessert. Since when is pie considered dinner?"

"Since my freshman year of college."

"You act like it's a burden to have dinner with your grandmother. Is there some reason you don't want to join us?"

"No," she answered immediately. "None at all."

"I'm sure she wants to, but she might not be available." Harriet came to the rescue. "She's going to be busy closing on her new property."

She whirled around to face her sister. "I got it?"

"Why else would I drag my date to your house on a Friday night?"

"I don't believe it. I thought for sure Little Guys would be staying put forever. Oh god, there's so much work to do." Overwhelmed by the warring emotions of relief, excitement, eagerness, and terrified dread, she hugged Harriet and then fell onto her couch.

"You could take a few minutes to celebrate." Harriet extracted a bottle from her liquor cabinet. "It's not like you can start renovating tonight."

Granny sipped eagerly from her glass. "But you should ask Dottie for help when it's time for renovations. In just a couple weeks, she's completely transformed the space she's in."

"You mean the space she was in."

"She didn't mention any work on the condo. She planned to sell it as-is," Harriet interjected before turning her attention back to a doe-eyed Patrick.

Granny froze, her tumbler halfway to her mouth. For the first time she could recall, Maddie thought Granny looked guilty.

"Of course that's what I meant. I must have misspoken." She gestured with her glass and hiccupped exaggeratedly.

"You're the most deliberate and plain speaker on the planet. You never misspeak. What's going on, Granny?"

"You're always so suspicious, child."

"With good reason. What are you up to? More importantly, what is Dottie up to?"

She squirmed a little, but Maddie couldn't enjoy making her share information she'd intended to keep a secret.

"If you must know, Dottie decided your new house needed a bit of a facelift. She's redoing the whole place, and she asked me not to tell you."

"What?" The room spun. Of all the ways she thc Dottie would make her life as a landlord hell, gutting her he without permission or approval and luring her grandmoth into an elaborate remodel and betrayal scheme wasn't one o. them. "Did you even try to stop her?" Maddie asked, though she was well versed in the futility of trying to change Dottie's mind.

"The work needed to be done, and she knew you didn't care about it. She wanted to take care of it for you and surprise you."

"That's quite a surprise." Maddie drained her drink and slammed the empty glass on her counter. Harriet, Patrick, and Granny all looked on in various stages of horror and concern as she dialed Dottie's number with one hand while refilling her glass with the other. "Get over here now," she barked and hung up without waiting for a response.

Within ten minutes Dottie sashayed through the front door, making her customary stop at the liquor cabinet before facing Maddie. For once she showed up without Carlisle in tow, but that offered Maddie little satisfaction.

"Anything you think you should tell me?" she asked. She wanted to give Dottie the chance to own up to her betrayal.

"That color does nothing for your complexion." She gestured toward her sweater. "And you really should give my salon a call. They could work wonders with your tresses."

She glowered at her for several seconds trying to regain her composure. "Not the right time, Dottie." She clenched her jaw to prevent herself from saying something she would regret.

"It never is. Trying to discuss aesthetics with you is like trying to discuss philosophy with a kindergartener."

"And getting you to respect boundaries is like trying to keep the Rat Pack away from the liquor cabinet."

Dottie gasped as if physically wounded, but she said nothing.

"Did you even consider asking for permission to remodel the house? Were you ever going to tell me about it?"

"That's what's got you so upset? The tiny—and might I add, necessary—touch-up? I'm just sprucing the place up a bit. Why is this such an offense?"

Let's pretend for a moment that you aren't painfully
are you shouldn't have done this. That sneaking around and
cruiting my grandmother to keep your secret isn't proof that
you knew this was wrong. The offense is that it's not your house
to remodel."

"Did you want to do it?"

"That's not the point."

"Of course it is. The work needed to be done. Unless you
thought the combination murder scene and elderly bachelor
chic was adding to your property value." Maddie's glare was
completely lost on Dottie. "If you're not upset that I stole your
design thunder, then what could you possibly be angry about?"

"It wasn't your decision to make."

"But the person who should have made that decision refuses
to set foot inside the property. Had I waited for you to tend to
the house, I'd still be living in an outdated murder shrine. What
was I to do?"

"If it was so awful, why did you work so hard to talk me into
renting it to you?"

"Carlisle and I needed more space to work in."

"Well, I hope you and Carlisle will be happy together."
Grabbing her jacket on her way out the door, she called out,
"Lock the door when you leave."

Dimly she heard her grandmother calling after her, but she
was too angry to talk this out.

CHAPTER TWENTY-FIVE

Maddie hadn't planned on going to the bar. She'd simply wanted to get away from her house and everyone in it. She wasn't sure what made her angrier—Dottie and Granny's secrecy or the fact that Dottie hadn't even consulted her about changes to the home she owned. True, she didn't want the property, and if she could legally unload it, she would, but that didn't give Dottie the right to overhaul something that wasn't hers. The fact that Dottie would undoubtedly make better design choices than she would was entirely beside the point. It was her house, and she should have been consulted.

And how could Granny justify lying to her like that? Her whole life, Maddie had been admonished to tell the truth, that her honor and her reputation were all she had in this world, and it only took one lie to tarnish everything. Yet Granny had lied to her for weeks without any remorse. She had no idea what to think about anything after that.

"May I see your ID?"

She jumped at the sound of the familiar voice. She hadn't expected to encounter a bouncer any more than she had meant to visit a bar. When she'd left her house in anger, she'd just started walking, paying more attention to the continuous loop of angry thoughts than the direction her feet took her. By the time she stood in front of the bar, she decided a drink would be at least as beneficial as walking a thousand miles in anger. What she hadn't anticipated was the addition of a Friday night bouncer, or that she would end up looking into the dark, kind eyes of Officer Murphy.

"Officer Murphy?"

"Miss Smithwick." Murphy grinned at her and held her hand out for the driver's license Maddie was slow to produce. She was still adjusting to the fact that Officer Murphy sat casually in front of her, her tight jeans and black T-shirt accentuating her lithe, lean body, smirking and patiently waiting for Maddie to comply.

"You're a bouncer now?" She maintained her habit of stating the obvious to Officer Murphy.

"Just for tonight. I'm helping Babe."

"Babe?"

"The owner. She called earlier to ask if I could fill in for her regular help."

Her relief disproportionate to her new understanding, she realized that Murphy hadn't dismissed her to take a call from her supermodel girlfriend and that maybe, impossible though it seemed, there was no supermodel girlfriend.

"The cats don't mind you being gone so soon after your recent absence?" She reluctantly handed over her ID (with its undeniable evidence that she was as photogenic as a yeti).

"They kicked me out. They fell in love with their babysitter, and now they want nothing to do with me." Murphy studied the plastic card in her hand as if she would be tested on it later. A small grin played at the corners of her mouth.

"Silly cats," Maddie muttered, simultaneously irritated and grateful that the line of women behind her cut their interaction short.

Once inside, it took a year to wind her way past the throng of prowling women and reach the bar where Kittens poured a steady stream of drinks (the majority of which seemed to be cheap beer). By the time she found an empty stool, her mood had tripled in foulness.

"You look like you could use a double." Kittens placed a drink on the bar in front of her, and she grunted her thanks.

But before she even had time to savor her first sip of bourbon, a voice beside her startled her for the second time that evening.

"Mind if I sit here?" Murphy gestured to the stool beside her but waited for her assent before taking a seat.

"Who's watching the door?"

"Babe's got it for a few minutes. I needed a break, and I thought maybe we could have that drink you changed your mind about." Murphy flagged down Kittens who seemed to know her order by telepathy.

"I changed my mind about dinner," she corrected and instantly wished she'd kept her mouth shut. Whatever Murphy was after, she didn't need to encourage it.

"I wouldn't recommend eating here." Murphy gratefully accepted the drink Kittens brought her, even tipping, though he waved off her efforts to pay. "But if you want to change your mind again, I know a few places around here with decent booze and edible food."

"Thanks for the tip." She actively ignored the second part of Murphy's statement. Hoping to change the subject, she asked, "You're allowed to drink on duty? Won't the lesbian riff-raff get in?"

"Perk of the job. I get all the free Coke and water I can stand, which isn't much." She checked her watch and rose. "I should get back to my post. Thanks for keeping me company, Miss Smithwick."

"You have to start calling me Maddie, especially if we're being friendly. I don't call any of my friends by their surnames."

"Except for me," Murphy pointed out.

"Only because you won't tell me your first name."

"Not yet anyway." Murphy winked, then smiled.

"You know, Officer Murphy, you're a lot less intimidating when you smile."

"I could say the same about you, Miss Smithwick."

"I'm about as intimidating as a kitten."

"And twice as cute." Murphy winked again, and as a record-breaking blush engulfed Maddie's face, she felt herself go weak at the knees, even though she was seated. "Especially when you blush."

"Considering I spend half my life in that state, that's a relief."

"If you ever decide to change your mind about dinner, you know where to find me." She winked once more and made her exit.

"Oh shit. I'm in trouble." She sighed and flinched when she turned to see a sour-faced Kat Russell staring her down.

"I don't get it," Kat said.

Clueless as to what she'd done to offend the scowling woman, she focused most of her attention on her drink. "What don't you get?"

"What the hottie at the door sees in you. She barely notices me, but she sees you and suddenly she's all smiles and flirtation." Kat flipped her brassy hair as if to emphasize the disparity between her beauty and Maddie's.

"It's probably my winning personality," Maddie offered, stopping short of comparing her likeability to Kat's surly demeanor. True as it was, she still wanted to talk to Kat about Terry, Lindsey and Leigh, which meant she should try to hold off on offending her for as long as possible.

"You come here a lot. Is this where you and Leigh met?" She already knew the answer was no, but she needed some way to get Kat talking about the victims. This seemed like a better option than just asking if she'd killed anyone lately.

"No. We go way back."

"So do we. You'd think we would have met before now."

"Well, we weren't always so close. We were neighbors first and then friends. And then more." There went the hair again, and Maddie ground her teeth.

"Odd that she never mentioned you."

"We had to keep things quiet for a while, until everything with Terry and Lindsey died down."

Unfortunate word choice, Maddie thought but let it slide. She was about to probe deeper but was interrupted.

"I thought she had better sense than to look for comfort in a bottle." At the sound of her grandmother's voice, Maddie's head snapped in the direction of the entrance.

Granny was by no means a prude or a teetotaler, but to Maddie's knowledge, she wasn't one to frequent bars. In fact, she had no memory of Granny ever visiting, mentioning or showing even the slightest interest in any of the numerous taverns the city had to offer. So what was she doing in a lesbian bar? And how had she found her?

"Of course she's here. I told you we'd find her in a bar." Dottie's voice carried across even the noisiest of rooms, giving her the answer to her questions.

Though she appreciated the fact that they'd come after her, she didn't see how arguing about their troubles in public would be in any way beneficial. But considering Dottie's penchant for manipulation, a public confrontation may have been a calculated choice. She wouldn't put it past her friend to swap privacy for a fast resolution to her troubles.

"Two trips to the bar in one week. She must really like this place," Harriet said, and Maddie wondered (not for the first or last time in her life) how things could get any worse.

"Three, actually," Dottie clarified. "We may need to stage an intervention."

"I don't know. It looks nice enough," Patrick, ever the optimist, chimed in. "And I bet the drinks are pretty good, or Boss wouldn't be frequenting the place." The three women who surrounded him stared at him in disbelief, and he threw his hands up defensively. "What? All I'm saying is she has high standards."

"She gets that from her grandmother." Granny beamed, apparently forgetting her earlier concern over Maddie's choice to take out her frustration in a bar. Maddie sighed, lamenting the speed with which she'd drained the glass in front of her.

"So much for trying to get away from my problems," Maddie muttered and tried to flag Kittens down for liquid reinforcements before the public airing of her private life commenced.

"This round's on me." Dottie extracted an American Express Black card from her Hermès handbag as she sidled up next to Maddie.

Granny settled herself on the stool Maddie vacated for her and leveled her Granny-est stare at Kittens (who took the old woman's order of Sex on the Beach in stride). Harriet and Patrick placed their orders as well, and Dottie looked to Maddie for some acknowledgment of her generosity.

"I'm not talking to you yet." She lifted her regrettably empty glass to her lips, straining to extract even one lone drop of liquid from it.

Clearly unimpressed, Dottie turned to Kittens and said, "She'll have another, and I'll have a gin and tonic, double the gin and skip the tonic."

"Don't be so pigheaded, Matilda." Granny paused the gratifyingly slow consumption of her titillating cocktail long enough to chide her granddaughter. "What did Dottie do that's so awful?"

Not trusting herself to speak without unleashing all the hostility she felt, Maddie scowled at her grandmother until the tiny cocktail straw she demurely sucked at was sufficiently mangled.

"You mean other than lying to me, sneaking around behind my back, disregarding my right to make decisions about my own property, taking my friendship for granted, and assigning zero value to my opinion? I guess she didn't do anything at all."

"It was for your own good, panda."

"And she roped my grandmother into her scheme. My unfailingly forthright grandmother, who I look to to know what's right. You're supposed to make the smart, moral, good choices, not get wrapped up in deceiving your grandchildren for the benefit of their manipulative friends. I don't even understand how you thought any of this was a good idea."

"Well, I don't understand why you think it's such a bad idea to put Dottie in charge of the renovations. She has the resources to fund the project out of pocket."

"You don't," Dottie chimed in.

"She has time to deal with designers and contractors."

"You don't."

"She has impeccable taste."

Maddie spun around to face Dottie. "Don't you dare say, 'You don't.'"

"At least you're speaking to me again."

She glowered at her but said nothing.

"You shouldn't let them treat you that way." An unexpected ally, Kat laid her hand on Maddie's arm, but before she recovered from her astonishment, another shock befell her.

"What the hell is this, Maddie?" Nadia stood behind her, her expression a dark cloud of jealousy. "Not only did you forget our date, but you're also out at a bar with another woman. Again." Her eyes flashed with an anger that sent a corresponding chill throughout Maddie's entire system. She could understand Nadia's irritation at her absentmindedness, but the intensity of her reaction seemed extreme.

"I'm not here *with* anyone. I came alone, and now I happen to be standing next to someone I have a passing acquaintance with. We're hardly laying the groundwork for romantic bliss here." She scooted a fraction of an inch farther from Kat, putting as much distance between them as possible (though given the crowd at the bar drinking in every word of her regrettably public argument with Nadia, that distance was negligible).

"You looked awfully cozy to me."

"Look around, Nadia. Every lesbian within a ten-mile radius is packed into this place."

"Not to mention family and friends," Dottie interjected helpfully.

"That's not cozy. That's crowded."

Nadia seemed to contemplate Maddie's point, but not enough to concede her argument. "That still doesn't let you off the hook for forgetting about our plans."

"In my defense, I was a little distracted when we talked this morning." Maddie hoped a reminder of the more pleasant start to their day would help her move past her anger. Judging by her stony gaze, Nadia wasn't going to be forgiving her any time soon. "I'm sorry, Nadia. I got a bit blindsided after Granny and I finished with Esther, and with that on top of the investigation—"

"You did not just try to use that stupid investigation as a reasonable excuse for standing me up, did you?"

"Not exactly," she offered meekly, remembering much too late that she was supposed to be taking the night off from crime solving to focus on their relationship. "It's just that Granny and I made some progress, and then Harriet had some news, but unfortunately so did Granny, and—"

"What about me, Maddie?" Nadia's voice rose in her anger. "You were supposed to be with me tonight, focusing on us, not thinking about your grandmother or your sister or Dottie or that stupid investigation. But you're so wrapped up with trying to figure out who killed Terry and Lindsey that you aren't even thinking about me, are you?"

"Lindsey killed herself," Kat jumped in.

"Of course I am." She ignored Kat's interjection but made no further progress defending herself thanks to yet another interruption.

"Is there a problem, Miss Smithwick?" Murphy appeared at her side, imposing cop persona in full effect despite her civilian clothes.

"Everything's fine, Murphy. Thank you."

"You know the bouncer?" Nadia sounded incredulous. "How often are you here?"

"Third time this week," Kittens chimed in and earned a stern glower from Maddie.

"She's a client," Maddie clarified.

"That explains so much." Kat seemed disproportionately pleased by Maddie's explanation.

"Just a client?" Murphy looked somewhat disappointed but refused to leave her side.

She would have apologized, but the suggestion that Murphy might be more to her sparked another jealous tirade from Nadia.

"You're so busy running around trying to figure out who killed Lindsey that I have to pencil in a date with you. When do you have time to get so close to clients?"

"I'm not the only one with a full schedule."

"Hello? No one murdered Lindsey," Kat said again. "She committed suicide."

Nadia shifted her attention from Maddie long enough to glare at Kat. "How is this any of your business?"

"Aside from the fact that we're practically sitting in her lap while we argue?" Maddie asked, earning an icy glare from Nadia.

"Lindsey made it my business when she stole my girlfriend, and if you think anyone other than Lindsey had anything to do with her death, you obviously didn't read her note."

"What did you just say?" Maddie asked, a dim awareness of something amiss forming in her mind.

"How slow are you?" Kat answered snidely. "She explained in her note exactly why she killed herself."

"And you read her note?"

"Duh, that's what I'm telling you."

"When?"

"What?" Kat's face morphed from smug superiority to budding panic in a fraction of a second, like she realized in that moment the mistake she'd just made.

"When did you have access to Lindsey's suicide note?"

"After she died," Kat said with as much confidence as a first-grader attempting to spell "triskaidekaphobia" in the school spelling bee.

"And who showed it to you?" Maddie asked, certain she already knew the answer.

Kat's mouth fell open, but the only sound that emerged was a low, plaintive groan.

"You were there, weren't you? You're the other person Esther overheard."

"So what if I was there? It doesn't mean anything."

"But it does seem awfully suspicious. Why would you be visiting the widow of your ex?"

"I was worried about how she was dealing with her grief. She wasn't the most stable person on the planet, so I decided to check on her."

"I thought you hated Lindsey."

"With good reason."

"But you thought you'd just overlook your painful history with her to make sure she wasn't feeling too heartbroken, is that it?"

"You don't know what it was like, watching Terry fall all over that bitch. It's not like she was even pretty. She was fat," Kat growled. Maddie decided against pointing out that fat and attractive weren't mutually exclusive.

"But what did you hope to gain by killing her? Terry was already dead. It's not like you were going to get back together."

"I tried to. I stopped by to talk some sense into Terry, to help her see how horrible Lindsey was, and that she'd be happier if she came back to me." Kat spoke as if she couldn't acknowledge Maddie's point any more than she'd acknowledged Terry's decision to move on. "But she wouldn't listen. She didn't leave me any choice."

"I somehow doubt your only options were reconciliation or murder."

"Desperate measures," Dottie chimed in, meriting death stares from both Maddie and Kat.

"I am *not* desperate," Kat growled.

"Aren't you? You've hurt everyone who's rejected you. Isn't that why you worked so hard to make Leigh look guilty? Because she chose Lindsey over you."

"I was there for Leigh after Lindsey dumped her. I comforted her and helped her get her life back together, but she still went running after her the first chance she got, and she ditched me as soon as Lindsey let her back in. What else could I do?"

"Almost anything other than framing your alleged friend for double homicide?"

Out of nowhere Kat grabbed Maddie by the hair with one hand, and with the other she smashed her half-full beer bottle against the bar. Cheap beer and glass shrapnel sprayed the

room, shredding Kat's hand and causing several people to pan
and flee. Murphy, Nadia, Harriet, and Patrick all surged toward
Maddie and the disturbed and bleeding woman who held her,
but she thrust her glass shiv at the entourage, keeping them at
bay as she retreated to the rear of the bar, abductee in tow.

"This is ludicrous," she heard Dottie say as Kat dragged her
through the bar.

She struggled to free herself but couldn't seem to gain her
footing well enough to slow their progress or release herself
from Kat's hold, and she shuddered at the bone-chilling thought
that she would perish in a lesbian dive bar.

CHAPTER TWENTY-SIX

The part of Maddie's brain that wasn't fixated on how Kat would kill her was wondering what her cop friend was planning to do about the crazed killer trailing blood and hostages all over the bar she was supposed to be securing. Surely, as a trained police officer and sworn guardian of a gay flock, she must have some sort of deranged lesbian contingency plan. But Maddie couldn't wait for Murphy to rescue her. And since neither Goliath nor Carlisle and her lethal umbrella were available, she would have to save herself.

Recalling the last time she escaped the violent outburst of a murderer, she asked herself, "What would Goliath do?" Just then a swarm of terrified lesbians surged past them, forcing Kat to loosen her grip on Maddie. She swiveled her head and sank her teeth into Kat's hand, sending her weapon clattering to the floor. Maddie, with the foul taste of blood in her mouth, dove to relative safety beneath the nearest pool table just as Kat launched a five ball at her and shouted, "All-State softball MVP three years in a row!"

Maddie watched, powerless, as the blur of bright orange whizzed past, heading straight for Granny. At the last second, Murphy dove in front of Granny, the ball making a sickening crunch as it connected with Murphy's head. Her would-be hero fell to the floor as another projectile zipped toward Maddie's loved ones. While Patrick pushed Harriet and Nadia behind an overturned table, Dottie thrust her sturdy handbag in front of Granny, saving her from grave injury.

"Is Granny all right?" Maddie called.

"Yes, but my flask will never be the same." Dottie extracted the battered vessel from her purse as proof of her suffering.

"Not now, Dottie," she hissed. "How is Granny?" As much as she wanted Kat to pay for murdering two innocent (if unsavory) people, in the moment she cared more about her grandmother's well-being.

"Spilled my drink, but I'm fine, child. Don't get distracted on my account."

"It would help if you weren't in the line of fire," she growled as the purple blur of a four ball flew by and shattered a pint glass to Granny's left.

With that, Dottie whisked Granny behind the bar where Maddie hoped they'd remain unscathed.

Finally assured that Granny most likely wouldn't end her night sprawled on the scuffed and alcohol-infused floor, suffering from a blow to the head, Maddie continued her ill-advised pursuit of a killer. In the plus column, Kat hadn't taken advantage of the commotion to slip out the back of the bar. The blessings ended there, however, as Kat had armed herself with a pool cue (with which she drove the remaining patrons from the vicinity of her makeshift armory) and had a full stock of ammunition from three pool tables. Apparently each table had started a fresh game in the seconds before the players fled the scene in terror, meaning she had a seemingly endless supply of projectiles. Still, Maddie felt oddly grateful that Babe had provided pool tables for her patrons rather than dart boards.

"How did you do it, Kat?" she asked to buy time. She hoped for both a distraction and an answer, doubtful she'd get either.

How did you get Terry to eat the brownies? And Lindsey to jump off the balcony? They couldn't have done those things willingly."

"Forget it, super sleuth. I'm not saying anything else that might incriminate me." Another ball flew past and hit a tap handle, spraying beer and eliciting a startled yelp from Kittens.

"Do you really think skimping on details now is going to help you?" Dottie called from her hiding place behind the bar, drawing her attention and her fire. She launched the cue ball in Dottie's direction, thankfully hitting the wall several feet above her.

"She has a point, Kat. You've as good as confessed to killing Terry and Lindsey, and you're attempting to assault a bar full of people, including a cop." Maddie's thoughts turned briefly to the now groaning Murphy. She hoped the only damage would be a hearty bruise, but she didn't imagine that nearly half a pound of hard resin colliding with her skull would leave her unharmed. But, she remembered as the nine ball shattered the mirror behind the bar, she had no time to worry about that now. "It's not like you'll be preserving your innocence."

"You really want to know?" Kat called out but gave Maddie no time to answer her apparently rhetorical question. "It's called a Glock, Brainiac."

"You have a gun?" Maddie's courage wilted at the thought of confronting a more lethally-armed Kat Russell. Not that her combination pool-softball blood sport was a picnic, but she thought she'd have far better odds of dodging a pool ball or surviving the hit from one of them than if Kat switched to bullets.

Kat cackled maniacally but otherwise ignored the question, barreling ahead with the details of coercion. "Terry laughed at first. She thought I'd never hurt her. But when I threatened to shoot Lindsey, she took me seriously. I gave her a choice between me or the brownies."

"It must have hurt to know she preferred excruciating death to being with you." Questioning the wisdom of her plan, she began crawling toward Kat.

"Shut up!" She launched another ball. "She loved me. She was just blinded by Lindsey. Even when I offered her another chance to end her suffering, she still refused to leave Lindsey. That's when I gave her the EpiPen."

"I thought it didn't work," Maddie called out, inching her way toward her target.

"That's because I replaced the epinephrine with succinylcholine," Kat said, as if that explained everything.

"Obviously that would be a problem." For the first time in her life, Maddie regretted pursuing a Liberal Arts degree rather than focusing on the sciences.

"She thought she was getting relief from her allergies. Instead she got a muscle relaxant. She couldn't have gotten help no matter how hard she tried. And she did."

"You watched her suffer and did nothing to stop it?" She was aghast at Kat's cruelty.

"She made me suffer first." She hurled another ball in her direction.

Too late, Maddie ducked and felt the impact in her shoulder. "But," she spoke through clenched teeth, "if you'd already gotten even with Terry, why hurt Lindsey?"

"Because she ruined everything, and still everyone wanted her. There I was, throwing myself at Leigh, but all she could do was cry over stupid Lindsey. If she was gone, we could be together. I wouldn't have any competition."

"So you pushed her off her balcony?" Maddie crawled around the pool table closest to her assailant. Kat's legs were only a few feet away from her.

"I needed to stop her from hurting anyone else."

"You know you aren't going to get away with this."

"No one's stopped me yet, and I've got plenty of ammunition left." To punctuate her comment, she launched three more balls across the bar.

"This is ridiculous, Matilda. Just hit her with a pool cue already."

"It's not that simple, Granny. She has a gun."

"Nonsense, child. If she did, she would have shot us all by now."

"Well, that's a comforting thought."

She spared a moment to glare at the bar her grandmother hid behind, paying the price when Kat landed another blow to her already throbbing shoulder.

"That's it." She grabbed a pool cue that had rolled to a stop a few feet from her. "I have had a seriously rotten night, and I am so ready to take it out on you."

Caught off guard by Maddie's unexpected forcefulness, Kat looked almost terrified when she swung the stick at her. She managed to deflect the blow with her own pool cue, but her defensive maneuver knocked her off balance, and she stumbled backward. Before she could right herself, Maddie used the cue to trip her, then following Goliath's example, sat on her chest, pinning her to the floor until a thankfully alert and still agile Murphy could take over. Kat kicked and shrieked but remained more or less under control (though hardly subdued).

"Finally," Maddie said, grateful for the backup that prevented her and Kat from engaging in the barroom equivalent of a swordfight.

CHAPTER TWENTY-SEVEN

Despite a lifetime of things not magically improving with the arrival of a new day, Maddie felt let down by life when she woke the following morning. Even as the sun streamed through her window, bathing the lower half of her bed in a patch of white light her dogs found irresistible, signaling another reprieve from the often brutal weather of October, the day already felt bleak. She glanced at the empty space in her bed where Nadia had spent the past few nights (and where she surely would have been that morning if not for the havoc of the previous night) and refused to succumb to self-pity. She had no doubt that, even if she and Nadia survived this most recent setback, their future looked dismal at best. Not that they'd discussed it. Once Maddie's well-being had been established and an especially perturbed Fitzwilliam gave them permission to leave, Nadia did just that. Maddie hadn't heard from her since.

"What now?" she asked the pups. "Does it ever get easier?"

For an answer Goliath rolled onto his back and wriggled on the bed as if to scratch an itch. Bart, meanwhile, army crawled to her side, leaned against her and rested his scruffy head on her shoulder. His snuffling sigh matched her own, and she kissed his snout in gratitude.

As she lay there, comforted by the warmth of her dogs, the events of the past week played in her mind. While there had been a few bright spots, so much of what had transpired—from Leigh's mounting tragedies to her rekindled (and apparently doomed) romance with Nadia to Dottie and Granny's orchestrated violation—had left her feeling drained. If she could have skipped even one of those events, she would be free to bask in her minor victories in her boring, mundane ways. After all, her life wasn't a complete failure, as evidenced by her business' imminent expansion. If she didn't have a surplus of reasons to wallow in misery, she would be celebrating, probably by revisiting the firehouse to plan and daydream about the future home of Little Guys.

"You know what, boys? We should celebrate anyway. You haven't been to the new space yet, and you will be spending a lot of time there once it's up and running. You need to familiarize yourselves with the new office space, pick out your favorite spots. I don't want to just spring it on you."

Slightly energized, she kissed Bart's head once more, scratched Goliath's belly and swung her feet over the side of the bed.

"Boys, we're going on a field trip."

Nothing rejuvenated Maddie or set her world aright again like focusing all her energies on her business—one area of her life that never ceased to satisfy her. And after the downward spiral of the previous night, she needed something positive and soothing in her world. Her business could do that for her.

Bart and Goliath loved walks, no matter the destination, as long as they were long, so she felt confident they would delight in the trek to their new home away from home, Little Guy's future headquarters. As they approached the building, with the sunlight glinting off its surface in what she found a particularly hopeful display, the boys' tails seemed to start moving in a more forceful demonstration of happiness. Either she was desperate, or she had hit upon the one location in the city that she and boys liked as much as their own home.

They walked around the perimeter, Maddie conjuring images of her business' future successes, the boys sniffing and wagging wildly, all of them lost in the possibilities locked within this piece of real estate, none of them noticing the approach of another person.

"I thought I'd find you here."

Maddie turned to find her sister smirking at her.

"Harriet, you shouldn't sneak up on people like that."

"I was worried about you after last night."

That Harriet had honestly addressed her concerns rather than tormenting her under the guise of sibling fidelity indicated just how worried Harriet was—that and the fact that she had come looking for her, twice in recent memory. Something had her sister worried.

"I'm fine. I'm not even the one who got hit in the head with a pool ball."

"But you are the one whose girlfriend treated you unfairly in front of a bar full of people."

She shrugged, unable to find the words she'd need to make Harriet stand down. "Don't worry about me, Harriet."

"Can't help it. That's what big sisters are for."

"I'm fine."

"For the record, I don't believe you, but I know you won't talk about it unless I put you in a headlock, and I'm too well-dressed for wrestling."

"Thanks. Did you know about the remodel?"

"Not a clue, and I'm just as surprised as you are that Granny kept it a secret from you."

"So I'm not being ridiculous and hard-headed about this?"

"A little bit but I get it."

"You think I should be happy that Dottie up and decided that her esthetic sensibilities were more important than my rights as a property owner?"

"I think you're getting pretty worked up about a house you didn't even want six weeks ago." Harriet hit her with the same raised-eyebrow, arms folded across her chest look she'd used in

capacity as big sister since Maddie was old enough to follow
r everywhere she went.

"I'm going to have to sell it eventually. I don't want to waste
money undoing whatever Dottie 'fixes up' in there."

"As if Dottie's design choices would somehow hurt you
down the road." Maddie kicked at the weeds withering outside
the firehouse but refused to concede Harriet's point. "Maybe
you should go see it before you make up your mind."

"No thanks."

"Why not? What's the harm?"

"I found my friend dead on the floor. It's not exactly a
welcoming environment."

"Maybe it will be once Dottie finishes. It would be foolish to
ruin your friendship over something as unimportant as a piece
of real estate."

"I hate when you're right."

"And it happens all the time, you poor thing." Harriet looked
like she was about to hug her but stopped short of actually doing
so. "Are you good?"

She nodded, ready to move on to whatever happened next.
Love it or hate it, she would have to deal with the house and the
changes Dottie wrought at some point. "Thanks, Harriet."

"It's what big sisters are for." She shrugged. "As long as
you're going to be okay, I have to go conquer the real estate
market. You should go see your best friend before you have to
be in the market for a new one."

"I will. I just have something else to take care of first."

"Anything to do with a girl?"

"Something like that."

"Hi." Maddie fumbled with her keys. She didn't know what
to say any more than she knew what she was doing there. "I
wanted to make sure you were okay after last night. And to
thank you."

"All in a day's work." Murphy opened her door wider to let
Maddie in. Miraculously her cats didn't dart into the hall, but
Stanley did take the opportunity to rub against Maddie's legs.

"I think helping to thwart a pool-ball launching murderer escape falls well in the 'above and beyond' category."

"I just wanted to make sure you were safe." Murphy shrugged off her praise.

"I am, thanks to you."

"You did fine without my help. Though, considering your tendency to inspire violent reactions in killers, I wouldn't dissuade you from taking self-defense classes."

"I'm staying away from murderers from now on."

"Famous last words." Murphy winked, sending her stomach on a roller-coaster ride. "I'm glad you're not hurt." Murphy looked at her intently, and she forgot how to breathe.

"Me too. About you. I'm glad you're okay." She fiddled with her keys again. "And since that's established, I should go."

"Or you could come in. Don't think I've forgotten about that dinner you owe me."

"It's eleven thirty in the morning, Murphy. It might be a bit early for dinner."

"Then I guess you'll have to come back another time."

"I guess I will."

At the next stop on the closure circuit, Maddie broke the news to Leigh. Though ecstatic to no longer be living in fear of arrest, she took the news of Kat's guilt about as well as could be expected.

"You're telling me Lindsey's dead essentially because of jealousy?"

"And a healthy dose of instability." Leigh would likely experience guilt over her role in Lindsey's death (insignificant though it was), but Maddie saw no reason to feed her self-inflicted remorse.

"And I really slept with a murderer? A murderer who tried to frame me for killing her ex?"

"And I thought my love life was complicated."

"Kittens is right. I do need to make better choices."

"Don't we all."

She felt a little guilty leaving Leigh in the wake of the news she'd delivered, but she still had damage to repair. She'd saved the most daunting reconciliation for last.

"Where's Nadia?" Granny asked as soon as she opened her door.

"At work." Maddie knew Granny wanted a more complete answer—possibly an explanation for Nadia's behavior and what Maddie planned to do about it—but Maddie was in no mood to dissect her perpetually lackluster love life.

"What about after work?" Granny pressed. "Where will she be then?"

"I don't know where she'll be," Maddie admitted.

"Because you don't want to deal with it, or because she's in time-out for bad behavior?"

"Or maybe because I know it's never going to work, so why delay the inevitable? Now can we please talk about something else?"

"Better yet, how about we take a walk?"

Granny didn't wait for an answer. She just bundled up and headed out the door, obviously expecting Maddie to follow.

"Don't think I don't know what you're doing, Granny."

"I didn't realize I was being mysterious."

"You're being obstinate."

"And you can thank me later," Granny called over her shoulder and picked up the pace, leaving Maddie no choice but to follow or risk angering her grandmother, a consequence she habitually tried to avoid.

"Fine. Let's get this over with."

She marched on with her grandmother, grumbling the entire way. Whether she wanted to or not (and she definitely didn't want to), she'd be visiting Howard's house. She held no illusion that she could avoid this indefinitely. Granny had made up her mind, which meant that sooner or later Maddie would have to visit the scene of her friend's crime. But that didn't mean she had to be happy about it.

"Are you trick-or-treating?" Dottie eyed her from head to toe upon opening the door.

"Yes. I'm dressed as a frustrated lesbian who's in the market for a new best friend."

Dottie pursed her lips. "Next year you should cut way back on the flannel. Maybe go as a sexy lesbian."

"I thought the point of my visit was a tour of the unauthorized remodeling of my house, not a fashion tutorial."

"Oh precious. It would take more than one lesson."

Dottie sashayed forward, Maddie hesitantly trailing in her wake for her first look at the transformation Dottie had carried out in secret. It was actually her first time inside the house since she'd found its previous owner dead on the floor not five feet from where she now stood. She hadn't wanted to return to such a horrific reminder, so she had let Harriet and their mother handle everything related to the acquisition of her horror house. When Dottie signed the lease, they'd done so at Harriet's office, and when she'd visited Dottie earlier in the week, she'd been barred from entering (not that her aversion to the space didn't offer as much resistance as Carlisle and Dottie).

But the space she stepped into now bore so little resemblance to the spot where Howard had met his end, she considered stepping back onto the porch to double-check the address. Though the basic architecture remained more or less the same (give or take a wall or two), the feel was completely different.

"This is incredible," Maddie admitted.

The work was still in progress—not even Dottie's deep pockets could speed the renovation process—but the environment had dramatically shifted. She turned slowly, taking it all in, and she could envision what the space would become much more readily than she could call to mind what it had so recently been. She felt the tension she hadn't even realized was there slipping from her shoulders

"I still don't understand, though. Why keep it a secret?"

"Because you would have mistaken my insistence on good taste as an act of charity and would have refused to let me fund the project out of stubborn pride. And even after I convinced you to make changes, you would have insisted on doing the work yourself, so I would have had to wait for what I wanted, which e both know I despise, and I would have gotten it piecemeal rather than the instant gratification I prefer. I didn't care for either of those options."

"So you lied to me instead." She wandered into the almost-finished bathroom, inspecting the fixtures and new granite countertop.

"For the greater good, puddin'. And since I know you love it, everything worked out. Admit it."

"It's beautiful, Dottie, but why didn't you hire my dad? You have half my family on the payroll already."

"And risk him telling you? I don't think so, dumpling. He would have shown you the blueprints on day one."

"But he would have done impeccable work and charged you less."

"Fret not, little one. I'll hire him when I overhaul the second story."

"You're planning more work? You've already done so much."

"Carlisle needs a decent space to share with her cats, and you know how I adore a good makeover."

"Especially when it comes to me and my belongings." Maddie glanced around again, taking it all in, considering what the finished product would look like. She nodded approvingly at the space, and for the first time thought of it as something other than a burden—she thought of it as hers.

Bella Books, Inc.

Women. Books. Even Better Together.

P.O. Box 10543
Tallahassee, FL 32302

Phone: 800-729-4992
www.bellabooks.com